The Island

By

A P Bateman

Author website: www.apbateman.com

Facebook: @authorapbateman

For the chance to win a signed copy of one of A P Bateman's paperbacks keep reading at the end of this book where you will find details on how to enter.

The Rob Stone Series
The Ares Virus
The Town
The Island

The Alex King Series
The Contract Man
Lies and Retribution
Shadows of Good Friday
The Five
Reaper
Stormbound
Breakout
From the Shadows
Rogue
The Asset
Last Man Standing
Hunter Killer

Standalone Books
Hell's Mouth
Unforgotten

Author's note. By all means, skip on and get to the story…

My grandfather wasn't a well man. He used to look out of his second floor window and cast his eye and opinion on all he surveyed. As a seven-year old I must have been extremely keen on my games because he once said, "That boy will never grow up, he'll always be playing." I certainly think that by the time I was ten, the year he died, playing still wasn't out of the ordinary for young children in the early eighties. Maybe it was the life he lived, forced to grow up quickly to work on the family farm. Then driving a Royal Navy ambulance in World War Two wouldn't have been too pleasant. It is worth noting though, that he was absolutely right. I have always played. Life moves on, and with it merely the need for bigger and more expensive toys. Whether that's guns or surfboards, boats, motorcycles or cars. And then even faster cars. I love that my two young children have reached the age where I can show them the things that really matter. Showing them how to fish, or use a bow and arrow or - and certainly among all of my friends only I seem to do this - how to throw a knife into a tree from various distances. Honestly, it's a life skill for I don't know what.

I remember my father teaching me to swim by pretending to plant limpet mines on the sides of enemy boats (the edge of the pool) or by shooting German soldiers (sorry) with harpoon guns (pointed fingers). The game has moved on with the age we live in and my children and I now rescue dolphins or seal pups snared in drift nets or retrieve sonar data lost to the bottom of the sea. It's certainly more fun than swim academy, that's for sure.

I only realised recently, when it was pointed out to me while on holiday, that back-flipping into a swimming pool is not normal behaviour for a forty-five-year-old, but that's the point – I haven't grown up and I bloody well hope I never do. The last time I looked life could be boring and hard enough without stopping the things you love.

Writing indulges me in my quest to refrain from growing up. That I live the characters, test that some of the things I make them do is possible and plausible. Yes, it can be hard work, there are pressures like in any job and sometimes the stress of maintaining sales figures, reviews and those relentless edits can be incredible, but the actual task of getting a story to unfold is a pleasure. I miss it the moment I type the last word of the final chapter. I hope it is something I will do for as long as I have breath.

So, I'd like to thank my wife, Clair. You have encouraged me to write, selflessly given me the time to do so, listened when I've not really had anything to say but desperately needed to say it and told me what to ignore and what to embrace. And you keep my anti-gravity boots grounded when they need to be. Well, almost. Thank you.

1

He was quite convinced that he was dead. There would, of course, be a half-life between one world and the next. He had unwillingly visited it before. Blown out of a vehicle by an IED in Afghanistan, he had survived when others had not. He had felt the sickening weightlessness; the confusing extra-sensory perception in which to view the bleary remnants of the world he was leaving. He could hear, but heard nothing; could see, but saw only light – shadows of brightness and glister. He had seen the tunnel opening before him, a void of darkness beyond; not the warm, comforting light that he had heard other people speak of when recounting near-death experiences.

He found himself within a white void, like that he had experienced previously, only broken, burned and bloody in Afghanistan, and the only direction, like then, was towards the darkness. Maybe that was all that awaited him. Maybe that was his lot. He had killed and done bad things. As bad as anyone can do. But he had done it all for the country he served, both in times of war and in times of peace. Perhaps his journey would be different to those who talked of out of body experiences. Perhaps they had been better human beings. He had never told a soul what he had experienced. Embarrassed, sometimes ashamed that his experience had been different, and that he would be judged accordingly. Maybe *his* tunnel led straight to Hell. If it did, then he would still have thought he'd done his best and his fight had been just.

This experience was different though. This was the furthest he had gone towards the black void. In Afghanistan, much had culminated in him being pulled back to life, back to the known world. These factors were not here. Not this time. There were no allied trauma teams working on him here, no fast transport in a Chinook to the state of the art hospital facilities in Camp Bastion. No shock of electricity to the system from a defibrillator, no nurse talking softly in his ear throughout, squeezing his hand and assuring him he would make it. No surgeon talking his team through what they were going to try, how best to attempt the removal of the dead soldier's bones and teeth and skull fragments from his tattered torso - turned to lethal shrapnel in a flash of blinding light and fierce heat. None of this accompanied him now, nothing or nobody tried to stop him leaving the void for the tunnel. He knew he was alone.

He was aware of heat. Burning him, tightening his skin. It felt raw. Then, as if to confuse his senses again, a coolness washed over him. The rawness multiplied ten-fold. But he could not react to it, could not move or look to take sanctuary. The tunnel started to recede and the light gradually grew brighter. There was suddenly a splash of colour to the light; where once there had been only white, there was a yellow hue, then starburst. A dramatic show of a million silver-white dots burning his retinas and washing the yellowness away. Sound returned from the void, a gentle white-noise which washed through his ears like an attack of tinnitus.

Rob Stone opened his eyes tentatively, hampered by the sun directly overhead. He tried to shade his eyes, but his arms would not move. He could move his head and neck fractionally, but not enough to see what was tethering him. Water washed over his legs, it eased the burning, but almost instantly turned to pain, the salinity searing at his flesh. His legs would not move, and nor could he roll onto his side. He was strapped down. Would he drown? The water reached his waist, washed underneath him into the small of his back. There was a chill to it there, his underside had not been heated in the sun.

He realised he was naked. He turned his head as far as he could and looked through squinted eyes. He was on a beach. Yellow sand. A scattering of large rocks casting shadows away from him. He turned his head the other way. The process was slow, like he was suspended in treacle. He stretched, felt a stab of pain in his side. His stomach was tender. His hip hurt too, sore in the salt water. He had been injured, but had no recollection of how or when.

He studied the sight in front of him. To his left was a large outcrop of rocks and beyond that, a headland. In the foreground, tiny crabs scurried sideways into the lapping shore break and a large seabird took off, great wings flapping slowly as it skimmed the water and headed out to sea and out of his field of vision.

Stone called out for help, but his mouth and throat struggled to form the words. He let out a gargle and coughed. This induced a coughing fit, but his mouth and throat were so dry there was no recovering from it. He coughed every few seconds, irritated that he could not stop.

Was he dreaming? He wanted to snap awake. He didn't think he had been anywhere near the coast recently. And certainly he had not been anywhere remotely this hot. But he did not know for sure, could not remember where he *had* been. All that he knew was he had not been here before.

Movement came with the sudden rush of tide. The water enveloped him, washed over his stomach and into his face. He took some into his mouth and swallowed inadvertently. Almost instantly, he vomited, turned his head and found that his opposite shoulder left the wet sand and followed. Natural preservation senses had done what he and willpower alone could not, but it started him moving. It took both strength and concentration, but he managed to roll onto his side and continued to vomit on the wet sand.

After an indeterminable period of time, Stone had no idea how long, he had managed to roll onto his stomach, rest on his elbows and was able to dig his toes into the sand. The water washed over him, getting higher on the pushing tide, but he was confident that he would not drown, would get his body working before it was indeed too late.

Stone noticed the soft flesh of the inside of his left forearm. Track marks ran along the vein, which had pumped and become prominent through the exertion. He had seen needle marks before. He knew he did not do drugs, but he had no idea how they got there. But then, *did* he do drugs? He had no inkling who he was, what he did. He remembered being a boy and then a soldier. Was he a father and a husband? A good man, or bad?

He did not know, but he knew the track marks were wrong. His fingernails were trimmed, his muscled arms plain – not decorated with tattoos. Plenty of scars though. He started the process of getting to his feet. He rested on his knees, longer than he cared to, but necessary all the same. He looked down at his chest and stomach. Muscled and defined, broad through to trim. Again, no tattoos, but a few white scars. A burn mark and pigment discolouration. He had been injured, but over time. He transcended from kneeling, but fell short of standing. His head light, his legs heavy. He fell forwards, but steadied himself on his arms. They were strong and pushed him back up quickly. Steadier this time, but still unable to stand. He was badly dehydrated. He imagined having to urinate after waking from what he imagined to be a long and un-natural sleep, but he had no need nor inclination. He was thirsty though, unimaginably so. A flash of memory, and he sees himself in a desert environment. He is wearing an olive coloured uniform dusty and ripped, a weapon – a compact assault rifle - resting on his legs. He is drinking water from a clear plastic bottle in one hand and sucking occasionally on condensed orange syrup from a sachet in the other. He is alternating from sachet to bottle, diluting and mixing it in his mouth. The memory drives his thirst insurmountably, he looks at the ebb and flow of the sea, surging from the shore break and for a moment he contemplates drinking it. Now he *knows* he is in trouble. He pushed himself up and crawled up the beach to the fringe of trees and foliage. His legs and feet become lighter and the feeling returns, after a few minutes and fifty-metres, he gets up and staggers, lengthens his stride, straightens his back and grows taller, like the evolution of mankind. When he reaches the jungle he is fully formed and dangerous once more.

2

Stone knew that without water he would not last long. It may well be possible for the body to continue to function and to go on for a few days without hydration, but the brain was another consideration altogether. The brain did silly things like tell the body to take a rest, take a nap, take a deep sleep. The brain told the body they could see something in the distance, or to climb a dangerously steep and unstable cliff as a shortcut, or that the scorpion underfoot was just another twig. The brain was a thirsty son of a bitch and needed water to make decisions. And a really bad decision only had to happen once.

It was hot. Tropically so. Although his experience of the tropics, or sub-tropics ended at Florida and Louisiana. He could recall desert and military uniform, and supposed it was Afghanistan or Iraq. He knew it had been hot, hotter than here, wherever *here* was. His memory was akin to recalling a dream. A tangible image, but one that dispersed to mist if dwelled upon for more than a mere moment.

The sun was high. Stone estimated it to be after noon, but he didn't know how or why he had come to the conclusion. There was an underlying subconscious to his thought processes. When he first awoke, left that no man's land, that void of light and the dark tunnel to the unknown, whatever its significance, he could not even recall his own name.

But he had started to recollect. Rob Stone. Robert did not seem to have any significance. It kind of lingered at the back of his mind, favouring Rob.

Not only was it hot, but the wind offered no respite from the heat, and what breeze wafted into his face was akin to opening an oven door. The shade of the jungle offered protection from the sun, but not from the heat. The heat became more intense, the air thicker. The jungle smelled of damp and mould. Of rotten vegetation and faeces.

He knew he needed water. His head thumped with a solid headache, pounding in time with his heartbeat. His head felt thick, his mouth dryer than cotton. He needed to ascertain where he was, and for that he needed to gain some height. The jungle seemed flat, and he could see no further than twenty-metres through the foliage. The rocky outcrop might elevate him enough to see further inland. He would walk along the beach, but first he bent down and dug up a handful of mud. There were tiny insects in the mud, but he rubbed it between his hands and started to smear it over his shoulders, around his neck and over his face. It would offer a little protection from the sun in lieu of clothing or sun-block.

And where were his clothes? Had he been partying? He couldn't recall. He felt he wasn't the wild partying type somehow. But then, there were the track marks in his vein. Maybe he was wrong. Maybe he partied like a rock star and fell of a boat and made it to shore before passing out. Maybe he *was* a rock star. He tried to remember, tried to draw on the depths and recesses of his mind and recall the day before, the day before that. Not only would the memories not come to him, but he could neither recall friends nor relatives. There was a woman. Auburn hair. She was tearful and thanking him, whispering into his ear. She kissed his cheek. As soon as he remembered, she was withering away. A dream unremembered. He closed his eyes, caught sight of a woman cradling a young man covered in blood, she seemed maternal, as if cradling her son. A sheriff's badge on her shirt. A sadness in her eyes, a sadness he could not imagine possible. He views the scene as a voyeur, then it is gone. Dispersed and unrecallable. Was this a recent event, or an image from long ago? It frustrated him to have no knowledge of this.

As he neared the outcrop of rocks, a jutting headland, he recalled a desk, a chair, a laptop. It's a workstation. Telephone, pens, notepad. The drawer opened, it's his own hand opening it, he's wearing a suit. The white shirtsleeve juts out from the black jacket. He is wearing an expensive looking watch, stainless steel, chunky. There are files in the drawer, a pistol on top, holstered. Is he a cop? He doesn't feel that fits somehow. The memory doesn't disperse, lingers for a moment. He lets it go, he will control this, he will attempt to recall it later. He looked at his left wrist. The watch is no longer there, but there is a faint tan line where it had been.

The headland is fifty-feet high. The gradient is steep. He can see his potential path, notes the fissures in the rock, the hand holds and pieces of jutting rock. He can see the lighter coloured rock, a seam running diagonally. He notes it is soft rock and the harder rock is pushing it out. This will create a fissure. Not now, but maybe in a thousand years. He doesn't know how he knows this, but he feels he knows how to climb. And he does. He climbs fast, competently and within ten minutes he is standing at the top. Surveying the scene before him, out to sea to his right and back in the direction he has come from. He is in no doubt he is on an island in the tropics. And he is in no doubt he is on his own. He cannot see all of the way around, but even supposing it is a peninsular, he knows he will have to survive without help, and maybe for a long time. He breathed a deep breath and said to himself, "As tough as it gets, as long as it takes…"

3

He knew that he stood more chance of finding water at lower level. Simple physics; water ran down hill. But the jungle floor was made up of soft earth and debris, and the water would contaminate easily, become nothing more than mud. And although water was of paramount concern, if he drank bad water he would become sick, dehydrate further and spiral quickly into helplessness. There would be no coming back. He would reach a point where he became unconscious or unable to move and then he would die. How did he know this? He was not sure, but he knew he had served in the military at some point, and each time he thought about a problem, the answer seemed to drift from a recess in his mind. It was like unlocking information. He seemed to have to ask the right question for the answer to come.

The centre of the island, if indeed it was an island, looked to be twice as high as the outcrop. He estimated it at just over one-hundred feet above sea level. It plateaued, looked to have less jungle on top. It seemed to be some thousand metres distant from where he stood. He was naked, carried no machete and it was hot. He was dehydrated. His head said go for it. His survival instinct, a primordial sense rarely awakened by most people in their day-to-day existence told him to hang back. It told him it could take a day or more to reach, and that was without getting lost. The earth rotates at a thousand miles an hour. He recalled being aware that when the horizon is not visible, people always veered left because of this fact. He may well miss the mount altogether. Where had he heard this? He remembered a Gunnery Sergeant, weathered and grey and as tough as hell. He remembered looking up at him, one of a number of men lying prone, heavy .50 calibre sniper rifles in front of them. The gunny talked of the curvature of the earth, allowing for the earth's rotational spin, the pull of gravity. That without wind, long shots dropped left and low. Left was always the easier path to take.

Stone looked further down the beach. The tide was rising, but there was still plenty of sand to walk on. The beach disappeared in the distance and Stone realised it was curving around to the left, around the peninsular. At the far end the sand was off colour. All the way down to the sea. He made his way cautiously down the other side of the headland. He faced the rock and took short steps. Kept his weight pressed into the rock. His genitalia got in the way of the steep rock face and he had to be careful placing his bare feet on the jagged rocks that jutted out. It was an awkward climb. When he got to within eight-feet of the sand he jumped and rolled and got back to his feet. The manoeuvre stabbed at his side, his ribs. The sand stuck to the graze on his hip. He looked at the wounds, still he was at a loss. He simply could not recall being in an accident. His head thumped beyond imagination. It pounded like a drum. He thought he could almost hear the thudding outside of his own head. As if it followed him, rather than came from within him and would be audible to a bystander, should there have been one. The walk took longer than he expected, but he realised that he was walking incredibly slow. He turned around and looked at his footprints. They curved greatly. He was not walking in a straight line. As he neared the discolouration he could see that it was wet. It was not a stream, but as he turned towards the jungle he noticed it inverted as a triangle, becoming narrower the further he headed away from the sea. At the earthen floor of the jungle, the water was visible. Twenty-metres into the jungle it was as if a garden tap had not been switched off properly. Another twenty-metres and it trickled, flowed even. Stone cupped his hand and made a dam. The water was brown. He rubbed it on his forehead and the back of his neck, resisting the temptation to drink. The jungle sloped upwards and he walked right through the water for another twenty- metres. Tiny scorpions scuttled either side of his feet, their red backs and black tails keeping his concentration focused greatly. He did not want to step on one inadvertently. At a point where the jungle steepened more immediately, Stone saw the water dripping from a ledge. He placed his hands underneath and the water dripped, pooled and washed the mud clean. He rubbed it on his face once more, then cupped his hands and waited. He slurped the water and it stung his lips, tongue and throat. After a few attempts, the water stung less and tasted delicious. He drank for what seemed like an hour or more. His vision seemed to noticeably improve, his head thudded less and he started to remember more about himself, but not how he had arrived. Not how he was naked and alone. After fifty or more leaky handfuls of water had reached his mouth, ran down his chin and quenched his thirst to the glorious point that he craved it no more, he kicked the earth and debris aside and sat down in the darkening jungle. He had remembered something significant, but when was this memory? And had it brought him here?

4

The bar is quiet. Sports heroes from thirties, forties and fifties America are captured for posterity and sealed in monochrome prints. They are not originals. This is a themed bar and the prints are on the walls of similar bars in Minnesota, Ohio, Illinois and New Jersey. Probably all fifty states for all Stone knew. Maybe not the southwestern states though. There was no Tex-Mex. The menu is Italian-American. Big subs, pasta loaded with cheese, steaks and chicken quarters, burgers as big as a softball – you can double up on the meat pate and triple on cheese for another four dollars. The pizzas are New York style and take up most of the table. But not Stone's table. He has a bowl of nuts and a cold bottle of beer in front of him. The waitresses are friendly, but they work for tips. No sense in docking your own pay by showing your true feelings.

He keeps looking over at the door as it opens. It's late summer and the evening air is cooler in the city. The air-conditioning is switched off and the door lets a distinguishable draft through each time it opens. The room is warm so it's not unpleasant. Couples and groups of people come in sporadically and each time the door opens they are greeted by the restaurant manager and shown to a booth. Stone watches and waits. He is used to waiting in his profession. He has lost count of the days and nights he has waited. Ready for something to happen, a scenario to react to and put the countless hours of training, the countless of rounds down the range to the test. Only then to stand to, hand over the watch and go off duty frustrated, unfulfilled, but at the same time, thankful his charge made it through his watch.

A woman walked in alone. She cast her eyes over the booths and discounted the twos and threes, the larger groups who were clinking glasses and handing each other menus. She's not joining in to make a foursome or add to the party numbers. She's meeting someone, but that person has either not yet arrived, or like Stone, she is unsure what they will look like.

The woman bypasses the restaurant manager, who is now busy directing waiting staff and has failed to notice her arrival. She approaches Stone's booth. "Hi," she says. Her accent is southern belle. Stone can't place it, but would go with South Carolina if he was encouraged to place a bet. There's a real unfamiliar twang to it though. "I'm Kathy, you must be Rob."

Stone is thrown at first. He has worked and socialised with countless colours and creeds, but he had drawn a mental image of his contact, and because of their mutual friend and the professional and social circles she moved in, he had not been expecting an Asian woman. For a moment he is ashamed to have expressed surprise, but he quickly moves on. You can't get it right all the time. It may account for the confused accent, a mix of Asia and the south. He squeezes his frame out of the booth and towers over her. He offers his hand and she takes it. She goes in for a double air kiss and Stone misses, catching her lips. "Sorry," he apologises awkwardly.

"Isobel said you were forward, and that I should watch you," she smiled. "Let's wait until the second date."

Stone waited for her to take a seat and he slid back in behind the table. A waitress appeared and asked if they'd like drinks. Kathy went for a cream soda, which surprised Stone, and he tipped his bottle a little to indicate he'd like another beer. Kathy slipped off her jacket and fastened her handbag. Stone watched, the blush subsiding from his cheeks at the thought of his air kissing faux pas. He can't put an age to her. Her skin is smooth and unblemished, there are no lines or wrinkles and her hair is as black as coal. Wet coal, glossy and rich. He is quite sure she is one of the most attractive women he has ever seen. The blouse is stretching over small, but perfectly formed breasts and her waist is no thicker than his powerful thigh. He is aware that he is staring.

"Haven't had a cream soda since I was a kid," he said. "If this were a date, you'd be the cheapest I've had in years."

"Thanks, just what every girl wants to hear," she said, somewhere between sarcastic and sardonic, but nowhere near sincere.

"Sorry, I didn't mean…" he paused. "Well, it's a hell of a lot cheaper than Cosmopolitans, that's for sure."

"I think we had better cut to the chase, don't you think?"

"Perhaps."

The drinks arrived and Stone clinked the rim of the soda with the neck of the frosted bottle. "Cheers," he said. "Sure you don't want an ice cream floater in that?"

"My dad used to bring me here. Well, to one of its sister restaurants down in Louisiana. I used to have a cream soda and he'd have one too. We'd have vanilla floaters in those, but I didn't think I'd carry it off tonight," she said. "He's dead and I felt nostalgic, that's all."

Stone hung his head, then looked at her. "Shit. I'm sorry. How about we start again? I won't kiss you on the lips again either."

"No?"

"No."

"Shame," she smiled. "I think Isobel still has a thing for you."

"Old news," he replied shortly. "Geography. We couldn't make it work. We gave it our best shot."

"She said you guard the President. That he's the one good politician we've had in decades and that you don't want to leave him to the wolves of Washington DC."

"Something like that."

"So how would you have time to help me?"

"Depends how long it takes," he said. "There's some appearances he's making soon. I requested I be re-assigned for a week or so. Nothing came up, so I've got gardening leave, so to speak."

"If you've got time on your hands, you could make more of a go of it with Isobel."

"Takes two to tango, not three."

"She's had a couple of dinner dates, that's all."

"Shall we get to what I can do for you?"

"Sure," Kathy said, a little taken aback.

"Well?"

"Look, sorry if I touched a nerve," she paused but Stone said nothing. He sipped a beer and stared at her impatiently. "Okay then. Are you familiar with the dark web?"

"Yes."

"You are? Well, okay, that kind of speeds things up a little. So what do you know?"

"I know it's part of the deep web, that mainstream search engines don't uncover enough layers to search it effectively. Much of it is encrypted and requires specialist software."

"In a nutshell, yes. The internet is like an onion and *Google*, *Bing* and the like take off the first layer. That's where the information is for most people to go about their day. They bank, book vacations, use social media, upload to *YouTube,* surf for porn - the straightforward stuff that is – and do just about everything they need to do. It's about five percent of what makes up the internet."

Stone nodded. "Child pornography, illegal gambling, black market, illegal financial trading lies in the layers underneath. The deep web and the dark web."

"And you've had experience with that?"

"An investigation I headed. The CIA contacted assets, exchanged and stole information in there somewhere. They operated an entire black-ops assassination program from the dark web. They shut down the operation after a congressman heard whispers of it, but a rogue CIA officer kept it going for his own ends. Along with this, I also uncovered a pharmaceutical company with plans to release a virus and sell the anti-virus for a colossal amount. Another case was for the sale of human organ harvesting."

"And you know how to use the dark web?"

"No."

She looked disappointed. "So how did you navigate it?"

"I didn't. I used a couple of specialist programmers. I struggle using my smartphone."

"I used a specialist programmer too," she said. "He was working for me, for my paper."

"What paper do you work for?"

"The Washington Post. I'm the senior reporter on the social affairs desk. The internet is changing society and in ways we are not ready for. Society, that is."

"So what has your programmer come up with?"

"Well that's it. He was absolutely banging off the walls. He said that the paper would have to quadruple his fee, that he had the story of the century. That there was a bestselling book in it for me, that the Washington Post could publish it and that he wanted half the royalties for that as well."

"Greedy guy," Stone said, then drained his beer. "So what was it?"

"I'm not entirely sure," Kathy shrugged. "He went missing."

Stone looked at her. Her beauty hadn't diminished any since he'd grown accustomed to her presence. He thought of her lips and how warm they had felt against his own, chilled from his cold beer. "Have you called the police?"

"I haven't. I wanted *you* to find him."

"If he's missing, the police need to be on it."

"Isobel said if anyone can find him, it's you. She also said the Secret Service have the means to find him…" she paused. "Even if he doesn't want to be found."

"The guy's trying to cash in big time. Why would he not want to be found?"

Kathy finished her cream soda. She made a noise with the straw as she negotiated the ice chips at the bottom of the glass. She let the straw drop from between her glossy lips and looked up at him. "Because I think he found out something else. He was keen to cash in and confident that the story would be big. And then I think he got scared. But I don't just think he found something that merely scared him," she paused, looked at Stone intensely with the darkest brown eyes he'd ever seen. "I think after a little more digging he found something that absolutely terrified him."

5

He had been badly dehydrated before and on more than one occasion. He recognised the signs. He was not sure where or when, but he recalled kneeling on hard-baked sand, a man in combat fatigues handing him a canteen and ordering him to sip slowly. He hadn't. He had gulped it down and had vomited the precious liquid. Another time a nurse had given him a white liquid in a thick beaker. He recalled it being sweet, but salty. Just short of so salty as to suffer reflux. The liquid had been warm and the nurse had said it was to prevent shock to his system. Stone knew he had been close to succumbing to dehydration here, wherever *here* was. But he had a water source now. He had a base. He stepped away from the stream and urinated. The sight was surprising, dark like Guinness. His system was flushing through toxins and impurities which had built up. He knew that his second drink would do him more good. After drinking his fill once more, he got up and walked down the tiny stream and met the sand and light once more. He felt invigorated. He was hungry, but he could ride that out. He knew he could function for many days without food – as long as he had water.

Stone looked both ways down the beach and made a note of the natural markers of the two headlands. He did not want to lose his water supply. However, the fringe of clean sand offered no visible food source and the jungle was dense and rank and he knew he should strike out across an obstruction-free beach and find a more suitable place to make a shelter or forage for food. Some flat rock might afford him some shellfish or seaweed and the coastline looked remote enough from risk of pollution that eating it raw would not bring him any harm. As long as he didn't eat vast quantities too quickly.

The sand felt warmer underfoot. He looked at the sun and assumed from its position that it was mid-day. He had earlier thought it had been afternoon, but the heat was increasing. He had no geographical insight, other than it was hot and the jungle denoted he was between the tropics of Cancer and Capricorn. Perhaps even equatorial. These were facts he knew. Facts imprinted from his past life. He just hoped he was right.

Stone cast his mind back to the bar and the woman in front of him. He knew her as Kathy. He knew the mutual friend Isobel. He could picture her dark hair, scraped back in a tight ponytail, a smile upon her face. He could not recall how they had met, but he knew they had been close. The thought of her comforted him, but the conversation clearly made him aware that whatever they had was now firmly in the past. He neither felt pleased nor sad. How could he mourn the loss of something he could barely remember?

The second headland was no more than a rocky groin that Stone could walk up, apart from the last ten feet which required hands, but no more than to steady himself and provide extra lift. At the top of the climb he was afforded a stunning view of a horseshoe bay with shallow reef and deep-water lagoons. There was a gentle shore break and part of the bay was exposed reef. He knew he would find food here, but it was impractical unless he either found another fresh water supply or a container to carry water in. He would simply burn off the positive effects of drinking to reach his food supply, and vice versa.

Although he had never, to his knowledge, visited the tropics before, he was aware of the ever increasing problem of plastic deposited in the sea. He was sure he'd seen a feature on television that tropical paradise was littered with bottles and containers and all manner of things which might help him. It was just a matter of time.

The climb down was as rudimentary as his ascent and he was on the sand and walking towards the exposed reef in a matter of minutes. There were tight shoals of tiny fish herded by baby sharks. A single shark would break rank and swim at high speed through the shoal. They took turns, each snapping a fish and returning to the edge of the shoal. Stone watched a shark come within a few feet from the beach. He saw another further up the beach. He contemplated diving on one. Would it be as simple as that? Would he get bit? Tiny details mattered, and the tiniest mistake could cost him dear. A bite would get infected. A fever would make him delirious. There was no help, no second chance. He decided that if the sharks did this, then they would do it again. Besides, shark skin was as tough as tanned leather and he had no way of cutting the flesh yet. He would need to find a sliver of rock or a fragment of scallop shell before he could think about the task of cutting a shark into sashimi. He walked to the reef and tentatively negotiated the sharp rock underfoot where small scallops and rock oysters lay exposed to the sun as the rising tide slowly covered the reef and returned them to feed and breed and do whatever else bivalve molluscs do.

He picked the white and brown shellfish and used the edges of the shells to pry them open. He smelt them, then when he discovered they merely smelled of the sea he prised out the flesh and ate them one by one. He wasn't a fan of raw shellfish, never saw the appeal of chilled oysters, but he remembered wasabi, soy sauce and pickled ginger making them a whole lot more palatable somewhere. Without the niceties of condiments, he would have to make do. After sliding a few down, he realised they simply tasted salty and were no different than eating undercooked poached egg.

The flash of movement out of the corner of his eye made him flinch. He didn't know why, but he thought a dark coloured bird was about to fly into him. He ducked down and looked up in time to see the object spin over and over, scything through the air over his head and out to sea. The object was black, and looked to Stone like a cross between a sickle, a machete and a fire poker. It crashed down into the shoal of fish and in an instant the sharks and fish were gone. Stone looked back in the direction it had travelled. He frowned, unsure if he was going mad, or if madness had already found its way into his mind.

The man stood tall and broad. He was extremely dark, his skin a shiny black. His hair was a combination of dreadlocks and afro. He glistened in perspiration and wore a loin cloth made from suede or softened leather. He carried a spear and wore a wicked-looking and curiously shaped sword on a leather thong around his waist. The sword was black and mottled, as if crudely honed from wrought iron, and rather than being straight and true, or indeed curved like a sabre. Its blade was a wavy design, the edge on both sides clearly denoted by a thin strip of silver roughly honed into the dark metal. The man hefted the spear into his hand like a javelin. The blade looked like a metal leaf, tapering into a broad tip and the blade looked to be fixed to the shaft by thin sinew or leather lashing. The man looked every inch the African warrior, and as Stone estimated the distance between them, he knew the man was both taller and heavier than himself. At a shade under six-foot and around a hundred and ninety pounds, Stone was built like a light-heavyweight boxer. He had the arms and fists to match, but he felt small in comparison. For a brief moment, he had forgotten he was naked.

The warrior was bathed in sweat, his muscles defined and the sunlight shone directly upon him making him glisten. He tested the weight of the spear above his shoulder, then started to jog towards Stone, closing the distance.

Stone sprinted hard towards the man. Already confusion was on his opponent's face, as the gap closed too quickly and he was forced to stop and recalculate his throw. Stone did not make it easy, breaking both left and then back to the right as he closed him down and raced to bring the gap down to nothing. The warrior spun the spear around, no time for a throw, he was going to use it as a lance. Stone bent down, scooped up a handful of sand and threw it underarm into the man's face as he neared, then dropped and shoulder-charged the man at the knees. The spear glanced the top of Stone's shoulder and he felt it slice open moments before he smashed into the man's legs. The warrior was bowled over, taking Stone with him. Stone grabbed the spear, ripping it from the man's grasp and rolled on the sand. He felt the sting of the sand in his wound, but came back onto his feet with the spear at the ready.

The warrior had reacted quickly to the attack. He had the sword out from the makeshift belt and sliced it through the air in front of him to maintain his ground and force Stone back.

Fighting, combat, whatever you chose to call it, is about the occupation of ground. You stand your ground and attack. You aim to occupy your opponent's space, force them to retreat and continue. After you have taken ground from your opponent multiple times, kept them on the back foot, the retreat, you start to beat them mentally. This was as true on the battle field as it was in the boxing ring. Stone knew this, but it looked like the warrior did as well. Stone lunged forwards with the spear and the man dodged and countered with the sword. Stone could see it was more of a long knife than a true sword, but the man slashed at the spear and a great chunk of wood was cut out leaving Stone in no doubt that the shaft would not last long if the man had too many chances at it with the blade.

Stone stared the man in the eyes. The warrior looked terrified, his eyes wide and the whites highlighted more so by the man's dark skin colour. Up close Stone could see the man was huge. He stood at least six-six and was easily twenty pounds heavier than Stone. He should not have looked so scared, but then again, Stone didn't exactly have a mirror handy.

The warrior lunged with the blade, but it was a bad move as Stone had the reach advantage. He used the tip of the spear to parry the blade, and swiped it back across the man's chest. The wound opened up and bled immediately, but Stone dropped the spear low and swiped back the way he'd come and caught the man's knee. The warrior slashed at the spear with the blade, but Stone snatched it back and as the blade of the man's weapon carried on past towards the sand, Stone jabbed hard and the spear went several inches into the man's gut. The man dropped onto his knees, realisation on his face. He dropped the knife and cupped the wound. Slowly, he turned his bloody palms upwards and steadied them, quite unhurried as if Stone was no longer there.

Stone almost recoiled as a memory, an image played before him. Standing over a young Taliban fighter, the same look on his face, the same bloody hands. The barrel of a rifle, bayonet fixed and dripping crimson. The pooling of blood as rivulets drained from the blade's blood groove and dropped to the dry, sun-baked earth. The look on the young man's face as the rifle draws back and then thrusts forwards, the bayonet travelling towards his neck. Stone shudders and closes his eyes momentarily. When he opens them, the rifle and bayonet are gone and the black warrior and the bloody spear are in front of him. Not a memory, terrifyingly real.

Stone stepped back a pace. The man went for the sword and Stone upended the spear and brought the haft down on the man's skull. He slumped down into the sand and lay still.

6

Stone had dragged the unconscious man to the fringe of the jungle. The man was heavy and the strain hurt his side. He wondered if his ribs were cracked.

The man was badly wounded. Stone was not concerned by the gash to the man's knee, but the stab wound to his stomach was not only deep but broad. He knew that it needed suturing, but the man was out of luck. Stone needed a fire to sterilize water, a container to carry water and he needed material. That was without sutures. He had the sword-like knife and could whittle some shards of wood and use them as staples, but unless he sterilized them by either flame or boiling water, then he would only cause the man more harm. But he had none of these things to hand. The best he could do was remove the man's loin cloth, soak it in seawater and press it against the stomach wound. He did this, bathed his own shoulder wound in the water, struggled to look at it, but could see it was bleeding less, already starting to clot and dry in the sun. When he returned, he pressed the loin cloth into the man's wound, tied some of the leather cord around to secure it in place, then he tethered the man's wrists behind a thin tree with the leather cord belt to be safe.

He had started to recall military service in Afghanistan. He had gone in to a compound to evacuate the wounded enemy for medical treatment.

First they bombed them, then they bandaged them, a soldier had commented. It mirrored the man before him. Maybe he should have simply killed him, but without the heat of battle it was murder. Stone wasn't about to run the man through, and he wanted to try and communicate with him, find out where he was and why the man had tried to kill him. But first he needed water, and he knew that if the man woke up, not only would he need water too, but the promise of it would get him talking.

Stone scoured the high-water tideline as he made his way back to the precious water source. He had seen footage on the television of beaches littered with flotsam and jetsam, but here there was only weed and driftwood. Not a container, plastic bag, bottle, flip-flop or fishing net in sight. Nothing. Not a single imprint of mankind.

The sand had dried and it was only by mentally marking out the two headlands earlier that Stone could be sure he was in the right place. There was no sign of water and when he found the point where he was sure he had entered the jungle; something became strangely obvious to him. He could not find his own footprints. He got down on his knees and studied the ground carefully, ran his hand gently over the sand. On the fringe of the jungle were clumps of palm fronds growing out of the dirt, their roots spreading out across the surface of the sand, as if they had rejected the beach and were blindly seeking out nutrient-rich earth. He picked up a frond and gently brushed it over his footprints. They disappeared, leaving beads of damp sandy clumps in their place. The ground looked the same as when he had returned. Maybe he was in the wrong place? No. He was sure, positive that his tracks had been purposefully cleared away. But why would the warrior do that? And why had the flow of water suddenly stopped and dried up?

Stone edged his way cautiously into the jungle. He kept his eyes moving; from the ground to avoid snakes, spiders and scorpions, to the area in front of him, also using his periphery vision as well as he could in the dark shadow of the jungle. He would stop every so often, his ears challenging a noise, his eyes daring movement. He wasn't necessarily remembering military training; these were primordial senses that seemed to come naturally to him.

The earth was damp, but there was no longer a flow of water. He climbed up the slope where it had trickled down. Nothing. No sign of a spring or overflow from a pool. Just damp earth. Strangely, the ground started to slope away. There was no evidence of mud or an area of dampness. The more he thought about it, the more he started to feel he was confusing the site. He turned around and made his way back down the earth slope, his feet occasionally coming close to tiny scorpions. He used the knife to hack down a thin, leafy branch and holding it in front of him, he brushed the ground in front of him like a travelling Buddhist monk. It was the first confident steps his bare feet had made since leaving the beach.

Back at the base of the slope, Stone thought about his earlier visit and walked to the tree that he had urinated against. The ground smelled foul, the impurities of his dehydrated waste reeking, even as it competed against the rotting jungle vegetation. There was no doubt about it – he was in the right place. But physics and geography meant that the stream of water that had saved him earlier should never have existed in the first place.

Back on the sand and in the bright, welcoming light, Stone surveyed the beach as he had done so before. He weighed his options, knowing it was both important to keep them open and have more than one. He could strike out the other way and look for habitation, or something of use that he could learn about his location. There were no ships or boats on the horizon, maybe if this was an island there would be shipping lanes on the other side. With some innovation he could make a raft or a smoky signal fire from leaves. It would take time, as he had to fabricate some makeshift tools first, but he was confident that if he could locate another water supply and consume enough food, he would both discover and make what he needed. There may also be more islands and he may well be able to swim and island hop his way to habitation.

The warrior. Why had the man attacked him? And where was this place for him to have met such a man? Stone could not stop thinking about this. He had left the man tethered to a tree. He knew deep down that he should have finished his opponent. Now he had left a man to fate, most probably certain death without medical attention and water. He had left himself wide open to fate also. What if the man had friends who could release him? There was also the possibility that the man could escape and come after him looking for vengeance. In showing mercy he had left a loose end and he may well have endangered himself because of it.

Stone climbed the rocky outcrop and surveyed the horseshoe bay. It appeared the same as before, except that the reef had been almost completely immersed by the tide. He could see a shoal of what he assumed where tiny fish in the shallows. No doubt the baby sharks would be shadowing and herding them as they learned to hunt. He reflected that he could try fishing for them, maybe with the spear if he could adapt the blade and fashion prongs in place.

Stone was feeling confident in his abilities. He was remembering more, but it was a subconscious thing. He knew things, rather than remembered them. He knew survival techniques, but they came to him as he thought about his situation. He couldn't reason with himself and set a mental task to remember the day he had been taught something specific, but he knew that he had skills and knowledge which was seeping out from the chasms of his mind.

Stone decided to test himself. He closed his eyes and tried to recall his college graduation. It was there. A warm day, bright sky. His mother and father proudly congratulating him on the sports field. His friends standing behind them gesturing to make him laugh. But he couldn't remember what he had studied. And he couldn't remember where. He shrugged. It was a hell of a lot more than he had been able to remember a few hours ago. He drew on the memory of Kathy in the bar. He could picture her. Her cream soda, her glossy lips, her satin black hair. Her sharp cheekbones, her eyes, dark and inviting. And Isobel. He could picture her, remembered meeting her at a buffet. She is wearing a smart skirt and suit jacket. It's business. Other men are talking in the circle, they are wearing ID badges and visitor labels. Still he is neither sad nor happy. She is clearly part of his past, but he remembers no more.

Tired, he decides to sit and look out at the open ocean beyond the bay. The water is green, a glistening emerald with dark shadows of deeper water in patches. Or perhaps it's weed or dark rock. He starts to think back to what this beautiful woman had said about the computer expert being terrified. Stone had thought Kathy's comments seemed a little dramatic. He closed his eyes again and tried to recall more of their conversation.

7

They had left the bar and travelled in Stone's red Ford Mustang. An original 390 GT, but uprated at great personal expense. Sixties iconic cool with modern technology. A cooling and electrical system that worked, Brembo brakes, racing inspired suspension and magnetic shock absorbers and an extra one-hundred horsepower over the original. It was Stone's personal obsession and a metaphor for living in the moment, one drawn on through tragic loss. Money was no good to you when you're dead.

Kathy was quite comfortable travelling with Stone. She had only just met him, but her long-time friend had personally recommended him. She was a good judge of character, or liked to think so, and Stone hadn't said no to her proposition. Not yet, at least.

"You live quite a way out," Stone commented. There had been a long pause which had broken into an uncomfortable silence. "I thought you'd be in a fancy apartment in DC. Chevy Chase, close to the political action."

"Well, the social affairs desk *is* a pretty web-based affair. I can do it anywhere. Whenever there's a big deal happening in town I stay with friends," she paused. "It's not *that* far out."

"Where are we heading?"

"Near Great Falls."

Stone nodded.

"You know it well?" she asked.

"I know there was an unofficial raceway at an old airfield out there. I ran this down there a few times. A *run what you brung* affair."

"Racing driver, eh?"

"I'm sure Isobel told you," he smiled. "She wasn't much of a motor racing fan."

"Her loss," she said quickly. "Another mile and take the next left."

Stone slowed the Mustang and worked the windshield wipers. A misty drizzle had started and made the street lights have a halo effect. The wiper blades smeared the glass, greasy from the road spray. The street lights became more sporadic and the houses more infrequent. Great pines lined the road and Stone could see that they grew thicker and the houses were built into clearings. After the left turn Stone kept the car at around forty-five, waiting for another instruction.

"Half a mile," she said. "Then look out for a road on the right."

"Really out in the boonies," he commented.

"Suit's me. I can walk with the boys. It's relaxing to be out the city."

"The boys?"

She smiled. "My babies."

"Oh, right," he said, quite surprised she had children. He took the right turning. "How far now?"

"We're here," she said. "On the right. Park behind the BMW."

Stone eased in behind a dark BMW X5 SUV. He looked at the house. It was a take on a log cabin but designed with modern elements. It looked expensive, and the car was in keeping with both the property and the location. He imagined plenty of other faux cabins spread out in the woods. Yuppie types enjoying the great outdoors, but with good road and rail links and supermarkets and coffee houses five minutes' drive away.

"How did you get into the city tonight?" he asked, eyeing the SUV.

"My editor lives a mile up the road. We had a breakfast meeting. He gave me a lift. I sometimes do that, then get the train back and a taxi up here. The station is only two miles away. I work from home much of the time, or travel to interview sources and contacts."

Stone nodded. "I suppose that works out well for your boys."

"I guess," she opened the door and stepped out onto the gravel driveway.

Stone followed her up the pathway and the four wooden steps to the decked porch. She unlocked the door and as she opened it she reached inside and flicked on the light. There was an almighty scrabbling sound on the wooden floor and two of the biggest dogs Stone had ever seen bounded into the hallway and charged at them. Kathy held out her arms and both dogs leapt up, tongues out, forcing her to close her eyes and turn her head this way and that to avoid a slobbery licking.

"My boys," she told him.

"No shit," he said.

"Not a dog person?"

"I guess. But these aren't dogs, they're wolves. Crossed with horses. Big horses."

She stood aside and they bounded past Stone like he wasn't there and charged outside. She closed the door behind them. "I'll give them ten minutes. They've been cooped up all day. They had a walk this morning. Sometimes I have a walker come round and take them out if I'm busy."

Stone nodded. He looked around the hallway as she kicked off her shoes and picked up the mail. She walked, stockinged feet into the kitchen. "Coffee?"

"Please."

"Cream and sugar, right?"

"Sometimes."

"Black and sour in the morning."

"What else did Isobel say?"

"Not much," she smiled. "Well, not *too* much."

Stone turned to the door. He could hear scratching. "Shall I get that?"

"Oh thanks."

When Stone opened the door the two dogs came in cautiously and stood in front of him. They both stared. He looked them in the eyes and held out his hand slowly. One of the dogs sniffed him, then sat down. The other looked indifferently at him. Both were in his way. He pushed the door closed and headed for the kitchen to where he could hear Kathy frothing the coffee. Neither dog moved and as he tried to get past them, the nearest dog bared its teeth.

"Just push them out the way!" Kathy shouted. "They're trying to assert their dominance."

"*You* push them out the way," Stone murmured under his breath. He covered his crotch with his hands and slowly eased past them, his thigh nudging the dog in the head. He managed to get past both dogs, but as he looked back, both were staring at him. It was not unlike his prom date. Both of the young lady's brothers had done the same thing. They looked just as mean and ugly too.

"You got past my boys then?"

"Just."

"Here, a cappuccino."

"Thanks. They're interesting companions."

"They were smaller when they were pups."

"They generally are."

She smiled. "As pups they were tiny. My partner and I bought them when we first moved in." She sipped some coffee, then added, "We split up and I bought him out."

"Of the dogs?"

"No, the house."

Stone smiled. "I figured that, just messing." He sipped the cappuccino. It was frothy and sweet and made with half a shot of espresso. He was pleased, he wanted to sleep at some point tonight. "How about you show me what you've got."

"Sorry?"

"The work the computer guy started on."

"Oh right, of course," she seemed flustered.

"I presume you have a file or something? That's why we're here."

"I'll take you through to my office."

The office was off the hallway and Stone could see the living area as he passed by the entrance. It had a sunken lounge with a big screen television about as thick as Stone's forefinger. The furnishings looked expensive. Kathy lived well, or had a lot of credit. Either way Stone thought to afford the house and interior, the BMW parked out front and use a dog walker when she was busy, she was over and above a senior reporter's salary. But he knew nothing about her, and face value usually had no value at all.

The office was a shrine to awards and achievements in journalism. Kathy's picture appeared in various magazine and newspaper articles, commendations and accolades. From a brief glance Stone could tell by the photographs that this was earlier in her career. She had achieved a lot, but as he cast his eyes over the walls without appearing too obvious, it would appear that she had either not catalogued recent successes, or had been devoid of them entirely. Social affairs, whatever that was, did not have the same career highs.

"My ego walls," she said. But she looked at the walls as if she was a third party. It was the first time Stone had seen a flaw in her, something he did not like. Vanity. She seemed to realize this and shrugged. "I don't frame so much now."

"No?" Stone ventured casually.

"No. Bread and butter gets in the way now. I have a lot of outgoings since Mark left. He saddled me with the mortgage. It was in my name, we used his inheritance as a deposit. I found out after he left that he'd re-mortgaged the deposit figure. He got all his funds out and I'm financed up to my neck."

"Nice guy."

"No. He wasn't. During my early years in journalism I worked freelance. I aim to do it again, but for now... Well, my work with National Geographic and a host of other magazines took me all around the world. I was away a lot, building my career. Jobs on news desks in TV writing reports for broadcasts brought me back. And then with the Washington Post, I put down some proper roots. We bought this place. Both thought it would be a great idea to get the dogs. Mark, my boyfriend, pushed for them, then left and never looked back. He said I should drive them to the pound."

"He sounds special," Stone sipped the coffee. It was milky and tepid, so he finished it quickly and placed it down on a coaster on the leather-topped desk.

"We seemed to get on better when I was away on assignment. Turned out he had a couple of other women on the go. We split a year and a half ago. I've no idea where he is, so I'm stuck with too big a mortgage and the car he financed in my name as well. It's depreciated like throwing a rock off a cliff, so I can't even sell it and pay the finance company back or hand it back and walk away." She held up her hands. "Anyway, you don't want to hear all that."

"Too late," Stone smiled wryly.

She laughed. "Okay, well I promise not to drain out on you anymore." She pulled out a drawer and retrieved a manila folder. Inside were papers and a USB drive. "This is most of what Peter Edwards, the computer specialist, found. He had more for me, but I haven't heard from him for nearly a week."

"And you called the police?"

"Washington police aren't interested. Murder capital of the US. They're only interested in crime statistics and until there's a crime, they won't do anything."

"But you lodged a concern?"

"Yes."

"Well that will be on file. I'll check up on it, get a second concern lodged. I'll need his details."

"Sure. I'm not sure if the missing person concern will have been filed though. The desk sergeant didn't seem to take me seriously."

"Which precinct?"

"Fourth district. It's the nearest to where the guy lived."

"On Indiana Avenue?"

She shrugged. "I guess," she paused. "No, that's police headquarters this was on Georgia Avenue."

"I'll take it straight to headquarters. I know the police chief."

"Friends in high places," she smiled. She opened the file, brushed against him with her shoulder as she took out the papers and spread them on the desk. "That's why I'm hoping you can find Edwards for me. You have the Secret Service resources behind you. Will you help?"

Stone turned the file around and slid it across the desk. "I'm here, aren't I?"

"What will your fee be?"

Stone looked up at her. "I'm not for hire. I'll help get you pointed in the right direction, that's all."

"For Isobel?"

He shrugged, turned his eyes back to the contents of the folder. "So tell me how far your guy got."

Kathy was stroking her ear absentmindedly. She smiled at Stone, perched herself back on the desk. "If not for Isobel, an old flame, then why? You won't discuss your fee. You don't owe anything to an ex-girlfriend, although you agreed to meet me when I dropped her name." She smiled at him, and for a moment he was lost in her eyes. They were like dark pools in the light, framed by the brightest whites Stone had seen. "I think I know why. Isobel said you were born in the wrong century. She said you should either have been the sheriff of a wild west town, or an English knight. You need to help, and you live for a challenge. The bigger the challenge, the more you feel alive."

"That must be it then."

"I'm upsetting you?"

"It's getting late. Do you want me to look at the file or not?"

"I *have* upset you…" she said. "I'm sorry."

Stone wanted to tell her that her telephone conversation with him yesterday had intrigued him. He also wanted to tell her that from the second he set eyes on her he was reeled in, hook line and sinker. He wanted to tell her how his chest pounded, his stomach fluttered and he felt giddy and adolescent all over again. That he couldn't remember seeing a more beautiful woman; that he already knew he'd do anything for her.

"Let's just take a look at what you've got," he said coolly. "How about another coffee?"

"Sure," she said. She leaned in and kissed him on the cheek. Her lips were soft, warm and moist. Her hair smelled of jasmine. Or maybe it was her perfume, he was unsure. But it was a smell which fuelled the senses, awakened desires. "And I didn't mean to offend you," she added, walking through the doorway.

Stone watched her leave; found himself staring at the open doorway sometime after she had left the room. He shook his head, willing himself to concentrate.

The sheaf of paper in front of him was a type-written report. He was unsure of much of the terminology but Peter Edwards had written an overview. He explained the internet as an onion. The top layer being social media, commerce and public services. Layered below this was websites with less detail given to the big search engines. Simply put, you pay for what you get and websites created without enough metatags built in, or with poorly thought out domain names – the search criteria to enable a search engine to find it – were in this technological no-man's-land. This was the surface web. And it accounted for only 0.03% of the internet. Then below these layers, purposefully made difficult to find by encryption and codes were institutions like government agencies, investment banks, stocks and shares linkage and military information. Designed as a secure internet, a mainframe that people with privacy and security at the forefront of their operations, only accessed by those authorised to do so. This was called the Deep Web. Under these layers rested the Dark Web, because things can get a whole lot darker here. The earth's core. Only highly technical encryption decoding search programs could break these layers, and the technology was changing daily. This was where the lowest levels of society's veneer rested. This was where international criminal networks could hire an assassin, where babies could be sold, sex slaves traded, child pornography made, used and bought and sold. This was where evil lurked, lived and bred. Where it thrived.

Stone skimmed across most of this. He recognised the Tor system, short for The Onion Router. He had read documents on the dark web before. As a senior Secret Service agent, he had been involved in operations using the dark web to find transcripts from people intent on carrying out attempts to assassinate the President and senior congressmen. There was a department of techs working on the dark web around the clock. Stone had been on the heavy end, a pistol in hand and his foot against the door. He had no real affinity with the tech world, but he crossed paths with it often enough. Once Stone could find where Edwards was going with his searches, he may be able to pull a few strings and have the techs spend a few hours routing out the searches in the Secret Service headquarters on H Street and 8th.

Kathy walked in carrying two coffees. "Here, cappuccino with a full espresso and not so much milk. You might need the caffeine because you won't want to put the files down."

"No?" Stone took the coffee from her, sipped it too quickly, pursed his lips to expel the heat.

"No. But it kind of depends where you read up to." She put down her coffee, spun the laptop around, put in one of the USBs and opened a file. "Edwards got this information from the Veteran's Association. It's a list of names of missing soldiers of Iraq and Afghanistan."

"MIA? There are none."

"Sorry, I mean missing veterans. Men who are out of the military but have dropped off the grid in civilian life."

"They do that. Some will be working security, contracting in the middle east. Others will be holed up in Montana shooting prairie dogs with an AR15 and living off the grid. Some will be homeless and will filter back into society, hopefully, at some point."

"And plenty commit suicide as well," she added. "But what that list represents are men who have simply disappeared."

Stone stood over her shoulder and looked at the screen. Again he smelled jasmine, and felt her warmth. He moved away slightly. "Quite a few."

She nodded. "Now, I'll let you read the files and scroll through the USB, but the next file is a list of missing veterans over the past five years. Programmed into the algorithm Edwards used, he has entered combat veterans only, not those who merely served in Iraq or Afghanistan in support roles, but walking patrol, weapon in their hands soldiers."

"Well, it will be a hell of a lot shorter," Stone paused, watched the file open on the screen.

Next to the name was rank, unit and service history.

"See anything?"

Stone studied the list.

"Yes. It's very short now."

"A pattern is forming." Kathy held up a hand and then opened the next file. "Now, the algorithm listed missing veterans over two theatres of conflict and two tours of service."

"I get it," Stone said impatiently. "But the more criteria he put into those algorithms, the shorter the list will get. Unless he used something more general to open it up again."

"Of course," she said. She glanced up at him, she was leaning across the desk and her hips were close to him. "When Edwards put in a search of decorations, commendations and notable achievements it changed."

"It would."

"Edwards was looking for veterans who had killed multiple times. Soldiers who had contacted the enemy and had claimed and verified enemy kills against their names."

"Why?"

"A culmination from an unrelated search," she paused. "I'll get to that later." She opened up the file and it filled the screen. "Now look at the names and details. See anything similar?" She opened another file and stood back. "Here are details of the last month's bank transactions before each of the veterans went missing."

Stone stared at the file in silence.

Kathy opened another file and ran the curser over another list. She highlighted it and looked at Stone. "Edwards changed tack and went for transaction beneficiaries of the account that deposited into the veteran's accounts," she paused. "Look at the occupations."

"And Edwards checked to see if these people are missing also?"

"He did, and they are."

Stone looked again at the names on the list, their occupations and the information taken from their bank statements. He did not need to look for long before making up his mind. He raised his eyes to Kathy. "Who else have you told about this?"

8

The sun was beyond its highest point, but the heat had intensified incredibly. Stone had a rough idea where north was, assuming that he was in fact still in the northern hemisphere. He could have known exactly had he still had his wristwatch. Placing the twelve hour on the sun would have enabled him to draw a median line from east to west. All he had now was dead reckoning, but as the afternoon wore on he could be more precise.

The loss of the watch saddened him. It had belonged to his father. His mother had bought her husband the Rolex upon his retirement. Stone's father, an accountant and frugal man had long coveted the watch, but would never have spent the money on such an unnecessary purchase. Stone's mother had bought the previously owned watch on finance, and the shop had sent it away for refurbishment before she had taken delivery. Stone's father had been delighted, but had died two weeks later. The watch had gone to Stone's older brother, an FBI agent who had later been killed in the line of duty. Stone had been given the watch at his brother's wake and had worn it ever since.

He looked down on the bay, shaking the thought away. He needed to remain focused. He was still naked, still had no idea where he was, he had no idea who had just tried to kill him or why. He needed answers and he needed to formulate a plan.

He stood up decisively and headed down the headland to the beach. He would check on the warrior and take it from there. Part of him hoped the man was dead. He could not afford to release a man who had tried to kill him. The emotion triggered a childhood memory. Stone could picture a farm in a lush and tranquil landscape. Rolling green hills, trees heavy with summer leaves and a slow moving river meandering through fields of waist-high grass ready to be cut for hay. His grandparent's farm in Connecticut. He had left the poultry pen open. A fox had savaged a goose and was at death's door. His grandfather cleaned the wounds and had given the goose the night in a separate pen with food of stale bread soaked in beaten egg and milk to see if it would start to recover. The morning had come and it was down to Stone, no more than twelve-years old to put the goose out of its misery if it had made no progress. *You started it, so you finish it,* his grandfather had said. Stone had prayed on his way down to the pen that the goose had succumbed to its injuries. It hadn't and it had been the first time Stone had killed. And the old goose hadn't given up easily.

Stone hesitated, wondered if he should simply cut his losses and walk the other way. *You started it, so you finish it,* rang in his ears. Well, he hadn't technically started it, but he had left the man injured and tethered. He would have to see it through. If the man could be saved, and it seemed he would not pose further threat to him, then he would try to help him. And if he couldn't… Well, it wouldn't be the first time, or the worse thing he had done. Afterwards, he would keep moving around the beach and see what he could find to help him. There had to be flotsam and jetsam on the tideline somewhere. There would be more scallops and mussels on other stretches of exposed reef and as long as he ate enough he would last a few days without water. If that time came, Stone was sure he would find more water. He would head into the jungle. The trees could only grow with water to sustain them. And rain water would pool at the base of the hill he had seen from the top of the headland.

Stone walked across the beach with more purpose. It was important to set plans, keep focus. A survival situation was overcome by maintaining a positive mental attitude. That was what Stone had been lacking. He knew he had been drugged and he had woken into a nightmare. Hot, dehydrated, confused, scared and disoriented. His muscles near paralysed, atrophic. Well, he was up and moving now, and his senses were sharper. He could recall more from his past, and was confident he would continue to do so. He could picture military training. Twice, no, three times. Strange, but as he tried harder to remember he recalled army basic training.

Manning a large artillery piece. Unloading hell onto the enemy in a hot and dusty land. There is a flash memory, he is tethered, dragged on his knees into a line. Tough, merciless men wearing rags and robes and ammunition pouches across their chests are beheading people in front of him. A weathered man, toothless and scarred, holds the sword up to Stone and grins. He will be next, the soldiers kneeling alongside him will be next…

Stone flinched at the memory, but he needed to recall it. The sand is crimson with dark blood and heads are scattered in front of him. Some are from women, most belonged to men, but there are children's heads amongst them too. Their eyes are open, all looking upwards. It strikes Stone that the eyes have moved there after being severed. There must be a moment, however brief, when the person knows something of what has happened to them, that the head knows it has been separated and all is lost. Men to both sides of him are whimpering, sobbing. Stone realises he is also. His legs feel leaden, his hands bound so tightly he has no feeling in his fingers. His heart is racing, beating so rapidly he feels he will pass out. He hopes he will, hopes to see no more of this. Hopes to feel nothing of it when it comes.

The first American soldier is pulled out from the line. He is scrabbling and kicking out wildly but the men are tough and strong and wiry. They are used to people reacting this way and have him pressed hard to the ground and lying motionless with apparent ease. Like a panicked goat before slaughter. Stone knows the man to be tough and strong, but he has little fight left in him. The man with the sword turns and smiles at the rest of the soldiers in the line. Stone cannot hear the background noises anymore. Only his own pulse hammering in his ears. The soldier is pulled up to his knees in one swift motion, a man holding each shoulder and pulling his tethered arms back like a lever. The sword is raised, poised over the man's neck, then raises higher still, the executioner ready to strike the deadly blow. The sword moves through its final downward arc. The blood covers all the men in the line. The soldier is still kneeling, but his would be executioner drops down onto his knees beside him, sword in hand, most of his head now gone in the shower of blood and bone and brain that has covered the prisoners. Grenades explode releasing great plumes of acrid smoke, bullets ping and thud and whoosh through the compound and every enemy is cut down as he runs, stands or takes shelter. The smoke clears and a group of men, heavily armed, communicating through throat mics and signalling each other with hand signals work their way through the compound. Wounded enemy fighters are dispatched without a second thought with silenced pistols or short carbine rifles. The surrendering Taliban are killed quickly and without malice –

merely humanely dispatched like cattle. Less than two minutes and the compound has been taken and secured. Stone feels like he is going to vomit. A large, fit man bends down, slices his bonds and hands him a bottle of water. He talks in a western drawl, pats him on the shoulder. Stone does not hear what the man had said, but thanks him profusely. He is crying tears of euphoria, utter joy and relief.

Three months and a lot of paperwork later and Stone is training again. He has transferred to Airborne Rangers and his goal is to join the elite Pathfinder and Reconnaissance Unit of just two-hundred men. Those same men who had rescued him. A special forces unit that did not officially exist but still managed a three hundred-million dollars a year budget from the Pentagon. A unit that made, developed and deployed the .637 calibre long range sniper system and made verified kills of over seven-thousand metres in Syria. The short-barrelled compressed cylinder rifle used a Sabo bullet system which separated in flight to release a hyper-sonic Teflon bullet. The unit also developed *SkyWing* – a silent electric-powered dual wing entry system that enabled free-fall from forty-thousand feet, but could take its operator over one-hundred and fifty miles against wind direction to the drop-zone. The system also housed all of the operative's weapons and equipment.

Without the rescue from the elite Pathfinder and Reconnaissance Unit, Stone would have died in

Afghanistan. He had trained and worked on nothing else until he won his place on their selection course. A gruelling thirty-week programme which saw segments of training in a hot zone. Stone had been transported unofficially into Afghanistan for parts of his reconnaissance training alongside serving operatives with the elite unit. After he had passed out and become one of six new recruits to hold the numbers at two-hundred, and only the nine-hundred-and-third Pathfinder and Reconnaissance Unit soldier to serve, he had gone back to Afghanistan for his second official tour of duty.

Working in the hills, mountains and valleys of the most hostile territory on earth, Stone had numerous 'contacts' with the enemy, and had avoided as many battles to move silently and unseen through their world to collect intelligence and make his own hostage rescues.

Towards the end of Stone's tour, a senior officer with the Pathfinder and Reconnaissance Unit dropped a card with a telephone number on it into Stone's lap. Afghanistan was drawing to a close for American troops and word was the Pathfinders were being side-lined in favour of missile-armed drones flown from a hangar in Nevada and boots on the ground when required from Delta Force and the Navy SEALs.

"The cowboys and Indians days are over now," the officer had said. "A man like you needs to learn new skills, but still make use of the one's he's already got. And above all, pass them on to others. Don't hang in there waiting for another war to happen, or wishing the one we had didn't end. The President inherited this one and won't be looking for another. He's too busy closing down this one and finding ways to pay for it. With your skills, you're halfway through the training for a new career. Call the number, drop my name and you're as good as in."

Stone had called and his transition from the Airborne Rangers to the Secret Service had been handled swiftly and seamlessly by the man in the Pentagon whose number was on the blank white card. A year later and Stone was running a team of fraud investigators in the treasury. A chance meeting with the White House chief of staff and Stone ended up on presidential protection duty. After three years' rotation Stone had taken over an FBI investigation which had been run by his brother. His brother had died on that case and Stone had taken over and solved it. It was a deniable operation, but the President had seen what he was capable of, and he had remained on a duty retainer to handle sensitive cases that found their way onto the President's desk.

Stone hesitated at the point in the sand where he had fought the warrior. The sand was full of tracks and scuff marks from their fight. And drag marks up to the jungle. He had now remembered substantial, but sporadic pieces of his past, but they were enough to give him confidence in his abilities. He knew now that he had lived a life unlike many, and that he could handle whatever was thrown at him. He had seen into his past and although the warrior had been bigger and equally as fit, Stone could see that the training and service he now remembered pieces of had ultimately given him the advantage.

He was hot, his skin and shoulders in particular, sore from the exposure to the sun. He would make more mud paste to block out the sun's rays. What protection it had once afforded had been washed away with perspiration. He knew he needed water and once again, it had become his priority. He walked up the beach, following the tracks made from dragging the warrior across the sand.

Stone could hear the buzzing long before he reached it. The sound of the flies sounded like a toy drone – high pitched and constant. He felt trepidation, knowing that it came from where he had left the man tethered. He felt a pang of guilt. The flies would have been attracted to the blood and sweat. The poor man would not have been able to fend off the swarm. Stone's stomach fluttered and his legs felt heavy, leaden. He pushed the brush aside with the spear and looked down at the man, his legs motionless and his hands still bound.

It was the eyes which shocked Stone the most. They were open, lifeless and staring upwards. Like the eyes of those unfortunate souls in the remote

Afghan village who had been beheaded in front of him all those years ago. And he was transported there again. Hot, exhausted, scared and staring at the decapitated head of another man, another time, another place.

9

Kathy had copied the data onto a USB memory stick for Stone. He had no cell service, so used Kathy's land line to phone and speak to one of the tech guys at home and get him over to Secret Service headquarters, or the "H" building as it was known. Stone wanted to work quickly on it, see if the tech guy could get into the bank transfer aspect further. It was a tenuous link, but he hoped the Secret Service Treasury Department could cover an angle and therefore he could keep up with the investigation. If it was decided that it did not fit into the Secret Service's remit, then Stone had a contact in mind with the FBI he hoped he'd be able to meet with and hand over. Either way, with what he'd seen he had told Kathy that it needed official involvement from the government. He had convinced her that if he could maintain contact with the investigation, or if he could get his contact with the FBI involved, then she would be able to follow with press involvement. It wasn't strictly his promise to make, but he was senior enough to pull the right strings.

He had told Kathy he would meet her late tomorrow morning at a coffee shop he used on 14th Street, close to the White House. She had a meeting at the Washington Post with the editor so it was mutually convenient.

Stone started the Mustang and glanced back at the house to see Kathy peering from behind a curtain. She dropped the curtain and disappeared from view. The two dogs were standing on their hind legs and watching him leave from the front door. Just like those damned idiot brothers on prom night.

He turned the car around, it's V8 reverberating on tick-over. A glance in the mirror before he accelerated away confirmed that the dogs were continuing their vigil. As was Kathy, who was standing in the lounge window talking on the phone. Stone couldn't see whether it was her cell or landline, but the hour was late. Perhaps she was calling Isobel in New York and thanking her for the introduction. Or maybe it was a guy. The thought made Stone shrug. He liked her, but what had it been? Four hours? He decided to put it back in the box, there was no room at the moment for a romantic involvement and who was to say Kathy liked him too? There were the glossy eyes. She beamed intelligence, but also a coyness that Stone had found so inviting. Then there was the smile, the fiddling with her hair or her ear, the leaning across the desk with her hips swaying towards him, the brushing against his arm, the kiss on his cheek…

He smiled to himself. He would be the first to admit that despite being what the majority of people would call a handsome man, he lacked all social skills in both dating and the signal reading of reciprocated attraction which preceded a date. He often looked back on assignations and thought, *oh yeah*...When it was too late, and too much time and history had passed he would see the signal, see that he had been given a romantic green light. He was looking forward to meeting her again, looking forward to coffee with her. But he knew that the reason for helping her, for listening to her in the first instance had been more than simply curiosity. Having come out of a relationship by mutual consent, he had floundered on the dating scene, allowing work to become an excuse. His work had taken him around the nation as the President defended his presidency on the campaign trail and sought his second term in office and Stone had concentrated upon nothing but keeping the most powerful man in the world safe from harm. A good man, and an honest politician, the President was now secure in his second four-year term. As his personal bodyguard, his go to man in a crisis, Rob Stone was now able to start thinking about what lay in stall for him after the man's presidency. It was unlikely another man such as the President would come along – the presidency was an increasingly tempting platform for unlikely glory seekers and billionaire's with no talent and dangerous opinions, but with a bank account big enough to cover the tab - and Stone had decided he would step away from protection and perhaps become an instructor in the Secret Service, or bow out of government service altogether. This had left him with uncertainty, and Isobel texting him to ask him if he would meet a friend of hers worried about the whereabouts of her source had filled a familiar void. He had enjoyed the prospect of a new challenge and was curious about the woman he had agreed to meet. He had attempted to *Google* Kathy, but no photographs seemed to exist in his searches. It was unusual, given that her wall of fame had been so full. He had tried the usual suspects – *Facebook, Instagram* and *Twitter*, but Kathy Newman did not seem to go in for publicity. He had eventually found some grainy images of her connected with older stories. She had changed since those pictures, especially her hair which was now cut short in a business-like bob. He wondered who she had been talking to. He glanced at his watch, the luminous dials showed it was after mid-night. The technician should be in the computer suite on the fourth floor by now and Stone would be there within twenty-minutes.

The lights glared in his rear view mirror, the car behind on full-beams. Stone dipped the mirror and eased off the accelerator. The road was as wide as a two lane despite the single yellow line running down the centre. The car's lights filled the mirror, the gap closed to single feet. Stone dabbed the throttle and the Mustang surged forwards and opened the gap to fifty feet. The car behind changed down a gear and closed the gap back up. Stone had no idea what the car was running, but it was powerful for sure. He was in no mood for a drag race and indicated right, eased over close to the shoulder. The car slowed too, pulled around and then matched Stone's speed.

Stone had spent too long in a world where reactions kept both you and your VIP alive. Too long to be caught out so blatantly. His sixth sense told him to brake hard and he did. The gunshot rang out and Stone saw the muzzle flash flare over the hood of the Mustang. The passenger tried to follow the Mustang through the weapon's sights, but couldn't get his arm back far enough. The pistol in the gunman's hand was way out of its arc of fire. Stone had his FN Five-Seven pistol in his right hand. He took his left off the wheel and dropped the electric window. It had only lowered five inches and Stone got the weapon out and fired a sustained ten-shot burst at the rear quarter of the car. The car surged forwards and the exhaust growled. Stone tucked the pistol between his thigh and the leather seat and flicked his headlights onto full-beams to light the way, and to distract and disorientate the driver. Then he floored it.

The Mustang roared and Stone pulled back out onto the road and gained on the car. It was a powerful Audi with a twin turbo-charged V8. It surged away from the Mustang as Stone worked up through the gearbox, but the sixties coupe held the gap as the speed entered three figures. The road was wide and straight and there were no other vehicles in sight. Stone knew the road remained straight for about a mile. He glanced at the speedometer. One-forty. The Audi was fast, but limited to one-fifty-five. The red button on the dash had two words scribed in a metal plate surrounding it: *Move It*. Stone pressed it and grabbed the wheel as the boost from the two nitrous oxide canisters in the trunk hammered him back into the seat and the dial on the speedometer went on fast-forward, hit one-eighty and ran out of digits to move any further. The surge continued and the Mustang shot past the Audi like it was braking harshly. Three hundred metres clear and Stone hit the brakes and held the middle of the road. The Audi started to brake, but slewed sideways before straightening up, the driver shocked by the turn of speed of the classic. Stone's carbon ceramic brakes stopped the Mustang in half the time and the Audi filled the rear view mirror. The inevitable happened and the big German sedan slammed into the rear of the Mustang and the two cars drifted and slid out of control travelling at least sixty miles per hour. Stone straightened the Mustang and the Audi slid past coming to rest in the centre of the road. Stone got the pistol back in his hand, the sights trained on the driver's window. The Mustang's headlights shone on the trunk, but the light was plenty enough to illuminate the driver. He was a white man with slicked dark hair and was wearing a dark suit. His pistol was finished in stainless steel and glinted in the light a second before Stone emptied the rest of the magazine into the door and the man started to dance in his seat before slumping forwards, his head slamming into the steering wheel and sounding the horn.

Stone got out, changed over to another twenty-round magazine. The tiny 5.7x28mm spear-tipped, boat-tailed bullets had incredible penetration capabilities and a flat trajectory. They had sliced through the door, the driver, the dead passenger's body and the passenger door. Stone advanced, his weapon trained on the body in the driver's seat, daring him to move. He didn't, and when Stone looked inside the car, he wasted no time in holstering his weapon. He wouldn't be needing it again in this company. He reached inside the Audi's shattered window and pulled the man away from the wheel and pushed him back into the seat. The horn ceased and the night was silent again. Stone looked up and down the deserted road. He took out his cell phone and cursed when he saw there was no service. He looked around and weighed up his options. He knew Kathy would still be awake, or at least in the ball park of being awake.

And she had great coffee.

10

Stone had felt the rise of bile in his throat, but supressed it. He could not afford to waste precious fluid. He needed water desperately and the lizard brain part of his subconscious was paying attention to the details. His humanity part, the conscience and feeling part, was trying to take in what had happened, was reacting naturally.

The man did not look to have struggled. Perhaps he had been unconscious, but Stone dismissed this when he thought of first seeing the head resting in the body's lap. The eyes were wide and scared and looked directly upwards. Almost as if they were focusing on the bloodied neck of the body above it. There was a great horizontal gash in the bark of the tree. It had been made with a sharp blade and with considerable force. The body, its hands still tethered, had been unable to shift or sag. There was blood splatter a long way up the tree. It had sprayed onto the underside of the leaves and had dripped back down like dew droplets in the morning. The head would have fallen and rolled. Stone was quite convinced it had been arranged as he had found it for visual effect. There was a lot of blood on the ground. Stone kicked at the debris of leaves and twigs and the flies dispersed, as did their incessant buzzing, but they soon came back; spiralling wildly in the dank air and pitching back on the body, gorging themselves on the blood.

He cut the bonds and the body slumped to the ground, the head rolling a few feet before resting still. He retrieved the leather plaited braids, knowing he would find a use for them, then took the makeshift dressing he had plugged the wound with using the loin cloth. He then turned and left the scene and returned to the beach. He had the knife and the spear with him and laid them on the shoreline with the length of leather binding as he entered the water. He washed the loin cloth and put it on. Part of him felt ridiculous, like he was auditioning for a Tarzan movie, but it was a relief to cover his nakedness and the material would have many uses now that he had the means to cut it and create cordage for traps or makeshift fishing net or line.

Back on the sand, Stone picked up the rope and weapons and struck off towards the next headland. He wanted to put in some distance between the body and himself. Not merely because of the macabre scene he had witnessed, but because there was somebody else here. Someone ruthless with an agenda unknown. Someone who would take the head of a man left wounded and helpless and tethered to a tree. Someone who had just committed a cold-blooded murder. Someone who, for all Stone knew, could be watching him from the cover of the thick jungle.

The headland was lower than the previous two. It was a swift climb to the top and Stone observed the bay ahead from above. It looked a treacherous terrain of sharp rock and jagged reef which was starting to become exposed as the high tide started to drop. His feet were sore from what rock and debris he had stepped on so far, and he was aware that what lay ahead should be treated as a last resort. To his left the headland disappeared into the jungle. Behind him lay the two bays he had already crossed. He reasoned that he should hole up somewhere for the night, and by the height of the sun and the fade of the light, he imagined reaching the scene of the murder at about the optimum time to rest up. It wasn't an option. The sky had started to turn grey on the horizon. The wind was light, but onshore. The greyness would reach landfall sometime tonight, hopefully bringing rain and some relief from the heat as well as precious clean water. But if it rained heavily, he would also need shelter. Even in the tropics, over-exposure to rainfall would make the cooling temperature unbearably cold.

Options weighed, Stone headed off the headland and into the jungle. He switched the long knife to his right hand and the spear to his left. The blade was sharp and heavy and would make light work of the foliage. The spear was ready not only to strike an attacker, but to push branches out of the way and hold thorns away from him as he eased his way through.

The going was tough. After the first fifty-metres, Stone turned and could not see the fringe where the jungle had met the headland behind him. The only sky he could see was directly above him. Patches of blue with scudding white clouds framed in the canopy of the jungle. The heat was far more humid and intense in here, and the slight breeze that he had felt on the headland had disappeared completely. The light was dim, and occasional shafts of sunlight cut through the canopy like searchlights. Stone rested against a smooth tree, listening. The only sounds were that of insects and small creatures scuttling on the jungle floor. His breathing was heavy and he sweated profusely. He knew he would need water soon. And food. Perhaps going back to the reef where he had eaten the shellfish would have been his best choice. He turned around, but felt disoriented. He was sure he had approached from the area directly behind him, but he had turned and looked at the shafts of light, walked to the tree to lean against and rest his legs. He couldn't swear to the direction.

He cursed himself. He was sure that the beach had faced south. That would put the median line of east to west at left to right across the beach as he faced the ocean. He tried to work out where the sun was, but all that he had to go on were the occasional piercing shafts of sunlight. He tried to recall what angle the shaft would have to run to indicate direction. He felt himself over-working the problem. It was getting late, the sun would be heading west, but what angle would the shaft take? Forty-five degrees running right to left. But the shafts seemed to hit him head on. Which way was that? He closed his eyes and breathed deeply. He needed to quell the anxiety. Needed to try and be rational. He did not need to work out the angle – he knew it already. He needed to put the light where he wanted it. He opened his eyes and calmly turned on the spot until the shafts of light shone from right to left. He now knew which way was south, and therefore the beach. It was all a matter of perspective. He needed to remain calm. No good decision would ever come out of panic or desperation.

And then, as if a gift from the gods, the canopy dripped with droplets of water and with each minute that passed the drips become stronger and heavier until they ran over the leaves and branches in rivulets. Stone sucked the water from the tree trunk he had rested against. The sky had dulled and he now lost his brief idea of direction, but he didn't care. He could feel the water flooding his system, making his kidneys and liver function more freely, slow his heartbeat and make his stomach feel wonderfully full. He still did not have anything to store or carry water in, but for the moment, his thoughts were filled only with taking in the gift and sustaining him for a while longer.

A memory flashed, but the terrain in this snapshot was deciduous forest. He was cold, but thirsty and there was a group of bedraggled soldiers in overcoats and ill-fitting boots. An escape and evasion exercise. Basic training somewhere, sometime. But it was enough to trigger his survival training. Snapshots of fire lighting, of shelter building and bush craft.

Stone looked at the trunk of the smooth tree, its bark running with water. He took the knife and dug the blade into the bark. He ran the blade around it until it met the initial cut. He then repeated the process a whole two-feet lower. Then he drew a vertical line with the tip of the blade and dug behind it, using the blade and his fingertips he removed a large, thin section of bark. It was like thick paper. He shaped it into a cone and then dug a hole at the base of the tree and shaped the bark into the hole. Satisfied it was both free from holes and in one piece, he pulled the edge of the bark sheet so that it touched the tree in the centre of a steady rivulet of rainwater. The bark visibly filled with clear water as he watched. The downpour continued and Stone spent the next thirty-minutes or so preparing another three water traps. When he had finished, the first one was over-flowing and he dropped down onto the ground and sucked it up, drinking his fill. He turned and looked at the other water traps which were well on the way to filling. His spirits were lifted and he cut three more sheets and made more wells. Next he worked on numerous sheets of bark quadruple the length. He laid them against a tree while he chopped a number of thin branches. He arranged them in a series of A-frames, sticking the ends in the soft earth and wedging them together using natural knocks and tiny growths of branches until they held. He then rested the bark sheets on top and draped them over the sides. It was raining heavily and Stone drank more water from the water traps and carefully made sure he left them positioned to continue filling. He climbed into the tight space of the shelter and was pleased with his handiwork. The odd drip came through, but it was otherwise extremely effective. He was starting to dry already. When the rain stopped and the jungle dried, he would gather what he needed to start a fire. For now, he was happy to be cool, but dry and thoroughly hydrated. He watched the drops of rain hit and bounce and splash on the surface of the water and his mind started to wander. He was coping with being here, thrust into this situation. But how did he get here, and why? He tried to recall the next meeting with Kathy. And then he remembered that things had started to get weird.

11

Stone looked over the rear of the Mustang in the dark. It had started to rain and the flashlight picked up the fine mist in its beam casting a searchlight onto wherever it shone. The impact had been substantial and had knocked out both rear light clusters and driven the chrome bumper deep into the trunk, which in itself, had pushed upwards into a pyramid. He stepped away, knowing it was likely that the impact would have twisted the chassis. Well, that was what insurance was for. He just knew that wasting the two men in the other car was going flag up something negative during the claim process. The thought made him smile.

The downstairs light was still on inside Kathy's house. Stone switched off the flashlight and walked up the pathway. The dogs met him. The same look as the two idiot brothers on his high school prom night. To his surprise they did not bark, just stared silently and menacingly at him. He looked at them as he drew back the brass knocker and hammered the plate fixed to the door. The dogs continued to stare at him. He had never known dogs like it and they unnerved him as the stared him out.

Kathy looked hesitantly around the corner of the corridor. Stone was backlit by the porch lighting. She frowned, then smiled when she recognised him. Her hair was damp and she was still dabbing at it with a towel. She was wearing only a satin ivory night dress. Sheer and revealing. Low cut. Stone felt his pulse quicken as she bent down and ushered the two dogs out of her way.

"Hi!" she said, as she opened the door to him. "I just got out of the shower," she paused. "Early start tomorrow. I just want to grab my jacket and handbag and go. What are you doing back here?"

Stone stepped in and closed the door behind him. One of the dogs stepped in between him and Kathy, leaned its weight against Stone's knee. "Did you tell anybody you were meeting me tonight?" he asked.

"No, why?" she frowned.

"Are you sure?"

"Yes. What's wrong? You're scaring me a little."

"I've got no cell phone signal," he said. "Could I use your phone?"

"Sure," she replied. She still wore the frown. "What's happened? Is everything ok?"

"Auto trouble."

"It's in my study," she said. "You know the way. Fancy another coffee?"

"Sure. I'm wired anyway."

Stone went on into the study. He called 911 and gave his name and details of his Secret Service seniority. He explained the scenario and asked the dispatcher for the police, coroner and fire service and left Kathy's address and number for a contact. He heard Kathy behind him and turned around as he replaced the receiver. She was standing in the doorway with two cups of coffee. She had put a red towelling dressing gown over her night dress. It was comfy and although hardly alluring, she managed to wear it well. Although it was far less thought-provoking than the ivory satin underneath.

"What do you need all that for, I thought you had car trouble? Has there been an accident?"

Stone walked over and took one of the cups off her. "I ran into some trouble. Two armed men. They shot at me then chased me," he said. "I can't help thinking it had something to do with your dark web story."

"Oh my god! Are you all right?" She had her hands held up to her face, then seemed to realise that merely by the fact that he was standing there her question had been answered. She looked a little more composed and asked, "Why would it?"

"Well, your computer guy identified missing war veterans with recent deposits made through the dark web into their accounts before they disappeared. The money appears to have been paid by the same source, albeit from a convoluted system of accounts and financial companies. Nothing a good forensic accountant couldn't untangle. But he was on to something strange, something potentially ruinous for someone with something to hide and it would appear, a great deal of money to spend."

"So we've stirred up a hornet's nest? Edwards and me, that is."

"And now me," Stone said. "Because both of those men are dead, and they will have buddies for sure. They'll want their vengeance. And for them to be on to you, to risk killing a government agent, then they must have backing. Hopefully just financial, and not political."

"Oh my god!" she exclaimed. "You killed them?"

"It was them or me."

She shook her head. "This is terrible. Why political? What made you say that?"

Stone sipped some coffee and shrugged. "Just a hunch, but those guys looked like spooks. Or former spooks. Just a feeling. The expensive car, the way they dressed. They wore shoulder holsters and carried identical pistols. Hoods don't wear shoulder holsters. They tuck a gun in their pants and if things go south they toss the gun and are clean. The evidence has gone. You can't do that with an elaborate shoulder holster, the clips and ties that attach to your belt to keep the weapon secure. And they were professional. Their drills were good, but I taught those drills and counters to the best the Secret Service has to offer. I knew what was happening just before it happened. Good for me, bad for them."

There was a knock at the front door and they both looked up. Stone went first. The dogs both stood between him and the front door. Neither one moved. *Give me a break!* Stone thought.

The man at the door was in his late thirties or early forties. He stood patiently, his identification wallet held open and pressed against the half pane of glass. Stone looked at it and opened the door.

"Detective Rawlins, homicide," the man announced and put the wallet into his inside jacket pocket. "Are you the reason I've got to write up reports all night?"

"You've seen the vehicle?"

"I have. Pretty efficient job. Damned car looks like Swiss cheese. Now, do you want to run me through it, step by step?"

"It's pretty straightforward really," Stone said. "I left here at around mid-night. The car picked me up at the end of the road, followed me, got too close and I speeded up. I thought it was some redneck wanting a drag race. I pulled over and the passenger started shooting. I fired back, gave chase and overtook them…"

"You overtook them? In a sixty-eight Mustang? That fancy pants German sedan had over five-hundred horses."

"You don't say," Stone said. "They took off the decals. I figured they wanted a stealth car."

"I saw the engine. Big V8, twin turbos."

"Figures. It had a good turn of speed."

"But not enough, eh?" Rawlins smiled. "Say, can we go somewhere with a table? I want to make some notes."

"Sure," Kathy said. "Can I get you a coffee, detective? We seem to be ignoring the basics of getting a night's sleep anyway," she smiled.

"Thanks. Black, no sugar," he turned to Stone. "Now, how about that table?"

Stone followed Kathy towards the kitchen. "Can we use the study?" he asked.

She turned and nodded, but her expression was aghast as she looked past him. "Rob!"

Stone felt the movement, sensed it in the air. He dropped low and moved to his right. As he looked back, Rawlins was clearing the pistol from its holster. He kicked out and caught the man in his knee, but it was a glancing blow and the man was still on his feet as he toppled to one side and fell into the wall, knocking a framed print to the floor and smashing the glass. Stone fell onto his knees and scrabbled up, one of the dogs getting in his way. He lunged at the man and caught hold of his right wrist, pulled hard downwards and took control of the weapon. The man was fast and kicked out. Stone twisted and the blow missed his groin and glanced off his hip. He swung a back fist and connected with Rawlins' chin. The man yelped and swung a punch, but Stone kept hold of the man's gun hand and blocked the punch with his right forearm. He barrelled into him, but Rawlins was strong and fit and pushed back hard. Stone reached for his own pistol behind his right hip in a soft leather holster. Rawlins pushed harder and the two men shuffled backwards and into Kathy, who was standing in the hallway apparently frozen to the spot. Rawlins dropped the pistol and it clattered to the floor. Stone let go of the man's wrist and pushed him hard in the chest. Rawlins fell into the other wall, clattered another print off its hook. Stone got a good guard up and shuffled forwards with a series of punches. Rawlins blocked and ducked and took a couple of hits, but he boxed back and caught Stone on the chin. For a moment Stone wobbled, but ducked and bobbed back up with his guard in place. He'd been scrappy in the confines of the hallway and the surprise had kept him on the back foot. He had a little distance now, and he would fight better now that he had chance to eye his opponent and study the man's guard and stance. Kathy bent down and reached for the pistol on the floor, but Rawlins lashed out and punched her to the floor without looking at her.

And that was the end of it for Rawlins. He was a dead man. He did not see the attack coming. A ferocious onslaught, leaving the man defenceless. Both dogs leapt on him and both dogs each weighed a hundred and twenty pounds or more of bone, muscle and sinew. And teeth. They roared and growled and their jaws gnashed and snapped. Their teeth ripped and tore and their claws held the man still while they did it. Stone stepped back, astonished at how quickly they had dominated the man. He looked at Kathy and her eyes met his briefly. For a moment he was sure she was smiling, but her expression switched imperceptibly and she looked as terrified as he'd ever seen a person. She held her swelling eye, transfixed on what the two dogs had done to protect her. She was shaking, her hands quivering. She was in shock.

It had only been seconds, but Rawlins was dead and the two dogs stepped back, licking their lips and padding around the corpse. The man's throat had gone. The spine was visible amongst the fleshy mess and he had bled out as he had writhed in fear and agony. The dogs started lapping at the thick clotting blood, smearing streaks through it on the polished wooden floor.

Stone stepped around one of the dogs and gently, and to his mind in light of what he had just witnessed, carefully placed a hand on Kathy's shoulder and guided her into the kitchen.

"I…" she hesitated.

"I know, me neither," he said. "They were protecting you. They're just animals at the end of the day. They did what came naturally."

She had wrapped her arms around her waist, comforting herself. "But why?"

"Rawlins, you mean? He wasn't a cop. Something wasn't right. As soon as you called out I knew. When he pocketed his ID wallet, I caught sight of his gun. A stainless steel pistol, leather shoulder holster. It was a custom Colt forty-five model 1911. Cops don't carry those and they rarely wear shoulder holsters these days. And those forty-fives were what the dead guys in the Audi were carrying. I only saw a flash of silver when he replaced his wallet, but at the time I didn't take it in."

"But how?"

Stone held up a finger to his lips to silence her and looked around him. "Get your car keys. We're going for a drive."

12

Stone was dry and fully hydrated, but he was incredibly hungry. He rested with his back to the tree and his legs tucked up. The graze to his hip was sore, but now significant bruising was coming out. This indicated that he had injured himself only recently, but still he had no idea how or when. The rain had stopped, but the jungle did not get any lighter. It had passed to night and although he could not recall having been to the tropics before, he seemed to know that the nights came quickly. He had no way of knowing the time, but it was a long night. In the height of the trees he could see the eerie glow of eyes, most probably large fruit bats. He did not want to risk injury climbing for one, but in the morning he would try to spear one from the ground when he had enough light to see by.

He slept little; permanently aware that somebody had killed the warrior and that same somebody could be hunting him also. He started to become paranoid about having his back to the tree. The same sort of tree that had borne the slash mark of the sword or machete that had taken the man's head. He had to calm himself, assure his paranoia that he was hidden, that the shelter would hide him from view and that the jungle floor, a sodden carpet of snagging overgrowth and fallen debris, would give away any would be attacker long before they got close to him.

He awoke with a start. He had not expected to sleep, and he experienced an unnerving vulnerability at having let down his guard. The light was brighter and shafts of light crossed his path and he knew he was facing south. He stepped out of the shelter carefully, stood and listened. The jungle smelled pungent, rotten. The temperature was hot and close. There was steam rising in places as the rainfall evaporated. He needed to press on, to get to the hill and see what he was up against, see if he was in fact on an island, or whether he would stand a good chance of following the coast to a settlement. Life was going to be too difficult in the jungle, the coast was making more sense.

Stone drank the rest of the water. The water traps would only spill and be difficult to carry, and water was best carried in the body. Never ration, always consume. He placed the sheets of bark on top of each other on the ground, dismantled the shelter and rolled them all up together. He bound them with the cord and fastened the roll over his shoulder. They were a precious resource and he was sure he would need them again sooner or later. He looked at the canopy, there was no sign of the fruit bats in the daylight. He had been sure that they were nocturnal creatures. If they were resting, then they should have been hanging from their perches now, and not last night in the darkness. There was no sign of them now and he had not witnessed them leave, but he would be ready for them tonight. Maybe he would see them come in to roost, if that was the term for what bats did to sleep.

He headed inland, supposing he had got the direction to the beach correct, and after two hundred metres of working his way through the thick undergrowth, the jungle started to noticeably thin out. He could see fifty or so paces ahead. The sky was suddenly visible; blue and cloudless. The sun burned the side of his face, but after the claustrophobia of the thick jungle, the searing heat was a blessed relief. His pace quickened, and the ground was dry underfoot. The freshness of the air was a relief also. It was still hot and humid, but the air was less heavy and the dank smell which seemed to stick in his nostrils and coat the back of his throat had gone. Already he was thirsty, and he knew that when the body felt thirsty then it was already dangerously dehydrated, so once again finding water was going to be his priority.

The ground opened up further and the trees gave way to pampas grass and clumps of thorny bushes. Banyan trees towered in sporadic growths and as Stone looked at a particularly large area of trees, he realised they were surrounding a large pond. He quickened his pace and as he neared, a flock of colourful birds took flight and his spirits were lifted at the thought of food and water being his for the taking.

He dropped the spear and the knife, took the roll of bark off his shoulder and jumped into the water. It was cooler in temperature than the air, but not by much. It was reasonably clear; he could see his own feet as he stood chest deep. He swam a few strokes, dived down and came back up rubbing the water around his face. With any luck there would be fish and crayfish to catch. He tasted some of the water on the tip of his tongue, and it seemed clear and clean enough. He sipped some, then drank heavily. He knew there would be organisms in it that should be boiled, but he did not have the resources and he needed to make his choices accordingly. It was more important to drink and hydrate his organs than to avoid what sustenance he could get and waste energy looking for or crafting something to boil the water in, only to fall ill due to dehydration.

He swam to the bank and was about to grab a branch to pull himself out when he realised it was a crocodile's snout. He froze in the water, his eyes staring at the green glass-like eye of the animal. Mentally he figured the creature to be on the wrong side of huge. He was in a quandary – the animal would be fast near the water, capable of snapping and lunging with great speed. But if the animal got into the water, then it was in its element. It would have the speed, agility, the underwater eyesight and Stone wouldn't stand a chance. One bite, one solid hold and it would spin in a death-roll and snap his limps in two. Stone kept eye contact with the beast, lowered off the bank and eased himself back into the water. Still he kept his eyes staring into the creature's lifeless eyes. He could see the reptile's nostrils flare as it breathed. Stone eased to the side. One pace, two, three… and then he lunged up the bank and rolled to his right as the crocodile lunged and snapped and he heard the jaws and teeth bite together just a few feet behind him. Still Stone kept moving, rolling and then when he rolled onto his stomach he jumped up and ran twenty-feet clear of the bank. He turned and saw the great creature, it's head backwards, its jaws high in the air. It held its chest high off the bank with its stubby front legs, its back in an inverted arch. It slowly lowered its head back down and rested still. It did not take flight into the water and it did not turn to seek a follow-up attack on the lucky prey. Stone saw the knife and spear on the bank and he walked cautiously towards them. He picked up the spear and the crocodile still did not move. Stone could see the beast looking at him, its left eye at the back of its socket as it watched, yet kept its head towards the water. It was keeping its options open, its escape into the water a mere fraction of a second away. Stone came up on it from behind. The animal could not see directly behind itself, but still did not move. Stone wondered whether its arrogance or lack of fear was simply due to the fact there were no natural predators. An evolution of confidence and indifference. Stone realised that the animal was at least twelve-feet long from its snout to the tip of its tail. It was black in colour with a light, creamy-coloured underbelly. The back was armoured with great jagged scales, raised and prominently high on both sides of the animal's spine. Stone raised the spear high above his head and as he got up to the tail, his feet either side of it, he threw himself on top of the crocodile's back and plunged the spear into the back of the animal's skull. There was a brief struggle and Stone released the spear, got his hands down onto the snout, forcing it closed and adjusted his weight over the animal's back. The animal struggled less, and Stone got his right hand away and onto the haft of the spear. It took all of his strength, but the spear drove deeper and the animal went limp. Stone got to his feet, but kept the spear in place. It had been a quick death, certainly quicker than his grandfather's goose all those years ago. And now his spirits were at the highest point they had been since he had woken on the beach yesterday morning. He had water and he had food. Now all he needed was fire.

Stone pulled the spear clear and walked around the animal. Near the bank he noticed two wooden posts had been driven deep into the ground. There were pieces of rope frayed at the base and he picked them up. It looked as if somebody had attempted to construct a trap. Perhaps they wanted to kill the crocodiles for their skins. Stone looked at what had been constructed but couldn't imagine what purpose it would serve. But he knew the frayed rope would make good tinder for a fire. He tried to wriggle the posts free, but they had been driven deep into the ground with a heavy sledge hammer, and he could not be bothered to waste his energy on them. There were smaller pieces of firewood around and he could simply pick them up. He caught hold of the animal's tail and pulled it back from the bank. It was heavy, at least two hundred pounds. He wanted some distance between himself and the water. Where there had been one, there would be others. He reflected, almost humorously, upon how lucky he had been swimming in the pond, but he needed to keep alert. And not just for other caiman or alligators or crocodiles, or whatever the hell they were. He needed to be alert for the person who had killed the warrior.

13

Kathy drove her BMW X5 and Stone rode in the passenger seat with his weapon drawn and resting in his lap. He was watching all around him for a vehicle following, or one waiting by the side of the road. He had put down the vanity mirror and angled it so that he could keep a lookout behind them.

Unsure what to do with them, and still repulsed at what she had witnessed in her house, Kathy had woken her neighbour, sold him a tale of a breaking story and asked if he'd take care of the dogs. The neighbour had been practically asleep on his feet, his wife calling down from upstairs the whole time to find out what was happening. Kathy apologised profusely, told the neighbour she was sorry and that she would make it up to them. Stone got the impression it had happened before, although not at such a late hour.

The crash site had been deserted. There was no Audi and no debris. No broken glass, no bullet casings and no traces of broken brake light clusters from a 390 GT Mustang. There were tyre marks on the highway, but nothing else. They could well be tyre marks from any other auto-incident, or rednecks lighting up their hot rods with burnouts. It was the most thorough job Stone had ever seen, and the political angle remained with him as well as the financial. The clear-up would have taken resources, mainly personnel, but that was difficult to organise in itself. And sending a man to assassinate them at such short notice meant some serious connections. If these were not men from a government agency, then they had to be ex-government agency employees. Perhaps ex-CIA. And in Stone's experience, ex-CIA personnel were often used when the CIA wanted deniability. If it walked like a duck and sounded like a duck…

Stone had got back in the BMW and told Kathy to drive them into the city. He had a cell phone signal now and he made a few curt calls. The first had been to his tech guy, but had gone straight to his voicemail. The next had been to the Secret Service Domestic Security Rapid Reaction Unit. Quite a mouthful, but not as difficult to remember as the acronym. He explained what he wanted and was told it would take two hours. After swearing profusely and making a few threats, a small team was sent to secure Kathy's house and await the arrival of the rest of the team. The coroner would arrive after the rapid reaction team turned up to sweep the entire house for electronic surveillance equipment. Stone had also told of his suspicion that the landline had been compromised in order for the 911 call he had made earlier to have been intercepted and impersonated. Again, he felt sure that there was either a rogue government angle, or that whoever was behind it was well connected financially and had employed ex-government agents.

His cell rang seconds after putting it back in his pocket. He took it out again. No number was displayed. "Stone," he answered curtly.

"Special Agent Stone, this is Agent Andrew Reece, duty officer."

"Nice shift you got yourself there, Andy."

"Yeah, whatever. It is what it is."

Stone knew Agent Reece. The two hadn't always got along, but it was currently amiable. Stone had some seniority with Special Agent status, though he never pulled rank more than he had to. Reece had taken the fall for a sting that had gone wrong. To lure a counterfeit and money laundering gang out of hiding, he had lobbied the higher echelons to use real money. A lot of it. The money went missing and the gang gave the treasury agents the slip, and although after a somewhat protracted inquiry there was no further comeback or suspicion resting on Reece, he was manning a night desk for the foreseeable future. So much so that he was talking of heading into the world of private security and flipping his middle finger at the Secret Service.

"What's the problem?" Stone asked. His attempt at humour hadn't seemed to have worked on the disgruntled agent.

"According to Ramirez's wife, you got him out of bed and into work around midnight."

"So? Tell him to call the union," Stone replied tersely.

"I guess he would if he could," Agent Reece paused. *"He stopped at a set of lights on Chevy Chase. Took a bullet in the head. Car-jacking gone wrong, the police have called it."*

Stone hesitated. He knew the man well, was saddened and shocked. "Was he still driving his Prius?"

"Yes."

"Kind of old and dented for a car-jacking, wasn't it?"

"Can't all drive Pebble Beach Spec Mustangs."

"Ouch."

"Sorry. No, you're right. Connected to what you've stirred up?"

"That's my thinking. Too much of a coincidence. He was a tech, but he was level three field agent trained. And all service personnel are required to carry a sidearm, due to the heightened terror alert. He wasn't going to fall foul to some junkie who fancied a new ride. And who the hell is going to steal a well-used Toyota Prius?"

"I'll send a team round to liaise with the police department."

"Thanks. Can you reiterate that the line was tapped and that they impersonated a dispatch operator? These guys have probably packed up and shut down, but it's worth checking junction boxes for signs of tampering as well as listening devices at the house."

"Okay. What is all this, Rob?"

"Trouble," Stone said. "Nothing but trouble."

14

Stone found the branches he wanted on the ground. He cut some of the seeding heads of the pampas grass and scraped the ground with the spear to gather the debris he needed. He chose to pick up fallen wood because it wasn't green and would burn better than live wood. Next he examined the spear and using the knife he hacked the last ten inches or so off the shaft and chopped it down to a fine point. The spear shaft was hard and dry. He split a fallen branch down the middle and cut a vee to the centre halfway through. He gathered some fine debris as tinder and piled it on the ground. He took the pieces of frayed rope he had found by the curious-looking manmade frame and pulled out the fibres until it looked like a large pile of hair. He then placed the branch on top, split side up with the vee above the tinder. He placed the point of the hard spear shaft on the vee and started to rub the stick between his hands, the point drilling into the vee. After a few minutes, the wood at the vee started to smoulder, and fine, burning saw dust spilled out onto the tinder. Stone stopped and blew gently. It didn't take, but he was ready for that. He spent the next half an hour or so repeating the process and re-adjusting the tinder and a piece finally caught. Stone got down on his belly and blew carefully, a steady stream of air to the base of the smouldering, blackening pile and the tinder burst into flames. He carefully placed small pieces of wood and debris on the flames, then after a few minutes he arranged larger twigs and sticks until he was confident it would take some larger branches and continue to burn without the risk of being smothered.

Stone turned to the crocodile beside him. It was a surreal scene, and for the first time since he had awoken on the beach, he smiled. Then he chuckled. He picked up the knife and figured the tail would be meaty and offer the easiest part to butcher. He had skinned a deer once with his uncle after a rights-of-passage hunting trip and imagined it would be similar. He found the skin tough, but the underside was easier to cut through and he managed to get a few strips of meat off the carcass. He cast his eyes over the ground around him and noticed a few rocks scattered in places. He found a flattish one and placed it in the middle of the fire. He banked the fire up on all sides and placed the strips of meat on the rock. He could forget about them now and turned his attention to digging some holes to line with the bark water traps near the fire. Then he set off to the pond and tentatively kept an eye out for his dinner's companions while he filled the traps with a large wrap of bark which made a useful, if wobbly bucket. The water traps would hopefully clear as the sediment and any living organisms dropped to the bottom.

Fire, water and food done, he looked for a suitable place for a shelter. The sky was a crystalline blue with a few wispy clouds. It did not look likely to rain, but it was the tropics and one could never be certain. The fire would provide comfort, but he had to treat his situation as hostile. A man had tried to kill him, and he in turn had been slaughtered. The murderer was still at large and Stone had to assume that his life was under threat. He would rig up a shelter in the fringe of trees. He would be far enough away from the crocodiles, yet able to survey the pond and open area. And he would hear someone approaching from his rear, the overgrowth and jungle debris would alert him of that.

He cut a number of metre-long sticks, fastened them with the cord and lined the frame with the rest of the bark sheets. It did not take long and he had a small and discreet A-frame shelter which would afford him a sanctuary from both rain and hostile eyes.

The fire was burning nicely and had glowing embers to each side of the rock. The pieces of meat were sizzling and had turned from a dull blue-white, like a raw tiger prawn to a brilliant white like steamed chicken breast. Stone cut into one and it was the same colour all the way through. He took that as a good sign and hooked all three pieces out with the knife and laid them on a piece of the bark sheet. He sliced another three pieces off the carcass and noted the huge quantity of flies that had gathered. The meat would spoil in the heat soon, and he would have to find a way of drying some of the meat into jerky or biltong if he was going to benefit further from the kill. He put the second helping of meat on the hot rock, banked up both sides once more with large branches and sticks and sat back to his meal. He was ravenous and devoured the first steak quickly. He had never previously eaten crocodile or alligator, or whatever the hell it was, but was surprised how good the meat was. A little like chicken and lobster in the same mouthful. It was good and he worked through the meat in no time. He drank plenty of water down, but it was lime green in colour and he noticed a few bugs swimming in the bottom. He didn't dwell on it, previously experiencing food poisoning and feeling that much of what people felt was psychosomatic. He felt he had literally thought himself ill in the past. He would maintain a positive attitude and wait for illness to strike. Hopefully it wouldn't, but if he did not maintain his fluids then he would become ill anyway.

He sat back and stretched. He was full, satisfied. He would wrap up the steaks when they finished cooking and eat them later. It was pure protein, so he would be hungry sooner than if he had eaten carbohydrate. He was starting to reflect how he had dominated the situation and had either found or created food, water, fire and shelter when he noticed how low the sun had become. There was less than an hour until dusk by his estimation and he was amazed at how quickly the day had gone. But he had everything he needed. He wrapped up the meat, left the fire starting implements next to the fire and made his way back to the shelter. He had no idea if the smoke from his fire had been seen by the person who had killed the warrior, but he was not going to take the chance of somebody seeing the flames in the darkness. The fire would soon die, and he was confident that he would cut some untainted meat from the crocodile in the morning. Then he would travel further and see if he was indeed on an island. If he was, then hopefully he would see more islands and set about making a raft or paddle board from what he could find.

As Stone nestled into the shelter with his cooked crocodile meat wrapped in the bark he settled down in the gloom and noticed the glowing eyes in the trees once more. The fruit bats, or whatever they were, had settled into the trees for the night, but he had not noticed them come in to roost. Their eyes were unnerving. He would try and get one with the spear tomorrow and carry it to his next camp. He could see the flies buzzing around the crocodile's carcass in the light of the fire. He hoped he would be able to salvage some of the meat, but perhaps the smaller fruit bat would be a safer bet.

He sipped a little of the water out of a sheet of bark. It did not hold much, and he noticed that it was leaking. He closed his eyes as he sipped the tepid liquid and pretended that it was coffee. The thought spiked a memory of drinking coffee with Kathy. He did not know how long ago, but the memory was vivid and fresh.

15

Stone had got the coffee on and poured a couple of cups. It wasn't as refined as Kathy's professional barista machine, but it was hot and strong and the cream was fresh. Stone had some seniority and UHT cartons did not make it up to this floor.

Kathy was pale. Her Asian descent gave her a little paleness, emphasised by her jet black hair, but grief and shock tended to have a paleness all of its own. Her hands shook a little too.

"God, that was horrible," she said. She did not look up from her cup, which she nursed between both hands.

"I've never seen much like it either," he lied. Stone had seen many things. Although he had to admit, it had been the last thing he'd expected. "Those dogs have your back, that's for sure."

"I don't know what to think," she said quietly. "I don't want them harmed, but… won't the authorities want them destroyed?"

"They were defending you."

"I know, but part of me even thinks it would be for the best," she sniffed, close to tears. "I mean, they killed a man."

"A man who tried to shoot me. A man who hit you, who would have killed you after he had killed me. For sure." Stone sipped his coffee and opened his laptop on the desk in front of him. He put in the flash drive and opened the next file. "How much of this have you read?"

"Most of it. Edwards had more. He was really excited about what he had. This was what was prompting him to talk about the paper publishing a book, or serialising a large piece."

"Did you get to talk about what he discovered?"

"No. He was cryptic."

"And it involved military veterans," Stone mused. "The money is significant. Our tech guys will get on to it. They handle all the Treasury Department's work, they're good at what they do. A team are on route now. If it can be found, these guys will find it."

"Where are they?" she asked.

"They will be here soon. A team of close protection operatives are bringing them in. They'll work from the computer suite downstairs. They have the most powerful hardware and the fastest secure internet connections."

"Why are they under protection?"

"The tech guy I called from your house was killed on his way in."

"That's awful!" she held her hands to her mouth. "Was it connected?"

"That's what we need to find out. Washington PD are on it and I've had a team of Secret Service operatives sent over to liaise with them."

"What happened?"

"Carjacking gone wrong," Stone said a little tersely.

"And you don't think so?"

"No."

"Why?"

Stone put down his coffee and turned back to the screen. "He had a pretty shitty car." He shrugged. "A family run-a-bout with scratched paint and dings all over it. Curbed wheels, the lot. A Porsche or a Range Rover is one thing, but a well-used Prius? Open-topped roadsters in the summer time are the main cars to get *jacked*."

"It's late summer," she ventured.

"It just feels wrong. Nobody jacks a Prius." He opened another file and stared at the screen. "Besides, the man was trained to a basic field operative level, which meant he had plenty of range time under his belt. He knew how to use a firearm, and use it well. Recent terror level alerts have made it compulsory for all of our support staff to carry a loaded weapon, at all times. On or off duty, and especially commuting to work."

"It can still happen."

"No doubt. But a carjacking is one thing, a professional hit is quite another."

"And you think it was a professional hit?"

"Yes. In light of what happened at your place," he paused as she flinched at the thought. He

113

knew she'd never see those dogs in the same light again. "I used your phone and I think they listened to my conversation with him and moved quickly. They have the resources and they have the motivation. Which means they know we are now in possession of the files and have probable cause to look into it further and shut down their operation. So we need to get moving on this and work out what Edwards had."

"And we need to find him," she said. "Which, in light of what has happened, seems less likely than it did earlier this evening. Finding him is our priority."

"If Edwards is still alive, then there's every chance he soon won't be…" The phone on Stone's desk rang and he picked it up. He spoke briefly then replaced the handset and turned to Kathy. "The tech guys are here."

They walked down the corridor and took the elevator down the four floors to the computer suite. Stone swiped his card to access the room. There were cameras covering all the angles and Stone knew that the footage was time-stamped. Stone's security clearance was at the highest level and he had access to most departments. Kathy was under Stone's umbrella as part of his investigation, but she was lucky to be with Stone, and lucky at the lateness of the hour. He may well not have got her in the building in the middle of the day. Not without a mountain of paperwork, at least. The building was quiet at night and there were less officials walking the corridors. The investigation was not yet official, and Stone had used a lot of resources so far. He would have a lot of talking to do tomorrow. But he had always found it easier to beg forgiveness than to ask permission. He did not like to think that his tech guy's death would help him, but if he was honest with himself it would seal the deal when it went before the chiefs. The Secret Service would be on it like a limpet until the end now. They didn't like to lose one of their own.

They turned around as a man entered the room. He was clean-cut and smart, but a little geeky. He was younger than Stone by almost a decade, and young enough to carry off a little quirkiness to his dress sense. To Stone he looked like someone wearing a school uniform, but under extreme protest. The shirttails untucked, the tie a little low. But it had been fashioned so, and as the man walked across towards them, Stone noticed the trouser hems were high and *Bart Simpson* looking up at him from one of his socks. *Comic Book Guy* was on the other and Stone imagined the man having time off for Comic Con every year. The man held out his hand, Stone frowned, shook it and stared at the man's tie. It was a novelty reference to MS-DOS computer systems. Stone lost interest before the punchline.

"Max Power," the man said. "I'm the team leader. Pleased to meet you, Special Agent Stone."

"You're shitting me."

"No," the man smiled. "I really am pleased to meet you. Your reputation is the stuff of legend."

Kathy smiled. Stone looked back at the man. "Max Power?"

The man smiled. "It's John, really. Maximillian is my middle name, after my grandfather. On my mother's side. Power was thanks to my dad. I got to college and suddenly thought *Wow! The girls will love this!* And did the 'ole switch-a-roo to my middle name. shortened it to Max, obviously…"

"Obviously," Stone interrupted.

Max smiled. "And there it was…"

"An instant hit," Stone smiled.

"Well, more or less. A bit less," Max said. "Well, actually, a lot less…"

"But it's an interesting anecdote," Stone smiled. "This is Kathy Newman. She's the reason you're here." The two nodded to each other. Kathy was smiling. She'd obviously enjoyed Max's anecdote a little too much. "We need to get down into the dark web."

"How deep?"

"As deep as it gets," Stone replied. He handed Max the USB and nodded to the file on the desk. "We have a missing computer and web specialist; we think as a result of what he found there. We need to find out the what, where and who behind it. It involves missing US military veterans and many of them had

116

deposits of between five and twenty-five grand deposited into their accounts shortly before they disappeared."

"By the same account?" Max frowned. "That would be sloppy."

"It looks to have come from a veteran's charity, though not one I've heard of."

"So what aspect of the dark web are we dealing with?" Max inserted the USB and started tapping keys. Stone barely saw what the technician had typed. "A charity wouldn't route accounts and transactions through layered web. They are on the surface, clean and accountable. Do you have your key-in card, agent Stone?"

Stone fumbled for his wallet. He pulled out an orange card similar to a credit card and gave it to Max.

"This will help you," the technician said, keying in the digits. "I'll route everything to your cloud which means you will also be able to view what I find on outside terminals." He smiled. "Plus, if I uncover a shit-storm, it will have your computerized fingerprints all over it. That will hopefully still allow me to draw a service pension." He handed the card back to Stone. "Here, tap in your user ID." Stone did so and as he stood back, Max's fingers went much the way as a concert pianist's. The screen flashed and the front page of a program, or what looked like an app appeared and Max clicked through to the search bar.

"We are interested in what these veterans were paid for. My guess is that Edwards, the computer expert, found something either shocking or potentially ruinous for somebody, hence his excitement and cryptic reasoning that his fee should change and that my paper could serialise a piece or publish a book about it," Kathy said, watching Max's progress intently. "Edwards was talking about it like he was wired."

Max nodded. The screen in front of him looked nothing like *Google* and his search keywords were written like strings of programming code. At least that's what it looked like to Stone. The searches were fast though, and Stone remembered hearing somewhere that the Secret Service's mainframe was as powerful as anything that the NSA or NASA had at their disposal.

Stone looked at Kathy. She was leaning on the desk studying the screen. The reflection played in her glossy eyes and seemed to make them sparkle. She was concentrating and pouted a little. Women simply shouldn't be this good looking. How the hell was a man to get things done in their vicinity? He was staring a little too hard, a little too concentrated when she looked up at him. She frowned at first, then smiled when he snapped back to it. The smile was warm, and her lips parted a little to expose brilliant white, perfectly straight teeth. Orthodontist work through her teenage years; nothing natural was ever that good. Stone looked at the screen, then glanced back and saw she was still watching him. The smile was coquettish and she leaned ever so slightly into him as she turned her eyes back to the screen. She was almost touching him now. It had been left up to Stone to close the gap.

16

Stone looked up into the trees but there were no signs of the fruit bats. He hadn't seen them fly into the trees and he hadn't seen them leave; but he had seen their sinister looking eyes watching him through the night. A reddish, amber glow that unnerved him and snatched at his chances of sleep, and with it brought fear of what else was out there, unseen and deadly. The death of the warrior had unnerved him. He was tired and his head throbbed like a bad hangover. He was thirsty again, almost constantly so. He recognised the signs of dehydration, and he knew he had not drunk enough, but the bugs and larvae had put him off and he knew he needed to purify the water somehow. He had been lucky, he had not been ill through the night, but if he continued to drink dirty water then it would only be a matter of time. Perhaps if he got the fire going and put in some rocks and waited until they were hot enough, he could drop them into the water traps and boil the water that way. Yes, he was sure that would work. A few rocks would raise the temperature adequately and kill the bugs and bacteria. He had a plan, and that was enough to raise his spirits once more.

Stone froze, suddenly aware of movement across the pond. The man stood at the fire and kicked at the embers. He was tall and fit-looking and wore khaki safari trousers and a vest jacket. He carried an old Springfield M-14 rifle with a large optic on top. Stone couldn't identify it from his distance of sixty metres or so, but the scope was a powerful wide-angle model with at least ten-times magnification. The rifle was obsolete, but was still in service with US Navy SEALs and Marine Recon snipers, and a favoured mid-range sniper weapon for the rest of the military. It was a heavy rifle with polished wooden furniture, but chambered in powerful 7.62x51mm NATO calibre. It was a semi-automatic weapon with a twenty-round magazine. Stone had been equipped with one for a three-month tour of duty in the Secret Service's advanced security detail; scanning rooftops as a counter-sniper and waiting for the President and his motorcade to arrive. He had spent plenty of time on the range with one and knew what it could do in capable hands. Which was why he was still sitting motionless and not intending to move until he watched the man further.

The man crouched and touched the ashes of the fire. He rubbed them between his thumb and forefinger and the dust crumpled and fell to the ground. The man took notice of the drop. Stone figured he was gaging wind direction and speed, as well as the temperature of the burned-out fire. He stood and took off his floppy hat, held it up to the sun and looked at the sky. Stone felt a shiver run up his spine and tingle at his neck. The man was a hunter. And Stone felt sure he was the prey.

The man's movements were minimal. He strode over to the crocodile's carcass, prodded it with the muzzle of the rifle. A cloud of flies dispersed and buzzed around his head. He crouched down, wiped a finger on the exposed meat and then sniffed his fingertips. He stood up slowly and looked at the ground around him. Stone noticed the machete attached to his belt. Could that have been the weapon to take the warrior's head? Stone was sure of it. The thought had crossed Stone that the man may be a rescuer. Someone who knew of Stone being stranded somehow and was searching. But the evidence of the camp would have brought on an attempt to make contact. Surely the man would call out Stone's name? Use a radio or cell phone to contact other rescuers?

The man would know that Stone was close. The kill was only hours old and the fire would still have some heat to the ash. Stone wanted to know for sure. Wanted to make contact. Wanted to see the man's intentions.

The man studied the ground and dropped down on his haunches. Stone watched, knew that the man was starting the process of tracking. He was searching for a tell. A broken twig, ground into the dirt to point to the weight of the footstep and the direction of the pressure behind it. Or a toe print. A pressing heel – something to give a sign to the next clue. Stone knew that some people were extremely good at this skill, and once they found a couple of tells, they would be off like a bloodhound that hit the scent.

Stone eased his way out of the hide and stepped backwards into the jungle, he had the spear and the knife, but had to leave the bark wraps and the remainder of the leather rope. He kept his eyes on the man as he walked. The man was tanned and weathered, his hair almost white. It wasn't grey, just so blonde it looked bleached.

From deep within the trees, Stone studied the man. He moved with minimal effort, a comfortable grace. He was now twenty-feet from the first tell, and heading towards Stone's shelter. Stone backed up again, his eyes not leaving the man or the clearing in front of him. He froze as the man shouldered the rifle and scanned the treeline with the riflescope. He could feel the crosshairs travel across him, but still he did not move. The man tracked the rifle well past. Stone realised that he was by now, both tanned and dirty and had somehow blended into the foliage. Movement was critical and a key factor in concealment. Taking the opportunity with the man aiming his weapon further along the treeline, Stone slowly and carefully lowered himself to the ground and kept his profile as flat as he could. The man sighted back along the treeline, then lowered the rifle and studied the ground once more.

Stone's breathing was calm, but his heart was beating so loudly that he would swear he could hear it, and that the man would too. His head ached, already he was dehydrated. The man was too, and he unfastened a canteen and drank thirstily. He had another on his belt. They both looked big, at least a litre and a half in each. Stone found himself craving a coke or lemonade, a cold beer or iced tea. He wondered if the man had sweet orange in the canteen. He tried to concentrate. He knew he should be thinking more about the rifle, and the man's intentions.

Stone shuffled backwards on his belly. He needed to get further away, but he did not want to go so far as to take his eyes off the man and lose him in the jungle. The man was concentrating on tracks where Stone had cut branches for his shelter. The footprints were jumbled and the man needed to find another tell.

Stone watched. He ignored the spiders and scorpions, the thought of snakes coiled and ready to strike at his feet as he continued to ease himself backwards into the thicker undergrowth. They did not matter, they would move out of his way, or they would strike. What mattered was the man, the hunter. He had found the direction of Stone's next point of travel and was striding confidently towards the shelter. The hunter had seen it and there would be little distance between them soon enough.

Stone was in a quandary. This was wild and remote terrain. Dangerous crocodiles, snakes, spiders, scorpions – who knew what else? Maybe this man was trying to *save* Stone. He had a rifle, but that could be for protection. The machete was merely a tool that was needed in a place like this. Maybe this man was trying to find the warrior, or the person who killed the warrior. He could be a local law enforcement officer or a park ranger, for all Stone knew. If Stone remained hidden, then he may never get out of this place. If he attacked the man, then he could be in worse trouble.

He was about to stand and call out, but noticed another man on the far side of the clearing. He was dressed in US Navy SEAL pattern camouflage. He carried a machete in his right hand and had a small rifle held loosely in his left. He was following a trail, by the look of it, and stopped to stare at the water. He looked around the clearing and froze when he saw the other man, just yards from Stone's position. He sheathed the machete and shouldered the rifle. He seemed to hesitate, then dropped to one knee and took careful aim.

Stone pushed himself up. "Get down! There's a man with a gun behind you!" he shouted.

For all his menace and tracking ability, the hunter jumped out of his skin, shocked at the sight of Stone. He hesitated, then turned around. There was a hail of bullets and the trees and branches were peppered with rounds as the other man some hundred metres or so distant, fired a burst that went wide as the hunter turned. Stone ducked his head as the bullets pinged and zipped and some ricocheted off the hard wood of some of the larger banyan trees. The hunter glanced back at Stone, turned his rifle and fired. Stone rolled and crashed his way through the undergrowth as the heavy 7.62mm rounds sliced through everything in their path. He kept moving and got to his feet and ran, several large trees now between him and the hunter.

The hunter had his weapon up and was more composed as he turned around and fired at the man across the water. He fired single shots, each one aimed carefully. He rose to his feet and advanced towards the other armed man, who looked to have taken a round and was on his knees. The hunter stopped firing and made his way carefully, tentatively out of cover and across the open ground. He skirted the pond and the fly-infested carcass of the crocodile and Stone watched him as he advanced on the small slope towards the other man. For a moment he was out of sight, in the low ground and then that's when it went noisy again. The man in the SEAL fatigues was up and charging down the slope, firing bursts of two or three rounds at a time and by the time the hunter got his weapon aimed, he had taken rounds in the chest and fell backwards. The SEAL kept moving, his machete unsheathed and scything downwards as he was on top of him. There was an audible wet-thwack of a noise and Stone saw the SEAL bend down and come back up with the hunter's head held high on the tip of the machete.

And then it got a whole lot worse. Because the SEAL looked directly at Stone from across the water and pointed at him with the machete and the hunter's head impaled on the tip and started to laugh.

17

Stone hadn't leaned in and closed the gap between himself and Kathy. She hadn't said much as she had driven them both to his apartment and he showed her to his bedroom, where he had then taken the couch. After a few hours' sleep, he had showered and put on some clean clothes and set the coffee machine to do its thing. Kathy had showered and was wearing black pants and a white satin shirt. She looked as gorgeous as he remembered from the night before, remembered from his dreams. She dropped her overnight bag on the polished wooden floor next to the coffee table.

"Coffee?" Stone asked.

"Please." She smiled sweetly, Stone guessed she was over him not reciprocating her blatant advance.

"Here," he said, passing her a cup. "Cappuccino. It's better than you'll have at headquarters today. He glanced at her bag. "We'll get you checked into a secure motel later."

A meeting had been set with the leader of the Secret Service Domestic Security Rapid Reaction Unit and with Max Power, who would have pulled an all-nighter in the computer suite. Whatever he had, Stone would send him away for a few hours to freshen up and grab a bite to eat, then get him back on it.

"What do you mean, headquarters?" she asked tentatively.

"To look into what has been discovered so far."

"But I have to go to work," she said, somewhat irritably.

"Not until we have carried out a threat assessment and assigned you some protection," Stone said. "You can't go home either."

"What?"

"Kathy, a man tried to kill us in your own home last night. Your place is undoubtedly bugged and has been under surveillance for some time. Your house is compromised. From this moment on, you are at risk and we can't assume you will be safe to simply carry on with your daily routines."

"And the Secret Service will provide all that?"

"No. But the FBI do. I'll look at this for as long as I can, but the feds will have to take this over. It's their skillset."

"But I don't want them involved!" she snapped. "I wanted you to look into this discreetly, keep the newspaper angle for me to write the piece or the book that Edwards deemed it to deserve!"

"Kathy, I've tried to help…"

"You blundered in and shot two guys to pieces! Now the whole Secret Service are involved!"

"So?"

"So? So it will be black-bagged. There'll be secrecy all over it, press orders and non-disclosure. I won't get my story! I need my fucking story!"

Stone glared at her. "You came to me, Kathy. I killed those two men because of what you, or at least what Edwards found out. You may well have been killed by the man impersonating a cop if it weren't for me and your stupid dogs."

"I know!" she snapped, then softened. "I know. Ok, I'm sorry. You were just helping, and it's not like you *had* to. I don't even know why you'd *want* to. I just…"

"Need to get it back."

"What?"

"Your career," Stone said. "I've seen the photos, seen the awards. Your career has stagnated and you're running out of time."

Her eyes flashed, and for a second were even more beautiful with anger behind them, but they softened and she nodded. "I'm on my last chance. Contracts might not get renewed unless my rating in the paper goes up. I'm on my ass with the mortgage and loan repayments and my résumé is dated in real terms so my employment options are limited." She sipped the coffee and put it back down on the counter. She wrapped her slender arms around herself and looked vulnerable, childlike.

Stone wanted to comfort her, but his inner voice, the one that always held him back, told him not to. It was the voice that had told him to stare straight ahead when a senator's wife had flirted recklessly with him. The inner voice that had refused a bribe when he had heard too much. The inner voice that had told him to step aside so that the love of his life could restart her marriage and give her child his father back. The inner voice that had kept him regimented and just, sanctimonious even.

And unhappy.

Stone reached out and hugged her close. She resisted for no more than a second and hugged him so tightly, so desperately he hoped it would never end.

18

Stone's heart was pounding, his lungs heaving. He crashed through the jungle desperate to put distance between himself and the man in the SEAL combats. His mind raced as he ran, but struggled to process what he had just witnessed. What he *did* know though, was that whatever the intentions of the hunter, the SEAL's were definitely murderous. The kill had been premeditated. No challenge given, no quarter relinquished. That man had killed the hunter and had taunted Stone with his prize. Was he the man who had taken the warrior's head? Stone was now sure of it.

Stone realised that during his escape he had dropped the spear. He had also left the leather cord and the water traps at the shelter. Only the knife remained, clenched in his hand, his knuckles white from gripping it like a lifeline. He knew he was heading west, because that was towards the end of the pond and he had run parallel to it. Only now, after fleeing and crashing through the undergrowth, ducking broken limbs from trees and dodging vast clumps of thorny bushes, he could not swear to his direction but did not dare to stop and ascertain his whereabouts. He simply had to flee.

There was a thunderclap of gunfire and the branches of a clump of saplings in front of him fragmented and splintered. Stone hit the ground and scrambled to his right. The vegetation was thorny and he winced as three-inch thorns stuck into him, the tips barbed, the stinging an indication that they were toxic. He pulled at them as he got to his feet and veered off to his left, deeper into the jungle. More gunfire, more plants and branches splintered. Stone knew the man was close, either firing at the direction of the noise he was making, or he had in fact seen him and was toying with him, shepherding him into a killing zone.

Stone reached a large tree, its trunk wide enough for him to stand behind unseen. He stood still, breathing hard. He listened, but the jungle was silent. Not even the animals made a sound, their world erupted by sound and chaos.

The first gunshot rang out. Then another. Stone both heard and felt the impact in the tree trunk. He had no fear of the 5.56mm round going through the tree, but the man would circle soon, and that would be it.

"Come on out!" The voice was southern. Deep south. Maybe as far as the Bayeux. "Don't mess with me, boy!"

Stone eased out slowly. The man was near, just a few paces. He had gotten in close. Stone hadn't heard him approach. He was worried. Scared even. He knew the emotion was uncommon to him. He held the knife loosely. The man smiled, nodded to it, then smiled as Stone dropped it on the ground.

"Just tell me what's going on," Stone said earnestly.

"You'll find out soon enough," the man drawled. "Now, get back the way you came, boy."

Stone turned and walked slowly back through the jungle. He was aware of the man behind him, but did not turn to look at him. He was making plans in his head, formulating order and possibilities. So far, he had nothing.

"Where are we going?" Stone asked. He slowed, but felt a sharp dig in his kidney. He buckled to his knees, turned, but the man had sprung back two paces already and had the compact M4 rifle aimed at him.

"You'll see," the man said slowly and spat just past Stone's ear. "Just get your ass up and keep walking. And work your way left a bit. You sure ran yellow, boy! Like a scared little girl! No clue where you were going, hell, you don't even know where you've been! Taking off through the jungle like Tarzan! Shit, I'd have loved to see you swinging on a damn vine!"

Stone grit his teeth. Partly because his bruised kidney was on fire, partly because he wanted to beat this guy to death with his bare hands and he realised he may never get the chance. The jungle thinned out once more and Stone could see the pond ahead of him. He gave the guy his dues, he knew how to navigate through the dense terrain.

"Where now?"

"Are you going to do the Tarzan yell for me, boy?" The man laughed. "I'd like to hear that!"

Stone turned around slowly and looked at him. "I'm not yelling like Tarzan," he said. "And I'm sure as hell not squealing like a pig for you either, you fucking redneck." Stone didn't take his eyes off him, and the man seemed to lose their staring contest. "I said, where now?"

"Get over there by the lake."

Stone turned and walked near to the bank. The water was green, but reasonably clear for the first few feet below the surface. He was suddenly thirsty. He looked behind him and saw the man looking at the trees above. He was turning, looking for something he'd either seen or wanted to see. He looked back at Stone and pointed with the rifle.

"Get on your knees."

Stone shook his head. "No, I'll stand, thanks."

"Trust me," the man said. "What I'm going to do, you'll want to kneel down and relax. Stretch your head out a little, even." He drew the machete, the edge glinted in the sun. "Don't be proud, take what it is. It's over. Turn around, do what I say and you won't feel a thing."

Stone turned around and looked at the water. It was still clear, inviting. He was so thirsty. He could see his own reflection. He could see something else too. Ripples on the surface. They shimmied his reflection slightly. His legs were shaking from exertion and adrenalin. He eased himself down onto his knees. The man approached cautiously. He stood to Stone's right, the machete in his right hand. He raised it above his head and held it there for a moment, then suddenly lifted higher, then brought it down hard.

Stone was already moving left and low. He pivoted and came up at the man's knees. He hooked his arm around the man's knee and pulled hard. The man's leg gave, his foot caught against Stone's leg and he was pivoted forwards and towards the water. The machete struck the ground, and Stone heaved with all his strength and stood up, driving through powerful thighs, engaging his core for maximum strength. It was a classic judo throw and worked on the push-pull principle. Physics did the rest. The man sprawled into the water and made a tremendous splash.

Stone stood and watched. He had seen the caiman; seen the ripples it had made on the surface as it glided gracefully and slowly towards him. Ten-foot plus in length and two-hundred pounds of muscle, teeth, bone and scales. He had taken his chance, played along, but the man had not known what Stone had seen. He hadn't known what else Stone had seen all those years ago and miles away in Afghanistan. He had witnessed men taking heads, had witnessed their arms poised above their victim's heads, then raised higher for extra momentum, that moment before they struck. Stone knew this, and had seen it in the reflection on the water.

The caiman was thrashing wildly, round and round, taking the man into a death-roll. Already, the man's limbs were like that of a rag doll in a washing machine. They had long since broken as the body had been spun at an incredible speed, and the man would be drowning by now. Stone was still transfixed. And almost as immediately as the attack had happened, the caiman disappeared with its meal and the water went still and tranquil once more.

19

Matters were going to get complicated. The hug had become a kiss and the kiss had become a frenzy of need and want that had succumbed upon the kitchen countertop in a writhing, thrusting few minutes of complete animalistic, uninhibited passion. It was the kiss which had done it. Kathy's lipstick was sweet and reminded Stone of summer punch, of deliciously ripe berries. Her lips were as soft as sliced strawberries. The best kiss he'd ever had. He soaked her up, her taste and smell, and it fuelled his desire further. Her scent was of jasmine and her neck had been soft and warm to his lips. They had moved to the bedroom, where the pace had been less frantic, though mutually pleasurable for both of them.

Kathy rested her head against Stone's muscular chest and slowly traced her fingertips over his torso, taking her time as she fingered his scars, like she was reading the pain of his past through braille. Each scar silently told a story. She was wrapped around him still, soft and moist. Her skin flushed red, her breathing still rapid.

Stone was relaxed. He had been out of the dating game for a while. He was relieved, and yet surprised it had happened in such a way. It hadn't seemed real, like watching a film where the scenario seemed unlikely. A simple hug, turned to so much more within seconds. He'd always thought such events to be implausible. He was glad to have been proved wrong.

Looking at his watch, Stone said, "We'd better get going."

"Again?" She smiled. "I thought you'd need a rest."

"I meant, back to the office," he said. "Max will have been working on it most of the night; we need to see what he's found."

"And the armour is back on, the façade back in place."

"What?"

Kathy rolled over, taking the bedsheet with her. Stone felt vulnerable, ironic in light of what they'd just done. He rolled his legs off the bed and sat with his back to her. She had stood, the sheet covering her. "You're guarded. You don't let anyone in for long. And then it's all business again. Rob Stone, the President's bodyguard. His number one agent. Is that how it was with you and Isobel? She said you were a difficult man to get close to. Now I can see why."

"I'm not discussing that with you," he said coldly. He got up and padded over most of his clothes to the bathroom. He looked back at her, naked and unashamed. "Get yourself dressed. It's *your* business we're dealing with here, not mine."

Stone closed the door and ran the shower. He turned the dial down all the way to cold water and stepped in. The spray was icy, but it suited his mood. He soaped up and rinsed. In a little less than a minute and he'd washed away not only Kathy's scent, but his irritation at her. He towelled off and wrapped the towel around himself.

She had struck a chord. He knew he lived for his job, but he hadn't expected Isobel to have discussed such matters with Kathy. He was surprised that Isobel had broken a confidence. But his anger hadn't been at the emotional or intimate details of their relationship; it had been at his relationship with the President. He was the operative of choice for the most powerful man in the world. He had once told Isobel this, and she had gossiped it to a friend. He knew, in that instant that there would never be another chance with her, that part of his life was over. And now he had fallen for her friend. And already, a day after first meeting her, she was commenting on facets of his character that had first driven the wedge between himself and Isobel. Either he had to change, or he had to hope he could enjoy his own company more. The latter would undoubtedly be simpler.

Maybe he could change a little. He was already considering stepping down after the President's term. He wasn't going to serve the men waiting in the wings. They had no moral fibre or integrity. Maybe he would see if he could start something with Kathy, use her words as a catalyst to improve himself. He smiled. Or maybe he could just enjoy the ride for a short while until it crashed and burned again. Such was his life; such were his relationships.

He opened the door and saw that her clothes were no longer strewn across the bedroom floor. Maybe she was cooking eggs, getting some coffee on. He pulled on his trousers and shirt, found his socks and smoothed out the black silk tie as he walked into the living room. The room was open-plan and Kathy was not in the kitchen cooking eggs. She hadn't got the coffee on either. She had gone.

Stone picked up his cell phone and dialled her number. He had called her once before, to arrange the meeting at the bar in response to her messages. Her phone went straight to voicemail. He didn't leave a message; she would know he had called by checking her cell phone's call history.

He was annoyed with her. Last night had shown that there were hostile forces with deadly intent who would not hesitate to kill, and whose resources were formidable. She was at risk, and putting herself in harm's way by leaving his company, the protection he could offer. He put on his tie and tucked the tails inside his shirt. He favoured a clip-on leather holster and tucked it inside his pants and fastened the clip to his belt. He holstered the FN Five-Seven pistol and clipped on the spare magazine pouch with its twenty-round magazine. Lastly, he placed his new Spyderco folding knife, with its wicked-looking serrated edged blade, in his pocket. He had carried a folding knife for most of his adult life, but had grown used to his brother's knife. Given to him by his sister-in-law at his brother's wake, he had recently lost it in Oregon. It pained him to be attached to trinkets and possessions, but like the Rolex on his wrist, a gift to his father upon his retirement, he had few, but they meant a great deal to him.

Stone lived on the third floor. He had chosen it, because of the number. Not that three was lucky, but because it was a six floor building. Safe from ground floor crime and attack opportunities, the third floor had escape routes both up and down and to the sides. Stone took the stairs and opened the door to the below ground parking. Another two flights and he was in the bowels of the building. The lighting was good – something he had addressed with the building management – and the whole level lit up as he stepped out from the permanently lit stairwell. His Ducati XDiavel S motorcycle rested on its stand next to the empty space usually occupied by his classic Mustang. The bike was a new purchase, part of his mid-life crisis. In Stone's mind, the only crisis would be in not being able to *afford* to have a decent mid-life crisis. He had nobody to consider, so spent what he earned and never lost sleep about it. His father had died two weeks after retirement with a heart and head full of unrealised dreams. His brother, an FBI agent, had been murdered in the line of duty leaving a young wife grieving and unable to move on. Stone had no dependents and lived his life accordingly.

He swung his leg over the frame, righted the bike and waited a few seconds for the oil to level out again. After he put on the open-faced helmet he started the bike, keeping his hand on the clutch, kicked up the stand and tapped the shift down into first with the ball of his left foot. The bike lurched forwards as he eased out the clutch lever and he was up from first, through neutral and into second before the end of the garage and the steep ramp into the street. Bikes had changed since he had first learned to ride, and as he bounced off the top of the ramp, he grinned as he accelerated harshly and the traction control eased his rear wheel back into line, allowing him to corner and put the power on all at once.

Stone usually made the ride in eleven minutes. Today he felt reckless. He was still angry at Kathy for putting herself at risk. He managed the ride in a little under ten. It took longer to get through security and ride the elevator up. He stopped and got two coffees and Danish pastries on the way at the second floor cafeteria. When he entered the suite he saw Max concentrating on the screen.

"Breakfast," he said. "Did you get anything?" Max swivelled round in his chair. His eyes were bloodshot. "You went home, right?"

"Nope," Max reached for the coffee and sipped some immediately. He eyed the Danish and Stone handed him the bag. "It's addictive. Digging, that is." Max took a mouthful and was halfway through the Danish with the second bite. He drank down some coffee and looked a little more relaxed, a little less wired than he had when Stone first walked in.

"Where's the rest of your team?" Stone asked. "They went home, right?"

"Compartmentalised," Max said through a mouthful of pastry flakes. He pointed to a window on the screen. "We are all on separate tasks, on individual machines. We have an open-chat window running. Most like the quiet so two guys are logged on in records and the girl just left for a few hours to shower and do what girls do."

"Which is?"

"No idea," he shrugged.

"So, the salient facts," Stone said. "Edwards?"

"I've got a list of his addresses over the past five years, his social security number, his tax returns and three cell numbers for him. I even have his licence plate number."

"That's good," Stone sipped his coffee and perched on the desk. "If we lodge it with the police, do an APB."

Max smirked. "Yeah, ok Kojak. Jesus, how old *are* you?"

Stone stared at him. "About ten years older and five promotions and pay-scales higher." His eyes softened. "Go on then."

"I got into his vehicle's tracker system. He showed finance payments on a Mercedes E-class coupe. It's a pretty sweet ride, I figured he'd need a tracker on something like that to satisfy the finance company and insurance. I have the GPS coordinates of where it's parked up right now."

"Nice." Stone caught Max looking at the second Danish pastry. He nodded for the man to go ahead. "And these payments?"

Max nodded, but a little less enthusiastically. "They trace back to a Panamanian bank, Anderson-Lucas, part of Anderson-Lucas Holdings."

"Doesn't sound very, what? Spanish?" Stone shrugged. "I think it's all Spanish down there."

"It is. República de Panamá. Bordered by Costa Rica, and Columbia. Columbia is officially South America. So Panama is Central America."

"Wikipedia?"

"Yes."

"Ok, so what about Anderson-Lucas?"

"British. Well-established as a bank, but has a dubious reputation in recent years. They bought out businesses in the last recession and sold them up. Financed the re-sell with large interest loans, sometimes funding three or four ownerships down the line. They broker so-called payday loans in Britain."

"Why *so-called*?"

Max shrugged. "It's a big thing there, the financial ombudsman is catching up, but rather late to the party. Two to four-thousand percent on a few hundred pounds and the people are paying thousands of pounds off a year for life," he paused to take a bite of the Danish and talked as he chewed. "The idea is to have a small loan until payday, but it seldom seems to work out for people that way."

Stone nodded. "So the payments trace back how far to this bank?"

"They've done a good job, or at least tried to. The money has gone through the British Virgin Islands, Switzerland, Andorra – the usual suspects – and culminated in Panama."

"To whom?"

"That's where it stops," Max said. "It's a number, not a name. I can't get any more."

"A numbered account? I thought those were practically non-existent since nine-eleven?"

"As part of the fight on terrorism, accounts have to be transparent. It's less common, but this account is practically firewalled in itself. I can't dig any further."

"We have an extradition treaty with Panama, don't we?"

"True."

"So I'll get the wheels in motion."

"But we have no crime," Max replied. "Extradition is for the extradition of known criminals to face trial. So far, no crime has been committed."

"We have missing people who were all paid from an account held at Anderson-Lucas, Panama. How many other banks do they own?"

"None. All their financial activity is via call centres in Mumbai and various internet sites. The money is released from the bank in Panama City."

"Then I'll go down there and have a chat with the director."

"It might not be as simple as that."

"Because?"

Max opened a window on the computer screen in front of him and pulled up a newsfeed. It was from the British newspaper, The Guardian. "Because Richard Anderson, CO of Anderson-Lucas Holdings disappeared on his yacht five days ago in the Caribbean. He was due to return to England next week for a Commons Select Committee Inquiry."

"What the hell's that?" Stone looked bemused.

"It's the way the Brits get things done when they don't have enough evidence for an arrest. Their former Prime Minister attended more than one over the invasion of Iraq. What happens is representatives from all political parties are selected to question somebody like Anderson, very publically and with the press and media recording, when they have been less than straightforward with the truth. It was almost a foregone conclusion that he would be hauled over the coals and possibly prosecuted for financial offences." Max finished the Danish pastry. "There's a lot of show-boating and the politicians relish the camera time, interrogating the person in the chair, but Anderson-Lucas Holdings have other concerns in the construction industry and electronics, and there has been pension fund discrepancies. As in, there isn't anything left in the funds."

"So he was finished."

"It would have been no surprise if he didn't show, and the press speculated that he would go somewhere the British have no extradition, relations or authority over. At least until things cooled and he started to put things in order. But for his whole family and yacht to disappear?"

"And who's left in charge of Anderson-Lucas Holdings? And who is Lucas?"

"Lucas is a misnomer. Early on, Richard Anderson wanted to look established, so he crafted a business persona. There is currently a struggle to see who is in charge."

"A power struggle." Stone mused.

"No. I think people are tossing the hot potato as soon as they catch it. It's a mess."

"And let me guess; there's no money left in the bank?"

"Exactly."

20

It wasn't the death of the hunter that troubled Stone. It wasn't the shocking display in the pond of the caiman ripping the man to pieces and his agonising screams prematurely silenced as he drowned, choking on the bloody water, his limbs ripped from their sockets as he was spun relentlessly. It wasn't even the death of the warrior, the look on his face, the severed head amid the flies and steaming jungle heat. It was the fact that the hunter had gone. His head *and* his body.

Gone.

Perhaps another crocodile or caiman had taken both. He knew alligators wandered for miles in Florida. Onto golf courses or into housing developments. But he would have seen one feeding back at the pond, or there would have been tracks and scrape marks from the beast's belly as it climbed the hill to the hunter's body. Maybe there were wild dogs or big cats here. The crocodile had been coloured black along its wide back, and Stone thought black caiman were indigenous to South America. So perhaps there were jaguar also. But a big cat like a jaguar would take either the head or the body. It would not come back on a shopping trip. And survival instinct as it was, given a jaguar's substantial size and power, it would have taken the body. A black panther? Stone was not sure whether the two were one and the same throughout South America. Merely coloured differently. But it was as he thought of the caiman and the insight of something remembered from the *Discovery Channel*, that he was confident that he was in fact somewhere in the tropics of the Central or South American continent. For all the good that would do him. But at least he had a ball-park location.

He stared down at where the dismembered body should have been. There were no animal tracks. No sign that an animal had started to feed. No sign that the body had been dragged. Stone got down and knelt on the grass and stroked his hands in the soil. The ground was wet, but when he looked at his fingers they were merely muddy, not red. He smelled his fingers. Three days without washing and he wished he hadn't. But he could detect a faint smell of putrefying blood and was certain that the site had been sluiced down with water.

He checked over the dead man's M4 rifle. There were five rounds left in the magazine, a sixth in the chamber. The SEAL had gone into the water with everything else, including the machete still in his hand, and Stone was going to pass on entering the water to look for that. He looked around the bank of the pond, but could not find the knife. He had not noticed at the time, but he assumed the SEAL had left it back at the tree Stone had hid behind in the jungle. He had a sinking feeling that if he indeed backtracked to the spot, then the knife would be gone as well.

For the first time since he woke up on the beach he realised there was so much more to this, so much hidden from him. Outside forces conspiring against him. And for the first time he also realised that he could take control of it. He was remembering more; Kathy, Max and the bank in Panama City. That Richard Anderson of Anderson-Lucas Holdings had gone missing in the Caribbean, along with his family and motor yacht. That was what he had been working on and this island, or stretch of coast could be in Central or South America – the black caiman would point to that – and it wouldn't be a million miles away from where a missing banker had been last seen, who was a wanted man and with missing money at his disposal.

Stone headed in the direction of where both the hunter and the SEAL had come from. The grass was knee-height and the air was both cooler and lighter than down in the jungle. He had only taken fifty paces or so when he saw the clothes folded and arranged on a fallen tree. A bottle of water and a bag of fruit rested beside them. Stone looked around, approached cautiously, then checked the pile of clothes. He looked all around him, but saw nobody. The clothes were familiar. A pair of black, lightweight suit trousers and a white shirt. Black leather shoes, thin black cotton socks and a black lightweight suit jacket. He looked around again, then drank all of the water and ate the fruit. There were two bananas, a prepared wedge of pineapple and an orange. They tasted delicious, like nothing Stone had experienced. Or at least, experienced for a long time. He remembered eating tinned peaches after days spent in the field on rations of oatcakes and water and it had been heaven in a tin. And he remembered the joy of a *Burger King* at Camp Bastion after a four weeks' reconnaissance in Afghanistan. The joys of taste and texture after a dry and tasteless palate. A Michelin stared chef could not have made a better meal than that *Double Whopper*.

Stone decided right there that he could fight the situation, or he could play along and learn more from it. If he could understand it, then that would take him towards controlling it. He put on the clothes. They fitted him well. He fixed the belt, noticed the worn indentations in the leather from the buckle. He was a whole hole smaller, and he realised that the belt was his. The clothes also. He picked up the jacket and saw the pistol in its holster. His own FN Five-Seven. The spare magazine was in its pouch. He checked over the weapon and the magazines, then fitted them to his belt. He then had second thoughts and took the pistol back out. He dropped the magazine and stripped the weapon down. He reassembled it, chambered a round and fired at the ground. A large clod of earth flew up and sprayed his legs with debris.

He was a round down now, but he was satisfied nobody had tampered with the firing pin and the weapon was working properly. Stone picked up the black jacket. He noticed that the lining was ripped. Two large pieces had been cut out and the silk had started to fray. He frowned and dropped it on the ground. As well as the jacket he ignored the tie – it was far too hot – and he left the shirt open at his neck and rolled the sleeves to his elbows. He looked around him again. He knew he was not alone – couldn't possibly be. But he had made a plan yesterday and he would stick to it. He would climb the hill and see what was beyond it. As he took a step forward something dug into his thigh. He put his hand in his pants pocket and felt a square of folded paper. He unfolded it, aware he was undoubtedly being watched. There were just a few handwritten lines, but as he read them, he felt intrigued, anxious and scared all at once. It couldn't be so. But he knew it to be true, had suspected something when he had seen the SEAL kill the hunter earlier. He scrunched the paper and threw it to the ground. Then, as survival mode took over his emotions and he knew he could have a use for a dry piece of paper. He bent down and reached for it. The paper was thick and already unfurling. The words bared themselves to him again…

Fight to survive

Kill to win
Win to leave

21

The ride out to Kathy's house took Stone about twenty-minutes. The Mustang was no longer there, having been towed to the shop where Stone had the original restoration performed. There was crime scene tape all around the house and a Washington PD officer was sitting in a cruiser outside the perimeter. Stone parked up the bike and took off the half-face helmet, hung it on the handlebar. He approached the officer and showed the man his ID.

"You got a partner in there?"

"No."

"You're here alone?"

"Yeah."

"Just sat on your ass at a crime scene?"

"That's what it looks like." The officer was in his forties, overweight and clearly hadn't had a promotion since joining the police department. He sneered a little, or maybe the bitterness of failure and the weight of life had stuck to his face permanently. "Just following orders."

"And they were?"

"What business is it of yours?"

Stone smiled. "It's a Secret Service crime scene."

"So what the hell am I doing here?" the man sneered.

Stone straightened up. Tapped his fingers on the roof. "I guess we needed donuts," he said, drumming his fingers louder. "I don't know; we don't have a department of fat, bitter, underachievers to guard our crime scenes as yet. Maybe we'll outsource it to private security someday, I guess until then we have to make do with the local police department."

The cop grabbed the door and went to barge it open. The sneer had gone, replaced by rage and he put his shoulder against the door as he opened it. The door opened, but only made it a few inches. Stone had his knee against it, most of his weight pushed into it. As much as the cop tried to push it, the door went nowhere. The man was flushed red, he gritted his teeth together and heaved. Stone acted as if he hadn't noticed.

"Normally when we ask for a crime scene to be secured, we expect a patrol, some basic security protocols," Stone said. He drummed his fingers on the roof like he was bored. "The thing is, if you're sat here, someone could get in a window or door around the back and either contaminate the crime scene, or remove crucial evidence." The cop looked up at him, stopped pushing on the door and sat back in his seat. He was breathing hard. Stone looked across the grass and nodded to the neighbour's house. "Did somebody collect the dogs?"

"What?" the cop asked, looking a little dejected, but a whole lot less angry. "I don't know anything about any dogs."

"The owner got the neighbour to look after her dogs." Stone stood up and stepped back from the car. The cop got out slowly and looked back across the roof of the patrol vehicle to the neighbouring property. Stone nodded towards the house. "Couple of big wolf things, the neighbour has them. Has the owner of this house been back yet?"

"Nope," the cop was calmer now. If anything he looked as if he realised he'd been foolish.

"Ok," Stone said. "Go do a sweep of the rear of the house and walk a few random patrols around it. Sit on the porch for a while, then sit round the back. Your patrol vehicle shouts that you're here from the front, you take care of the back and sides." He turned and walked to the neighbouring house and climbed the steps. He looked back and saw the cop walking dutifully around to the rear of Kathy's house. He had worked with local police departments for as long as he'd been in the Secret Service. It was inevitable. But also inevitable, was their contempt at knowing that the Secret Service answered to no other agency and could commandeer any department, organisation or law enforcement body within the United States. It never stopped local law enforcement trying to assert themselves though, and Stone felt he'd taken it pretty softly on this guy. He had taken a police chief's career and pension before and not lost a minute's sleep over it. He had found in his work that even when tasked with protecting the President's life, some people just couldn't let go, couldn't float with the tide for a few days. There was always someone who had to stick a wrench in the cog and threaten to crash the entire machine.

Stone cupped his hands against the glass and looked inside. The house was empty. There were no furnishings or anything to show anybody was living there. He thought back to the previous evening. The man on the doorstep, the woman shouting from downstairs. Why would they have been living there with no furnishings? Had they been in the middle of a house move? Kathy would surely have known if that had been the case. He started to feel uneasy.

Around the back of the house Stone saw the thick tyre marks on the grass. He walked up to the deck and looked inside the kitchen window. Empty. He had moved enough times to know it couldn't be done that quickly. There was always cleaning to be done, boxes to shift, furniture to move. The tyre marks and the size of the tread would denote a large vehicle, maybe a removal truck, and the parking was better here than around the front where the ground had been laid over to garden and parking for two mid-sized vehicles.

Stone took out his cell phone and dialled Kathy again. Voicemail. He dialled the service desk and asked to be put through to the Rapid Reaction Unit, the team who had secured the property.

"Agent Yates speaking."

"Ernest, Rob Stone."

"What, you don't like voicemail or something?"

"What?"

"I've rung round the clock. You have a half dozen messages. And about twenty missed calls."

"Sorry, I…"

"Forget it," the man was curt. He was a New Yorker. The Bronx. There never needed to be an explanation. Some would say he was curt; others would say he was rude. He was neither. It was a geography thing. *"We had a team secure this woman, Kathy Newman's house. Nothing."*

"Nothing?"

"Nothing." Yates paused. *"At least it was meant to look that way. No body. No blood. No DNA, except for yours. And your set of prints. On the desk, the door handles and on a couple of coffee cups."*

"Impossible."

"No. There was a hell of a lot of bleach though. Or traces of it. Industrial strength, spray gun would be my bet. Toxicology will come back on that. And there were some dog hairs, but no dogs."

"The dogs went to the neighbours."

"My team leader went there. No dogs. No people, no furnishings, no trace. Again, cleaned with industrial bleach. No DNA."

"But there were people in that house last night!"

"Did you see them?"

"Yes."

"Did you go in?"

Stone felt a wave of heat wash up his neck and into his face. "No. I waited. Kathy spoke to the guy on the doorstep. His wife was shouting downstairs. *Who was it? What did they want?* That sort of thing."

"But you didn't go in."

"No."

There was a pause. *"My guess is the house was already empty, boxed up and cleaned. After you left they finished cleaning the last things like door handles, the thresh holds and were out of there. I'll get some enquiries done, find out who owns it, whether it's rented, who leased it, that sort of thing."*

"Ok," Stone paused. "While you're at it, do the same thing with Kathy Newman's house."

"You can't ask her?"

"No," Stone paused. "No, she's not answering her phone and I don't know where she is."

22

"I don't know where she is. I don't much care either."

Stone looked at the woman in front of him. She was fifty, a red head and Stone could tell by the lines of her cat's bum mouth that she smoked heavily. He could smell the smoke and nicotine on her clothes, saw the yellow stains on her fingers.

"When did you last see her?"

She was irritated by Stone's presence. She had a paper to run, more important things to do than to talk to a government employee about a waning reporter's absence. "A week," she paused, skim-reading a sheet of copy in front of her. "I don't know, ten days?"

Stone took the copy out of her hand and for a moment she looked ready to explode. "Ms Kowalski, let's not do this. You *will* tell what I need to know. How difficult it becomes is down to you. Ten minutes of your time, a call from you to your personnel department, then I'm out of here and on my way. Or, I'm going to have to pull some strings, shut your presses down for a day, have you suspended for non-compliance of an informational request aiding a government inquiry. Your assistant editor will enjoy the challenge of sitting at your desk for sure…"

"Ok! I get it!" she picked up the phone and asked someone for time sheets and payroll details.

She looked back at Stone. "Kathy was good. But that was a long time ago, and to be honest, it was before she was with us. I hired her on a wave of great achievements. Those days were gone before she took up with the Washington Post. I suppose it eats at you, but there comes a time when you have to get on with it. You can't let it get to you forever. We all have family problems, but in this game you can't languish. The stories are there; they won't wait for you."

"Break-ups can be tough," Stone commented. He'd had enough experience.

She frowned. "Break up? What are you talking about? She hasn't had a partner since she's been here. I'm talking about her father."

Stone remembered the bar, the cream soda. Her comment about nostalgia. He nodded, understood. "He died, I know."

The editor sat back in her seat and frowned at him, it bordered on sympathy. "Do you actually *know* anything, Agent Stone? He isn't dead. He's in a nursing home in Virginia. Kathy used up all of her leave – compassionate *and* holiday. The paper even granted her a short period of time to get things in place, move him to Washington DC, or one of the suburbs. Kathy has barely filed copy since. We were going to let her go next month, the board have had enough. She just beat us to it, that's all."

"What is wrong with her father?"

"Age and Alzheimer's. She could have just left him; it's not like he would have known. What good has it done? The old fart is sat there chewing on his carpet slippers and Kathy Newman has squandered her talent and career sitting with him and talking to someone who doesn't know who the hell she is anyway."

There was a knock at the door and a young woman walked in with a file. She handed it over to Kowalski, smiled at Stone and walked back out. The editor perused the file, then handed it over.

"Here, keep it. It's a copy anyway. She hasn't been in for twelve days. Nobody's spoken to her either. If you see her, tell her she's fired."

"Tell her yourself." Stone stood. He took the file and looked down at her. "That old guy with the slippers. That was your Dad, right?"

"What if it was?" she asked, her tone hostile, defensive.

"Well, I hope in between bouts of coherence and complete periods of blankness and despair, Kathy's father is proud of her for hanging in there. For doing what it takes and putting family before her career. I hope your father could say the same." Stone saw a flicker behind the woman's eyes, a break in her harsh façade, but he said nothing more as he turned and walked out of her office.

Stone checked his cell phone again as he reached his motorcycle parked on the street outside the Washington Post's offices. He hadn't received the messages from Yates. A call to his network provider had drawn a blank. He had called Yates, who had read back the number. The correct number. Stone never left a personal greeting message on his voicemail, choosing the network carrier's setting instead, but he hoped Yates had misdialled. Otherwise someone else was picking up his messages.

He called Max, who was sounding tired. "Just checking the coordinates for Edwards' GPS were still at the location you gave me."

"They are," he paused. *"Kathy just called, I checked and the vehicle hasn't moved. She'll meet you there."*

"What?" Stone cursed. "You've heard of operational security, haven't you?"

"Sure. What's the problem?"

"I'm not entirely sure of Kathy's credibility. I need to check further."

"Shit, sorry. I just thought…"

"What?"

"Well, last night. You know? With the whole ear-stroking, hip swaying thing. I thought you were close. I thought if you weren't, you soon would be."

"From the man who actually changed his name to Max Power to score girls?" Stone cursed inwardly. He shook his head. Max was right. They had been very soon after. Now he felt bitter, like he'd been played. "How long ago was this?"

"An hour."

Stone swung his leg over the Ducati. He reached for his helmet with his other hand. "Ok. Look, check up on the house. Find out what the deal is. The neighbouring property too. And when you've done that, run a full background check on Kathy Newman."

"Sure. I can like, sleep when I'm dead and shit."

"That's the spirit."

"What's the problem with Kathy?"

"I don't know. Yet. Check out her father too. I gather he's in a nursing home in Virginia."

"East or West?"

"I don't know."

"Hell, why don't we throw in the entire eastern seaboard?"

"If it makes it easier."

"Ouch. You're mean."

"I get meaner. You done it yet?"

"I'm on it." Max hung up.

Stone called Yates. The agent sounded terse. Or maybe he'd just won the lottery. It was hard to tell. *"Hey, you called back."*

"I've *called*. Don't tell me you've left another message?"

"I have."

"On this number?"

"Your caller ID just showed up. You're in my phone book."

"Shit. My phone is compromised."

"Come back, I'll organise a handset and new number. A burner."

"I will, but I need to be somewhere."

"The house. The neighbour's place, that is. Empty for seven weeks. If that broad took the dogs round, she knew it was a set-up. The real estate agent even checked the place and showed a couple round it two weeks ago."

"Could this couple have been the same one who took in the dogs?"

"I've got people looking at it, but don't expect much. A call from a burner, a viewing and no further contact. I wouldn't hold out much hope."

"But Kathy would have known." Stone said flatly.

"Yes. Where's the broad now?"

"I don't know. But I think I know where to find her."

23

The Ducati could really move through the traffic. Stone kept it up around seventy, weaving around slower cars and between the lanes. The brakes were powerful but smooth and the traction control was a revelation compared to the *slight mistake and you die* handling of the Honda VTR 1000 he last rode ten years ago. The bike which nearly killed him and put a break on his motorcycling for a decade. He only found out that the biking fraternity called it *The Widow Maker* after he'd crashed. When the road joined the two-lane, Stone dropped a gear and saw one-hundred-and-thirty before settling down to a hundred as he headed east towards the Chesapeake and the small, picturesque town of Churchtown, south of Shady Side.

Stone remembered the Chesapeake well from his childhood. His family would rent a beach house near North Beach for two weeks every summer and both Stone and his brother would swim and go crabbing and fish and get sunburned all day long. When Stone was fourteen he would act as his older brother's wingman with teenage girls as they ventured into the town and onto the boardwalk to hang around the arcades and hotdog stands. Andrew was two years older and having a cute younger brother didn't hurt, especially if the girl he liked had a younger sister in tow.

Stone had left the I95 and passed through Upper Marlboro where he had remembered a particularly hot day and a river flowing into a small lake at Mount Calvert. The brothers had rigged up a rope swing high in the boughs of a tree and had taken turns to drop the twenty-feet or so into the river. The rope swing went down well with the local children and had still been there on subsequent trips. Stone remembered his brother fondly, but as always, felt saddened by his death. Sometimes he tried to forget everything, to avoid feeling that way, but he reasoned it was better to remember the good times and take the sadness that accompanied it. The same went for remembering his father. Otherwise, what was the point of it all? He had come to realise that there was no cushion in life and that experiences, good or bad, made you what you were.

Stone was still hustling along. Overtaking traffic and using third and fourth gears with their savage acceleration and massive torque braking. The bike was a cruiser-come-street-racer and had such massive acceleration that many fairing-clad Japanese sports bikes would struggle to match it up to a hundred. The air was cold and his thin suit offered such little resistance to the wind that the speed had turned late summer to winter against his skin. As he reached the outskirts of Churchtown, he slowed the motorcycle and within a few minutes driving at the speed limit he started to warm steadily.

He turned onto Shore Drive and counted the house numbers. The house he was looking for was a ranch-style single storey with a wooden porch and a small garden front and back. The silver Mercedes E320 Coupe was parked on a chipping drive to the side of the property.

Stone parked just past the plot and took off the helmet. He hung it on the handlebars and opened his jacket. The FN pistol was within easy reach. He looked all around him, studied the cars in the street for drivers and passengers, the driveways for anyone watching him. The street was deserted. Behind the houses opposite he caught glimpses of the sea, sailboats and rigging. Seagulls calling and swooping up and down.

The house did not look well maintained. Although many houses had a chic shabbiness about them – whitewashed, faded blue accenting paint, washed-out wood stain – the other houses had better lawns, tidier plant beds. This house had overgrown grass and the windows were encrusted with salt and dust. The longer Stone studied it, the more out of place it seemed. He climbed the steps to the deck and porch. He could see the mail on the hall table. Someone was here, recently. But not long enough to open the letters. He tried the door, but it was locked. He walked around the deck and made his way past a few overgrown vines to the rear. The door was ajar. It seemed wrong somehow. Stone had the pistol in his hand and was checking his side and rear. He looked back at the door and gave it a gentle push with his toe. The door creaked open and he eased his way into the kitchen. There were coffee cups and a plate with toast crumbs and a smear of butter on the edge of a knife. He reached out and touched the kettle. It was warm, close to hot.

Stone had no idea of the provenance of the house, but he suspected it was the computer and internet expert's bolt-hole. The area would have indicated that perhaps it had been a parent's home and he had inherited it. The street looked child-free, sedate. A place where people with a little means came on vacation or lived out retirement. It wasn't The Hamptons, but it was certainly more exclusive than Jersey Shore. The Chesapeake was a sailor's dream, and elderly people had the time to sail and play with boats. It would explain why the property hadn't shown up in the man's background search. Edwards most likely had not properly sorted out the deeds, or perhaps another family member owned it.

Stone had a bad feeling in his gut. He had felt it before. It was seldom wrong. He raised the pistol and trained the sights on the doorway to the corridor. The motion was slow and careful, measured. He knew what he was going to find. At least the context of what he was going to find. Edward's car hadn't moved and the man had been off the radar for some time. Kathy couldn't find him and had unanswered questions, needed the information he had. Now Stone could see a picture building. Who better to find someone than an agent with unlimited resources and the weight of the Secret Service behind him? He felt played, as he had done after last night. Only then, he'd had a happy ending. Or two. There was no gain here.

He rounded the doorway and tentatively stepped through onto the wooden boards. It wasn't laminate, these were old fashioned planks. Most likely reclaimed timber from a ship or an old foundry. Dried over hundreds of years. The result was they creaked. Badly. Anyone waiting for him to show himself had prior warning and lots of it. A continuous announcement of his direction and his intentions. Stone upped the ante and ran. He swung the pistol into the first room on his left. It was the master bedroom. Edwards, or at least Stone assumed it was him, was lying face down on the floor. There was a bullet hole in the back of the man's head. He was dead, or at least beyond help and that's all Stone looked at. He backed away, kept his weapon up and ready and checked out the rest of the house. It took another five minutes – the house was a three bedroom and fairly compact. But Stone took his time, he had learned the hard way once before. He walked back into the master bedroom and looked at the body. The blood had yet to congeal, indicating that it was minutes rather than hours since Edwards had breathed his last breath. The blood had pooled on the wooden floor, filled the gaps between the planks. Stone realised they had to have been modern tongue and groove, to have filled and not simply butted up to each other. He noticed things. Not all of it relevant. Still, they matched the older planks of the hallway well. He holstered his pistol and squatted down beside the body. There were two bullet holes under his left shoulder blade. A professional. Both had plugged the heart after the initial headshot. There was little blood around these two holes, indicating the man had already been dead. They were grouped well, but the distance would have been less than eight feet. Still, a good display of marksmanship. He looked up and saw the exit hole of the initial headshot in the stucco wall. There was splatter across the bed and on the window pane. Stone could see boats outside, through the crimson mist on the window. He conjured a picture in his mind. Edwards walking into the bedroom unaware. He would have to have trusted the person behind him. Or been keen to get to know that person better. The promise of sex would have done it. Maybe there had been some kissing to build the excitement, heat the passion. Full of anticipation, pulse raised, leading the way into the bedroom. Then, a single shot to his head, two follow-ups to his back, straight through the heart.

Had Kathy found Edwards after all?

Stone pulled the body over and ran his finger across the cadaver's cooling lips. He dropped the head back onto the floor and looked at the colour, the waxy smudge on his fingertip. He sniffed it. A distinct smell of summer fruits, of cherry and raspberries. Stone wiped his finger on his knee, rubbed until all trace had gone. He had smelled and tasted the same lipstick on his lips last night.

24

Stone looked around the house. He searched using a tier system. First he looked for the obvious. Edwards was a computer expert and there was no way the man would be here without tech. There was nothing. No smartphone, no tablet and no laptop. There would always have been a smartphone.

The next level of the tier was sideboards, drawers and cupboards. The wardrobe, the airing cupboard and also the bathroom cabinet. Finally, Stone removed his jacket, rolled up his sleeves and took off his tie. He was going into the backs of the kitchen units, taking out the drawers and moving the bed. He would remove the bath panel, check the toilet cistern. After an hour, he was convinced there was nothing here. He would speak to Agent Yates and see if the man could get a team in to remove floorboards and get a thermal imager and x-ray machine onto the walls.

Stone checked the body over. He ran his hands over it, delved into the pockets and came back with a tear-off of white lined paper, no bigger than a post-it note. It had been folded twice. There were a series of numbers on it. 0900 8000. He looked at it, then took out his cell phone and dialled. There was a little delay and then the dial tone went blank. Perhaps it was a bank account number. There were specialists in the treasury who could check. But it was a single line, and without the bank code or bank name he didn't hold out much hope. He tucked it into his pocket and finished patting down. There were car keys, but no wallet. Stone took the keys and headed outside. The car was new but you wouldn't know it from the inside. There were empty fast food wrappers in the rear foot wells, cigarette cartons in the door pockets. The passenger seat was littered with papers, and receipts. The glovebox looked the same, only full. The car smelled like a miasma of tobacco and greasy meat, of stale sweat and old coffee. The upholstery was stained and the leather scuffed. Stone bunched up the papers and took them back to the kitchen where he spread them out across the table. He had a flashback to his father at the end of the tax year. An accountant for small businesses, the house was always full of receipts and files as business owners had left it too late and Stone's father barely slept for the week leading up to the tax deadline. This wasn't quite in the same league, but Edwards had certainly been far from organised.

He scanned most of it, piled the receipts, turned everything over – he'd learned long ago that people often write important things on scraps of paper, and unimportant things on the back of items of huge importance. He stopped when he saw the simply scribbled name – Kathy, followed by a telephone number. He recognised the area code. He picked up his phone and scrolled to Kathy's number. The two numbers were different. Stone dialled Max and paced over to the window while he waited. There was a glimpse of sailboats and blue water, but he had to peer between two neighbouring houses to see. He wondered how much more expensive the seafront properties would be. Most likely they didn't come up for sale that often. The neighbourhood looked well-established. Everybody probably knew each other.

Max answered on the fifth ring. Stone felt sure it was about to divert to voicemail. *"I need sleep."*

"Later. I have another number for Kathy," Stone read it out and waited for Max to get a pen. Finally, he confirmed he had it. "Look, see if you can get a location on it. I think it's a cell, the code is…"

"West Virginia," Max interrupted. *"I'll check. Have you thought any more about what I said?"*

"What?"

"I left a voicemail message."

Stone's blood ran cold. "Look, my phone has been compromised. I'm picking up another when I get back. What was it?" He hoped Max had not divulged too much.

"The house you met Kathy at is a rental. But not by her. It's been vacant, like the neighbouring property for six weeks. Those houses aren't too popular. The developers attempted to recreate a wilderness and that's what they got. With cell masts and train links. There's a serious Lyme disease issue out there, caused by deer with ticks. Plus; many

houses have been hit with termites. Like eaten through. Word has spread and there's a glut of empty properties all through the valley. Nobody's buying and landlords don't want any comebacks. And let's face it – Lyme disease isn't pleasant for anyone, let alone the kids needed to fill those family homes."

"So Kathy wasn't meant to be living there," Stone mused. "And the neighbours were never there, for anything more than appearances, that is."

"Weird."

"You could say that," Stone mused, then added, "I found Edwards."

"Cool."

"Not for him," Stone said. He turned back from the window, folded the piece of paper with the telephone number on it and leaned against the countertop. "He's dead."

"Oh." There was a pause, then Max asked, *"Did you get his laptop?"*

"He didn't have one. No tech at all. Not even a smartphone."

"That's bogus. If he's a geek, he's connected. End of story."

"That's what I thought," Stone sighed. "But there's nothing here. They've cleaned house." Stone could tell Max was working on something, the sound of keys tapping and a mouse clicking. "What are you doing?"

"Got that number. It's a cell and it's not a million miles from you."

"Where?"

"Calvert Cliffs. It looks remote. It's around twenty-five miles down the coast. I'll send you the address…"

"Don't!" Stone snapped. He softened his tone. "My phone is rogue. Don't text me on it and for goodness sake don't leave a voicemail. Now, give me the address and zip code and I'll write it down." Stone scribbled on a sheet of tattered paper. He read it twice, then folded it and put it in his pocket. "Do me a favour. Call Agent Ernest Yates on the reaction desk and get a CSI team out here. Then call the local cops and ask them to secure the scene."

"I will. What happened to Edwards?"

"Shot. Up close, professional."

"Well, be careful. There's nothing much out where you're heading but woods, sand dunes and dirt track."

25

Night was looming. Stone felt exposed, the white shirt didn't help. It was as opposite to camouflage as you could get. Unless you were in snow. But it seemed to be part of the game, and he knew if he played along he would discover more. He felt good with the M4 assault rifle in his hands, the pistol on his belt. It made him feel secure, more secure than the spear had at least. But the best thing about his discovery was the luxury of socks and shoes. His feet were covered in tiny cuts and scabs and he hadn't realised how slow his progress had been barefoot until he had taken his first few confident steps with his shoes.

He had finished the water and fruit, but had kept both the empty bottle and plastic bag, squashing the plastic bottle flat and tucking it into his trouser pockets along with the clear plastic bag. Both were handy for carrying water. He had no idea where to go, or whether he was being watched, but he was confident that his progress was being monitored. The neat pile of clothes, and the fact that his own weapon and ammunition had been with them, meant that there was a protocol of some kind. He would know soon enough.

His side still hurt. The bruising was coming out and his hip was sore against the fabric of his trousers. He could not remember the injury, but he appreciated from the bruising that it had been recent, and that meant it had happened shortly before he had found himself here. He looked at the track marks on his forearm. There were five or six holes running into one another and they were raised and swollen. They itched too. For the first time he gave thought to what they meant. Obviously some kind of drug had been administered to render him unconscious. He had little knowledge of drugs, but either that, or something in addition to it had played havoc with his memory. He had no swelling, lumps or pain to his head, and no symptoms of a concussion. Some kind of drug had been used. But what of the other needle marks? How many types of drugs had been administered? Everything he had been remembering pointed towards an organisation with experience, resources and an agenda. What if they had used a truth serum? *Sodium Thiopental* was effective. It contravened the Fifth Amendment but he had heard of it used by the CIA against Taliban fighters in Afghanistan and on terror suspects in Guantanamo. *Chloral-hydrate* or *Ketamine* would have knocked him out, but the dosage would have to have been large, and he was probably lucky to be alive. He'd been taken to the edge for sure.

He felt the chill run up his spine, linger at the nape of his neck. What if he had been coerced to talk? To compromise the President's security schedule or operating procedure? Is that what this was about?

Suddenly Stone had more reasons to leave. Until this point, his strategy had been to survive. That was all he intended to achieve. Play the long game and make it back to safety and civilization. Take few risks, plan well and adapt. Don't rush. Think. That was the way to survive. But now? Now he wanted to get out of here as soon as he could. Get word to the Secret Service; counter any damage done by his possible coercion. Career-wise, he was finished. If he had talked; he was done. If he couldn't be one-hundred percent sure that he had not talked; he was done. Past victories and triumphs only went so far, and never truly put the account in credit. But Stone cared about national security. He cared about the Secret Service, and he cared about the President and the man's family. He wanted to pull up the shutters, put down the barriers. He would risk it all, like he had before, to get the job done. And right now, the job was to get out of here and raise the alarm.

He looked at the orange sunset behind him. Another hour and it would be dark. He needed to hole-up somewhere. To his left, he saw a belt of pampas grass and a circle of trees. Behind him, that same kind of circle ringed the pond with the caiman. Perhaps this was a similar pond. He imagined in the rainy season a string of ponds would join together, the banks swelling with rain. There would be less competition for fish or turtles or frogs, or whatever they sustained themselves on when one-hundred and seventy pound murderous men weren't tossed in for lunch.

As he approached, he noticed the eyes of the fruit bats again. Only now, after everything he'd seen today, he wasn't convinced. He walked under the canopy of trees and looked up at the eerie glow. It was so obvious now. He would have shot one down, had he not wanted to waste a bullet. He could see the glow, and in the half-light of dusk, he saw the box. Dark coloured, probably green or brown in the light of day, and no bigger than a paperback. The plastic unit emitted a beam of infrared light, invisible to the naked eye, that the camera saw by at night. From directly head on, the glow of the infrared lights was visible. The more Stone looked, the more pairs of glowing 'eyes' he saw. He had seen these cameras before – originally used by hunters to monitor the patterns and behaviours of game like wild boar and deer – they were now increasingly used for covert security surveillance. The units downloaded onto an SP card or a USB stick, but Stone would have bet his life that these units were wireless enabled and that somewhere a router was picking up individual feeds where they would be displayed on a monitor.

26

The Ducati didn't like the sand. The road was largely worn asphalt patched at irregular intervals with cement, which had expanded or contracted in winter frosts and the summer heat, and had separated and crumbled. Stone supposed a well-meaning resident had patched the potholes with cement not realising that it would break down as the pliable asphalt expanded and contracted around it. Maybe this had been done back in the recession. One of them. But it was the sand that was most hazardous, the onshore wind had whipped up the sand from the grassy dunes and spewed it onto the road. Sheltered from westerly winds by a thick belt of trees to his right, the sand had nowhere else to go. Maybe the same well-meaning resident occasionally shovelled it back onto the shore side, but they hadn't been busy lately.

The Ducati was a powerful beast and shod with a set of smooth road rubber. It was a planted machine, capable of leaning to within inches of its frame through a corner and powering out onto the straight on a wave of torque. It was heavy and had not been designed to go off road, and each time a patch of deep sand drift lay in his way, Stone had to throttle back, keep a high gear and almost freewheel through at a crawling pace. He would then accelerate until the next drift and slow down again to repeat the process. It took all of his concentration. And Stone liked to concentrate on more than merely the road ahead. He needed to be aware of a situation, aware of escape routes, of threats, of distractions. The road was becoming his entire focus. The last time he had felt this way, an IED had taken out his artillery unit on his first tour in Afghanistan. Stone had been the sole survivor and seriously injured.

He brought the motorcycle to a halt at the next bend. The road had been relatively straight. There had been the occasional break in the dune and there were houses on both sides of the road. He guessed the dune-side houses cost more with their waterside location and sea views over the Chesapeake. The houses were few and far between though. Some were older houses, basic. Old money. Or no money, but had been owned for a long time. Others had been bought, developed with no expense spared and sold on for millions. They featured a lot of glass and chrome and teak and were box-shaped. The older houses were timber-framed and largely painted powder blue and eggshell white.

Much of the land was national parkland. He had seen several signs indicating various species of birds, amphibians and snakes. Another sign was for turtles in freshwater lagoons and a sign warning people not to interact with egg-laying or hatching turtles on the shore side of the dunes.

Stone took out the note of paper and his phone and checked his progress with *Google Maps*. He was close. That was, if the cell phone belonging to the number hadn't moved in the meantime. He dialled Max and waited. Again, he answered after five rings.

"Are you there yet?"

"Nearly." Stone turned in his saddle and looked back down the road. A car was pulling into the driveway of a shore-side home. It was grey, too far away to see the make and model. "Is the cell phone still there?"

"Wait," Max paused and Stone could hear him punching keys. *"Yes. It's registered to Mike Newman. Ring any bells?"*

"The editor at the Washington Post said Kathy's father was in a nursing home in Virginia. It could be his. Have you got anywhere tracing her father? Do you have a name?"

"I do now. I'll search Mike, or Michael Newman and see where it gets me. I've drawn a blank until now. But to be honest, I've got a hell of a workload and…"

"Well don't waste time talking to me," Stone snapped and ended the call. According to the map on his phone the house was the next on the left. A shore-side home. Stone started the motorcycle and accelerated steadily over the sand.

He got a good glimpse of the sea, glistening and clear, as he rounded a bend and steadied the bike through the gateway into the short drive. There were no gates, but there looked to be the remains of a weathered gate tucked to the side. The paint had worn and flaked and the timber looked rotten. The house was a single storey wooden beach house. Stone hoped the wood had been taken care of better than the gates had been over the years. He imagined that the winters were harsh, the Atlantic not far from the mouth of the Chesapeake - storm waves pounding, wind onshore, salt spray and rain blasting into every crack of wood.

There was an old Jeep parked up in front of the house. It was a fifteen-year-old design, full of dents, rust and holes, and at odds with the neighbourhood. This was a premium neighbourhood, if a little casual and lifestyle-focused. Many were basic homes, but all were expensive. The vehicles he had seen so far in the driveways were premium brands, some a few years old, but mostly there had been a pattern. It could have been a maintenance guy's vehicle, or a maid's, but it wasn't the vehicle to go with the million-dollar view.

Stone turned the bike around and switched off the engine. No matter where he parked, he always parked facing out. Warzones and close protection had taught him the importance of a quick getaway. He could hear the waves on the shore, a tiny shore break and the surge and ebb of the tide. Gulls dipped and rose on the wind and the calling was incessant. He hung the helmet on the handlebars and dismounted. The driveway had initially been spread with gravel, but much of it was now sand with tufts of beach grass poking through in clumps. He skirted the house, watching the windows as he walked. He wasn't watching for anything other than movement, and for this he used largely his peripheral vision. It caught movement - just the slightest change in light and mass and shape - better than staring directly at one particular spot. It was how the best bodyguards saw a change in the crowd, a weapon aimed or a person dashing out.

The movement came from the kitchen window. Just a shift to the side. Like a nosey neighbour in suburbia. Stone kept walking and rounded the house. He was out of view of the kitchen, and he quickly ducked down, scurried back the way he'd come and climbed the deck. The front door was locked and he stepped back and lunged a front kick at the lock. The wood splintered. Soft, worn and weathered wood. The door crashed in and Stone drew the pistol and paced four good strides into the house. As he'd suspected, he'd been watched from the kitchen then that person backed out and made their way into the lounge, no windows to the side to witness him back-tracking.

The woman looked stunned, her mouth agape as she stared at the gun in his hand. She was similar looking to Kathy, but a little more wholesome. She was a little heavier, curvier and her hair was more natural. Longer, wavier. Still as black as jet though. Her Asian features were less prominent, clearly mixed race. She recovered, closed her mouth. Stone lowered the weapon.

"What have you done to my door?" she shouted, then shook her head and shrugged. "Oh, forget it. My god, am I glad to see you?" she said. "Isobel gave me a picture of you. I've been trying desperately to get in contact with you. You don't pick up your voicemails, or you're not returning my calls. I'm Kathy Newman. I don't think we have much time."

27

Stone thought of the things Kathy Newman – or the woman he'd initially thought was Kathy Newman – had said on that first night. She had known that he was the President's man. His go-to agent in the Secret Service. At the time he had been surprised that his former girlfriend had divulged as much to her. Now, he was sure that she hadn't. Isobel would not have betrayed his trust gossiping about what he did in the Secret Service. She would have told her friend that he might be able to help, and she would have helped set up a meeting, which she had, calling Stone to ask him to consider meeting with her friend.

It made sense now. Stone had been the victim of a counter intelligence operation by agents' unknown. They had tapped and monitored his phone, diverted his calls, done the same with Isobel's phone in New York, listened to conversations and drawn a plan based on the data they had recovered. They would have watched him, followed him, learned from him. They had probably got into his emails via Isobel's. He knew they had taken control of his cell phone and listened to and deleted his voicemails. When Kathy Newman had contacted Isobel with her dark web story and her missing computer and web expert, they had inserted an agent to impersonate Kathy Newman. They had the upper hand then, and they'd had it ever since.

He shifted in the grass, but kept his movements slow. The pistol was comforting in his hand. It was close to bring to aim.

The first gunshot rang out, the bullet piercing his crisp white shirt just left of dead centre. The bullet travelled through the back and into the jungle beyond. A second shot sounded and found its mark next to the first. Stone did not move. He was laying deathly still on the ground.

Minutes passed and the gunman emerged on the fringe of the jungle. He held the rifle relaxed in his hands, his finger off the trigger, the muzzle towards the ground. Good weapon drills, experienced. It was all but dark, a hunter's moon low in the sky. The gunman stood over his target. He rested the rifle against the same tree that had blocked his target's head from view, bent lower to inspect his kill.

Stone was up and behind him, the grass he had covered himself with falling off him as he stood, the pistol aimed at the centre of the gunman's back.

"Don't move," he said quietly.

The gunman flinched, then regained a little composure. He shook his head disbelievingly, smiled. He went to stand up but Stone jabbed him so hard in the spine with the muzzle of the pistol that he let out a howl and fell forwards onto his stomach. It was a substantial blow, would have moved the vertebrae a little, pinched the spinal cord. It would take a chiropractor some work to straighten the man up again. Nevertheless, he knelt up slowly, wincing at the pain and tugged at the white shirt which Stone had stuffed with pampas grass. The trousers too, attached to the shirt by the belt, which Stone had weaved through the tears he'd made in the shirt. "Very clever," he conceded. "They were right about you. Jesus, you outsmarted me with a fucking scarecrow…"

"I want some answers," Stone said.

"Don't we all."

"Where are we?"

The man laughed. "We're in hell, my friend. Or heaven. You take your pick on how you feel about killing."

"It's some kind of game."

"It's all a *game*, man!" The man swayed, Stone stood back and kept the pistol on him. "Life's a big fucking game, man. At least here you get to live it!"

"Are you a soldier?"

"We're all soldiers, man. Except you, that is. You're the Secret Agent! You're the bodyguard!"

"What do you know about me?"

"Odds on favourite! I thought I had you!" The man turned, but saw that Stone was too far away to attack, to close to miss with the pistol. "You're the man! They said the betting went mad with you. Stratospheric. They said the requests came in thick and fast. Especially after they saw all that Tarzan shit

191

you pulled. And that thing with the alligator? Fucking awesome! First you kill one and eat it, then you throw the SEAL team guy in and get the poor son-of-a-bitch eaten alive! That fucker was hard core. SEAL Team Six! He was on the crew who killed Osama Bin Laden! Said he took the shot, but I didn't believe him. I bet there are twenty guys saying they all nailed that fucker!" He winced with a stab of pain, and looked at Stone seriously. "Now they are sending all kinds of requests. The bidding has gone crazy!"

"Bidding?" Stone asked. He noticed the man was wearing an earpiece. He raised the pistol and stepped forwards. The muzzle was close to the man's face and steady. Stone snatched the earpiece out of his ear and pulled the wire. The small receiver unit pulled out through the neck of the man's T-shirt. Stone stepped backwards a pace. "What requests? Who?"

"The internet, man. What else? All those dark web sickos! The people who are paying to watch us kill each other." He tried to move, but felt a stab of pain in his spine and dropped involuntarily, like his legs had no feeling. He rolled onto his side and looked up at Stone. He seemed high, he had definitely taken, or been administered something. "The dark web is full of people like that. First it was snuff-movies, some poor East European girl drugged up and taken every which way by a group of rapists, before they strangle her or something nasty. Most likely the killing was faked, but even *that* shit is illegal. Then there's child porn. Plenty of sickos eat up that shit. But this? *This* is new. Or as old as time. You make up your own mind. This is what they lived for in ancient Rome. Gladiator games, man. Spartacus and shit. The rich *love* this crap! Arab and Russian billionaires. New money Eurotrash, rich Americans. You're famous, man! You're the President's man, the best of the best. Well, that's what they want to find out. They're requesting some serious shit now! But it will cost them. You're going to get a war on your ass!"

"Who is doing this?" Stone stepped forwards and caught hold of him by his jacket. It was an old and well-worn olive military jacket. The kind many homeless veterans wore. He jammed the pistol under the man's chin. "Who is behind this? Tell me, I'll help you get away."

The man laughed. "You don't get it, man."

"What?"

"We're *all* a part of it." The man closed his eyes. "We *all* agreed to it. And we all fucking *love* it."

"You agreed to do this?"

"What else was there?" The man opened his eyes, they still looked dilated, like he was high. "We took the money and agreed to the terms. I was homeless, I didn't know where my next meal was coming from. Now I have luxury buffets, cook-outs

193

and barbecue. I sleep safe. I just have to come out here and hunt some bozo down every once in a while. I have money going into my bank, I'll *buy* a life with that."

"One payment."

"What?"

"Each missing person has had one payment made into their accounts, shortly before they went off the radar. From a numbered account in Panama. A bank whose boss has disappeared and left the bank in turmoil. I don't think he's coming back."

The man looked confused. "That's not true. We get paid the same amount monthly. Regardless. Then we get a bonus if we win our bouts. There were ten of us, in the beginning. We took turns to hunt some guy or other, but then came the requests to battle it out with each other. The betting was raised and our fee was meant to have gone through the roof on account the hunts were going to be tougher." His confusion passed as he gave way to anger. "It can't be true!"

"Take it up with your boss. But I imagine when you've all killed each other he'll be bugging out of here with a fortune in his bank. Wherever the hell that is." Stone motioned him to get up. Just a sweep of the pistol, but the guy got the message. He started to stand but fell back down, his eyes drawn to the arrow shaft protruding from his chest. Stone ducked down.

A second arrow found its mark below the first in the man's stomach. There was less resistance there, just flesh, muscle and cavity. The arrow almost went completely through, but the flights remained in view. The arrow had penetrated the liver. The blood was dark and thick. It had already reached the man's lips. Stone reached out and caught the man's hand. He heaved and pulled him towards him to safety, as a third arrow flew over him and struck the tree. The arrow was made from aluminium and the shaft bent as its velocity halted instantly. Stone could see the arrow head was broad and sharp.

"You're fucked, man," the man said, his voice wet and bubbly. "That's The Saracen. He's a Yemini, an Arab." He gasped in air, quivered as he rushed his words. "He's a master with a short bow. They think he was with ISIS, executed hundreds of people in Syria and Iraq using his bow. Your only chance is to get him in close. Those Arab fuckers can't fight for shit. They rely on knives and other weapons. They can't take a fucking punch, especially in the mouth." He heaved for breath, shuddered. "I hate to think I've been screwed over. The others will too…"

"Where do I find them?"

The man looked at him intensely. "They'll find you…"

Stone watched the life quickly leave the man's eyes. He tugged at the jacket, but the two arrows made it impossible to remove. He pulled the body over, caught hold of the bloody arrow shaft that was protruding the most and yanked it through. It was difficult and made a wet, squelch as he pulled it clear. He pulled the second arrow out in the same manner, all the while scanning the moonlit ground ahead of him. He could not see the archer, or The Saracen, as the man had called him. He got the jacket clear and hastily put it on. He ripped at the dummy he had created and pulled off the trousers. As he put them on, his feet pushed out the grass stuffing and he fastened them quickly. He couldn't locate the holster and spare magazine in the gloom and cursed inwardly, but he still had the pistol and he tucked it into the back of his pants and picked up the M4 rifle. The dead man had a rifle with a scope, but it was a heavy calibre hunting rifle and at best, would only have three rounds left in the flush magazine. He ignored it and took the man's water bottle.

An arrow whipped past Stone and clattered into the belt of trees. Stone turned and looked in the direction of its travel and saw a figure, lightly silhouetted in the moonlight duck, down behind some cover. He brought up the rifle and fired off a round, a little lower. He kept the rifle sighted and waited. He doubted that he had hit the man with one shot, but it wasn't his sole reason for firing – he had wanted to slow the man's pace, give him something to think about. The act of stopping the enemy's momentum was the biggest part of combat. Courage is often beaten by self-doubt, given enough time. And if someone is given that time to doubt their own ability, then they will start to consider their own mortality. Stone fired again. The time had been about right for someone to take stock, attempt to take a look. A bullet landing near them would give them something else to think about. They would also worry that their enemy was advancing on them, out manoeuvring them, flanking them. Stone counted off ten seconds and fired another round. He then ran through the belt of trees at a sprint for fifty-metres, dropped low and re-sighted on the cover he had last seen the figure behind. He waited. He may well have hit his target. But he was sure he hadn't and was sure he would be served well by waiting. He backed up to a tree and rested the weapon against its trunk, the open sights on the clump of cover where he had last seen The Saracen. Lower down was a thin branch which would provide a steadier aim point. Being lower to the ground was more preferable, bringing his profile and size as a target down considerably and making him more difficult to hit, so he crouched down and flinched as the arrow struck the tree just above his head. He fell backwards as a second arrow struck a point two feet lower – right where his body had been. He got the rifle up to aim, but a third arrow struck the weapon's frame and glanced off into his shoulder. Stone cried out and dropped the rifle. He fell backwards, the arrow protruding from him and when he rolled the shaft bent and gouged the wound, sending a searing pain through him that felt like fire and ice all at once.

He crawled on the ground, thrashing his legs to get him behind a clump of trees before another arrow found its mark. He could not believe how fast the man had launched the arrows. And then he thought to the dead man's words; *he's a master with a short bow*...

The pain was unbelievable. He was sweating profusely from it, and not just the heat and exertion. He felt the tip, which was just below the surface of the skin. The tip had struck the bone. Stone hoped that the tip had not broken off or that shards of bone had not shattered. He dug his fingers into the wound, clasped the tip and pulled. It was agony, but a short sharp dose of it. He looked at the tip and the wicked-looking point looked to be intact. He threw the arrow down and drew the pistol from behind his waistband. He had no time to see to the wound, no time to look for the man. He simply took off through the jungle to put as much distance between The Saracen and himself as possible.

28

Stone could feel the blood seeping from his shoulder. It did not hurt quite as much now, more of a constant nagging throb, but he was focusing on getting away and that was taking his mind off the pain. At a particularly thick belt of trees he chanced a look and saw that most of his left arm and side was covered with blood. He needed to staunch the flow and he needed to take on some water. He had dropped the bottle, lost the plastic bag and had left the dead man's water canteen near his body. All he had was the FN pistol in his hand and the nineteen rounds it still held. But he had also kept hold of the man's earpiece and receiver.

He tucked the receiver into his pocket and put the earpiece into his ear. There was a blast of static and then he heard a voice. Calm, collected. Female.

"He's approaching the slope. The terrain gets thick. Swing right, that's east, and the gradient is much less steep, relatively open." There was no reply. Stone had noticed that the unit had no throat-mic. Maybe The Saracen's was the same as well. *"Your arrow supply is low. A drone drop will resupply you at the top of the slope."*

Stone slowed his pace. He tried to visualise the man branching off to outflank him. He had reached the base of the slope. It only looked to be a hundred feet or so, but he knew that even the tallest mountains looked like nothing from the bottom. He looked at the ground above him. It was thick with foliage and debris which had washed down after the rain. He climbed twenty-feet through the thick brush, then turned and ran back down the slope and branched off to his right.

"The target is heading south! You will have to finish your climb now and traverse the top of the slope. Take the slope down at the southerly-most point and you should come out just behind him. Will redirect the arrow resupply until you get into a better position. The drone is ten minutes away. Repeat, ETA of drone-drop ten minutes. Location to be confirmed."

Stone wasted no time veering off to his left. He was putting maximum distance between himself and the man he knew as The Saracen. He crashed through a tremendous network of spiders webs, their sticky gossamer covering his face and neck. It creeped him out a little, spiders not being on a list of his favourite things. Then he remembered something he had heard long ago, and started to gather up as many webs as he could. He pressed them into his wound, using his fingers to manipulate them inside. It hurt like hell, but he gathered more and pressed them in and around the opening. The bleeding was staunched quickly. Not only did the webs soak up the blood, they contained a coagulant property, the same that turned the web from liquid to its cotton-like state as it left the spider. It would clot the wound better than anything modern medical science had at its disposal. Stone pressed on.

"I have lost sight of the target, but he is in quadrant four-fourteen. If he stays on his bearing, he will emerge in the open ground at the foot of the hill. He's done a double-back. We have assets on the ground getting ready for body removal. They will not engage, will hold position at the other side of the clearing, but he must not see them. Drone-drop re-supply of arrows will take place at the first spinney of banyan trees. Break for the clearing early. We have no cameras until the clearing. Do not kill off-line. If you capture, you will need to get the target to a good location for maximum bidding."

Stone stopped and pressed himself against a tree. His lungs were heaving and his head thumped with dehydration. He caught his breath as best he could, visualising The Saracen's progress. By his reckoning, the man would be almost level with him by now, but a hundred yards or so closer to the clearing. Stone kept the pistol ready in front of him and headed north. It was only a guess, but the shafts of light shone through the jungle canopy from right to left. It was not yet mid-day by his estimation, and he was learning to use the jungle and not fight in vain against it.

Ahead of him, an arrow knocked against the undrawn string and the shaft resting on the arrow rest,

The Saracen eased himself slowly through the undergrowth. Stone could see him and beyond the man the light was brighter, the clearing already having opened up. Stone moved carefully, each pace timed with The Saracen's own to minimise the noise. The gap had closed to forty-metres or so. Stone had a good shot, but he wanted more. Needed more. Needed a way out. He looked at the trees above the man in front of him, looked into the trees above his own head. There were no glowing eyes, no sign of a camera or a transmitter. The voice had declared the area a dead zone. Stone smiled to himself. That was exactly what is was. Or was about to be.

The Saracen was dressed entirely in black, in Arab trousers and a modified robe. He had a turban-style head dress that partially covered his face. Stone had encountered similarly dressed fighters in Afghanistan. He wore a quiver on his back, and Stone could see only two arrows poking out of it. The bow was short and dramatically recurved. It looked to be made of wood and horn. On his belt, Stone could see the Arabian *kanjar* – the classically curved middle-eastern dagger. This one was about eighteen inches long from tip to haft and sheathed in a silver scabbard.

Twenty-metres out, The Saracen drew his arrow back and swung to his right looking directly at Stone. As the arrow released, Stone hit the ground, suddenly aware that the man had known he was there and was most likely watching from the corner of his eye. Stone pushed himself back up and aimed his pistol, but saw the man drawing another arrow directly through the pistol's sights. He rolled away, but The Saracen did not release. Stone knew that the archer would fire the moment he stopped moving, but would already be estimating a moving shot and getting ready to shoot accordingly. To counter this, Stone stopped and rolled back, catching a glimpse of The Saracen adjusting his aim. Stone fired. The Saracen ducked, and Stone stopped rolling and fired again. Both shots missed and the arrow released and grazed a tree, clattering off into the undergrowth. Stone kept the pistol on the man and got to his feet. The Saracen had his last arrow in his right hand, the bow in his left. He knew he wouldn't make the shot. His eyes raged, framed by the wrap of material trailing off his head dress.

Stone nodded to the ground and the man dropped both the arrow and the bow. Stone stepped closer. Six-feet now separated them. The Saracen sagged, deflated. He had been captured and was accepting his fate. Stone was about to start questioning him when the man moved. In a flash he had spun around on one leg, kicked the pistol from Stone's hand and had the *kanjar* drawn and slashing towards Stone as he completed his spin. Stone dodged left and backwards and the dagger scythed past him, whipping the still air with an audible swish. The man's eyes looked devilish through the slit of material. He was advancing on Stone, swiping the air backwards and forwards, the blade travelling so fast that the silver edge seemed to track through the air like a child's sparkler at night.

Stone kicked out but the blade slashed across his shin and he grit his teeth and cried-out as he heard the blade strike bone. He shuffled forwards and the next time the blade flashed, he smashed the man's forearm with his own and punched, but the blow was blocked and the man swiped a backwards fist that connected with Stone's jaw. The man was already bringing the blade downwards as Stone stepped backwards again, but this time he backed into a tree and had no place else to go. The Saracen saw his chance and lunged towards Stone's stomach, but caught his foot on a tree root and tripped. Stone pushed the blade aside with his left hand and hammered his right fist onto the back of the man's neck. He dropped down and straddled the man's shoulders, raised his fist again and hammered down on his neck. He kept going and didn't stop until the man went limp. Stone's one-hundred-and-ninety pounds gave him at least a twenty-five-pound advantage over his opponent and he used every single ounce of it. He had both heard and felt the vertebrae just above the shoulder blades dislodge after the fifth blow, but kept on hammering a few more times driving it out and snapping the spinal cord. The result was unmistakable. Every part of the man relaxed and lost rigidity. Not even a breath or groan was emitted from the lifeless body as it slumped to the ground and rested completely still.

The Saracen was dead.

Stone slumped down the tree, exhausted. He closed his eyes and breathed deeply. He needed water desperately. He checked the body and underneath the robe was a litre canteen, which he drank and finished in one go without drawing breath. It was warm, but clean and tasted wonderful. He bent back down and checked the body over. Attached to the belt was a coil of string, which upon closer inspection, Stone recognised as a spare bowstring. The string was made of hundreds of strands of fibre, no thicker than a hair, that looked to have been waxed and twisted. Each end was woven into a loop and in the middle of the string it looked like cotton had been wrapped repeatedly to provide a reinforced back stop for the arrow. Stone pocketed it, then noticed some plastic ties looped on the man's belt. He took them off and looked at them. Then he thought of the last words the woman had said through his earpiece - *We have no cameras until the clearing. Do not kill off-line. If you capture, you will need to get the target to a good location for maximum bidding...* Stone thought what could have happened, how it could have turned out. Captured and taken to the clearing, where The Saracen would have awaited instructions as bids came in from the dark web.

And then Stone had an idea.

29

Stone had seen the car through the bay window behind Kathy Newman's shoulder. It passed the open gateway slowly. It was the same shade of grey as the car he had noticed pull into a driveway earlier. He was sure it was a Ford Taurus. Not the kind of car that fitted into life around here. Nobody would drive a new Ford sedan. A new BMW or Mercedes maybe, or even an older premium marque, a few facelift's back as to create a statement that they did not need to upgrade, that life had more to it than the attainment of this year's model car - such as sailboats, and even bigger sailboats than their neighbours. The only Fords out here were pickups and soccer mom SUVs.

He watched the gateway, but the car had driven on. Perhaps it was a rental.

"*You're* Kathy Newman?"

"Yes."

Stone looked her. He could see how scared she was. She had softer features than the other woman he knew as Kathy. She was nervous and didn't look like she had slept in days. "You are friends with Isobel." He stated. "Tell me about her."

She looked perplexed. "What do you want to know?"

"Where do you know her from?"

"High school."

"She never mentioned you."

She looked hurt, momentarily, then regained some composure. "We lost touch."

Stone noted she had cared. He said, "She was best friends with a girl in college." Again she seemed hurt. Stone saw a distance in her eyes. "Do you know who I mean?"

"The one who went on to join the FBI?" She seemed uninterested, a little jealous even.

"Yes."

"Liz," she said. "Elizabeth Delaney. I didn't know her."

"You know what happened to her?"

Kathy nodded. "She died."

"How?"

"In the line of duty," Kathy said. "That's all Isobel said. She was cut up for a while, still is."

"That was before I got together with Isobel," Stone said. "Or *just* before…"

"Well, do I pass?"

Stone had been swayed not only by her answers, but by her expression. Isobel had moved on since their high school days, and this woman wasn't as comfortable with it as she tried to appear. Stone had once been in a bar when his good friend announced a mutual friend would be best man at his wedding. Stone had thought he'd been fine about it, until he caught his own reflection in the mirror behind the bar as he was talking about his friend's wedding plans. The reflection had told a different story. It hurt to be second best. "I guess. It's been a trying couple of days," he said to her.

"Tell me about it," she said. "But I think I was right when I said we don't have much time."

"What makes you say that?"

"I was followed here," she said. "Or near here. I gave them the slip about ten miles out. Or at least I hope I did."

"Are you sure you were being followed?"

"Absolutely."

"What kind of vehicle?"

"A Ford sedan, grey. New looking."

Stone looked at her. He was wary what to believe. "Kathy, I'll be straight with you," he said. "I met a woman who looked a lot like you. She impersonated you, in fact. She obviously had good intelligence both on you and on myself. I was fooled by her. She wanted to find her computer expert, Edwards…"

"*My* computer expert," she interrupted. "A web expert to be more precise."

"For searching the dark web?"

She nodded. "He's one of the best."

"Was. He's dead." Stone stared at her, using it to gauge her reaction. He added, "He was shot at close range."

"Oh my god!" Kathy held her palm to her lips. Stone noticed she wasn't wearing any lipstick or chap stick. Not like the woman who had left traces of berries on Edwards' lips.

"There was no tech at the scene. No smartphone, no tablet and no laptop."

"Then it was stolen. Edwards was always connected. He had an iPhone, the big new one, was always scrolling through feeds and searching the net. And he carried his laptop in a kind of weird looking case. That material hard core sports cars and street racers have all over them." Stone frowned at her. "You know? Like a black weave."

"Carbon fibre?"

"Yes, I think so."

"So what was Edwards working on?"

"Hang on," she said. "Who was this person impersonating me?"

Stone looked at her again. He watched her eyes for a flicker. In his experience people looked one way when they lied. It was to do with the side of the brain used for spontaneous lying. When that person lied, they looked the opposite way. Both sides can be used, but not by the same person. Stone needed a control answer to see where she looked. But he'd already had it. She had said that both her and Isobel had lost touch. The truth was, Isobel had moved on, grown closer to her college friends and left her high school friends behind. Kathy's eyes had darted right. They hadn't done so since. He trusted her. "I don't know, but she was good. She had a wall of photos with awards, achievements in your name."

"Mine are in a drawer."

"Mine too."

"What else?"

"She had two big dogs."

"Dogs? I hate dogs. I'm a cat person."

Stone frowned. He could not understand why the woman had the dogs in the house. And it struck Stone that the man impersonating the cop could have been from another organisation. Unless he had been sacrificed. "She had a story about how her partner had left her with the dogs, the house, the SUV," he said. "That she was in debt."

"Well, that's true. I'm crippled with debt. My father is in a home and I'm paying for it until his health insurance steps up. But there's been problems…" she trailed off. "I have an apartment. Or I did until the block was burned down. I hate soccer mom SUVs. So she's hardly mirroring me."

"Whose is the Jeep outside?"

"My dad's."

"He's in a nursing home in Virginia."

"Yes," she replied. She seemed surprised that he knew.

"The apartment, was it arson?"

"It was."

"Do you think it was to do with what you've uncovered?"

"It wouldn't surprise me."

"So whose place is this?"

"My dad's. It's been in the family for years. He inherited it from his mother."

"Your dad is white American? This isn't a Chinese area, especially not for him to have inherited."

"He is. My mother was *Vietnamese*. She died three years ago."

"I'm sorry."

"For what? For my mother's death, or being generalist about racial stereotype and race?"

Stone shrugged. "Both, I guess. Your dad was a Vietnam veteran?"

"Lord no! How old do you think I am?" she smiled. "He was a merchant seaman. He met my mother in Australia. She was an illegal immigrant there, boat people they called them, she managed to stay in the country. My father met her in Darwin when his ship had to put in for repairs, and he managed to get her back and into the United States."

"You were telling me what Edwards was looking at," he said. "What was your story about?"

"It was about betting and online services," she said. "It kind of snowballed. I was investigating illegal gambling within the United States. Each time I uncovered something substantial, it opened up something else. When I got Edwards involved, he unravelled more than I bargained for. More than we both did, I imagine."

"Like what?"

"I started to look at the sex industry, but as a story it wasn't cutting enough. I mean, everybody knows that you can buy flesh. And then there's the child pornography and paedophile thing, but I wanted something new. Sure, I was planning to give my findings to the FBI, but I needed to unearth what was becoming a huge story, finish what I started."

"But the sex industry isn't about betting."

She smiled at him, a little coyly. "Oh my, you have a lot to learn. How many men could a woman take on at once? How big a phallic toy could be used before a woman actually passed out from the pain, or pleasure? How…"

"All right," Stone held up his hand. "I'm just an innocent country boy. Apparently."

"People bet on everything and anything. Big money too. Live internet feeds, live gambling. And then there's the pay-for-acts. The winning bid gets what they wanted to see performed." Kathy waved a hand. "It was always going to go this way. But Edwards found a whole new scene. We started with snuff movies, but it escalated. Pay-for-murders and executions. The winning bid gets what they want to see performed. Live."

"Jesus…" Stone said. He wasn't usually blasphemous, but he was at a loss for words.

"It started in Syria. There was a group, I suppose they fought as ISIS or ISIL. They were pretty savvy, tech wise. Many of them were from Europe. They used the dark web to film beheadings, and then it evolved into killing people in a certain manner requested in return for money. They raised serious funds, but not all of it went on equipment and resources and fighting their cause. Much went to Russian mafia and Saudi sympathisers, weapons dealers mainly. The people they were in fact working for. Half the Islamic extremists are just thugs working for some organised crime ring or another." She shrugged. "What better way to get your weapons sold than to keep a war going? A huge amount of this money went out to Swiss and off-shore accounts and appeared to stay there. Whether it was going to be used for their cause, or whether they decided it would be a better life for them, I don't know. Edwards has…" she paused. "Or *had* the information."

"It needs to get to the Pentagon. That information is crucial."

"That was always the plan."

"And now Edwards' technology is missing and there's nothing to point to this information."

"It would appear so," she said. "But the whole Syrian thing shut down suddenly. It's not happening now."

"Air strike," Stone ventured. "That or they were killed in battle. But an airstrike would seem the most logical answer. No survivors to carry it on and nobody to start up a new venture."

"That would make sense."

"But you found out more," Stone prompted her. "The details of missing veterans."

"Exactly."

"But I don't get it. I don't understand why the woman who came to me, who impersonated you, threw all of this out there to me."

"To reel you in?" Kathy said quietly. "To get your trust. Was she flirtatious?"

"A bit."

"Did she come on to you?"

"A bit," Stone felt himself flush around his neck. "Nothing too much," he lied. For a moment he pictured the woman naked in front of him, the things they'd done. He'd been a fool.

"I bet she tried it on," she said. "I bet she got close enough for you to smell her, make you want her…" Stone didn't reply. She studied him, looked as if she was going to say something, but shook her head. "But what didn't she already know?"

"She needed to find Edwards…" Stone said flatly. And he'd led her right to him. Not directly, but through the corruption of his cell phone. The missed calls, the deleted messages. "Now he's dead and everything he had is missing." He bunched his fists. "Shit! This is all on me!"

Kathy remained silent. She started to pace around the lounge. "There has to be more. There has to be another angle."

"With Edwards out of the picture and his findings gone, there is no story. But she had details, she showed them to me."

"If she was among the people who are behind it, then she already had enough information to appeal to you. This could have just been a carrot. They could have lifted the details, enough to entice you, and reel you in. Finding Edwards was their intention."

Stone nodded. "But there has to be more," he said, then looked at Kathy and closed his eyes. "Oh, no…"

"What?"

"Hand me your landline," he said tersely. He took out his cell phone and looked up Max's number. Kathy handed him the handset and he dialled, tucking his cell phone back into his pocket. The phone rang once and was answered immediately. Stone thought it unusual. "Max? Rob Stone. I'm on a landline at the house on Calvert Cliffs."

"For goodness sake!" Max snapped. *"It's all gone crazy here. I've tried to call you, but your number has been disconnected. A virus has wiped out practically everything the Secret Service has on our database. Security protocols, lists of security threats – organisations and individuals who have threatened, or pose a threat to the President, intelligence from*

other agencies, both domestic and overseas. But treasury accounts were emptied first," he paused for breath. *"Millions of dollars in operating capital, ring-fenced fund accounts and special project money. As well as treasury assets. You've got to come in, Rob. Like yesterday."*

"Are they recalling agents?"

"Not exactly."

"What do you mean?"

There was a long pause before Max lowered his voice. *"The virus was spread when you logged into the mainframe from an outside network. It's been pin-pointed. I've been sequestered to work on specifics, all of the tech boys and girls have jobs to do. But it's finished. Nobody knows what this virus is, but it's eating things up. I think it's too late, I think the Security Service's technology side has been irreparably crippled."*

"But Max, I haven't logged in," Stone tensed. He reached for his wallet, flipped it open and looked for his log-in card. It wasn't there. He felt a shiver up his spine and a wave of heat wash over his face at once. "My card's gone."

"We used it to log on. When you were here with Kathy."

"She wasn't Kathy," Stone said, thinking of the passionate encounter with the woman in the kitchen, the bedroom. Then she'd left while he was in the shower. "My card has gone, she must have stolen it," he said lamely.

"You'd better come in," Max said. *"They've asked me to inform them if you call me."*

"Who are *they*?"

"The whole top floor."

"Shit," Stone paused. "I need time. I need to look into this further."

"Agent Stone, I can give you an hour or so. But this is as big as it gets. Effectively, Parks and Recreation have more computer processing ability than the Secret Service right now. The NSA and CIA are here, and they're taking over."

"Have they put out a clear indication that they suspect me, that I'm wanted?"

"Reading between the lines, they're dropping this on you whether you did it or not. It's been a pleasure working for you, your reputation is legend around here. But that's also enough reason to be unpopular as well. With the upper floors. The lower ones too. I know you haven't done anything, but getting a good lawyer lined up before you come in wouldn't hurt your prospects," he paused. *"There's more. One of the other technicians was given the task of looking into your bank accounts. There's a lot in there, seven figures. I know it's none of my business, but I imagine you're not aware of that kind of balance."*

"No," he said adamantly. "There's always a months' salary in there at the lowest, two months' worth at the highest. I've also got ten-grand in a savings account." Stone was sweating. He felt nauseous. He was silent a long while. "Thank you for the heads-up, Max," he said quietly. "I'll see you sometime. Good luck with your computer virus."

"Thanks, I'll need it. We all will. I've never seen anything like it. A ruthless son-of-a-bitch. Named after the Greek god of war…"

"Ares…" Stone said, looking up.

"The very same. You know your Greek mythology." Max remarked.

"No," Stone said. "But I know about Ares." He ended the call and placed the handset on the coffee table. His blood ran cold. There was something about this, something personal. Using his card to log into the computer mainframe pointed the finger at him. He could prove his innocence, he was sure of that, but it seemed a personal affront. He would have a task ahead of him explaining the money. He'd been on those teams, and he'd played *real* hard ball. Again, he could argue through the set up, but he could be looking at years to prove his innocence. But it was the fact that the virus released into the mainframe had been named Ares. It was a step too far.

The Ares Virus was designed as a weapon of mass destruction, a hypothesis into what a fast-acting, violent flu-like virus could do in a military arsenal.

What predominantly came from the Ares project was Aphrodite, the cure or anti-virus. A medical breakthrough had been made and Aphrodite's application into other areas of medical science meant cures for the common cold and every known strain of flu. It also drew cures for AIDS decades closer, as well as Ebola. It was as close to a cure for cancer as medicine has come. A rogue CIA agent hatched a plan to steal both virus and anti-virus and release Ares while a partner within a pharmaceutical company marketed Aphrodite. A plan worth billions. Isobel Bartlett, a senior researcher on the project, stole the formula and was hunted by an assassin working for the rogue CIA agent. The case Stone was investigating, a disbanded assassination program, crossed paths and he managed to keep Isobel alive and keep the virus out of their hands.

"Trouble?" Kathy asked, her expression one of concern.

Stone looked at her, then caught the sight behind her of the two armed men moving tactically through the gateway. "Yes."

30

"We have you online. Good work. Multiple cameras ahead, above and to your right. Good visibility."

Stone, dressed in The Saracen's robe and head dress stooped down and picked up the quiver full of arrows. The body on his shoulder weighed about one-sixty-five. He could bench press and squat more, but he was exhausted and dehydrated. He wobbled, but steadied himself in time. The Saracen's body was dressed in Stone's black trousers and the olive military jacket. He had fashioned a hood from The Saracen's vest and wrapped and fastened it around the head. The body's hands were behind its back, fastened with two pairs of plastic cable ties.

The woman spoke again in his earpiece. *"Is the target dead?"* she paused. *"Look to your right if he's still alive."*

Stone looked to his right. He looked back to the single banyan tree in front of him and carried the body over to it. He eased it off his shoulder and stood it upright. It took all of his strength, rigor mortis was yet to set in and the cadaver was still pliable, but awkwardly soft to handle. Stone used the spare bowstring and tied the body in place by its shoulders, threading the string under both armpits. He backed away, turned and walked fifty-feet before pulling an arrow from the quiver.

"What are you doing? Death in the field is one thing, but bidding is coming in for an execution! Wait! I've got Miami on here for a quarter million for you to cut both of his arms off. London wants to see him castrated first, they're up to a hundred grand. Go for castration, he may bleed out if you take the arms first. Either way, there's enough smaller bets on the slate to make beheading the conclusion. We'll see if there's a raise from enough bidders to make it a slow one."

Stone looked at the bow. It had been a while since he had used one. His whole adult life in fact. He fixed the arrow to the string and pulled back. A searing, stab of pain tore through his left shoulder, he could feel the wound seeping. The bow was powerful and he was surprised how difficult it was to draw. He aimed, released, then cursed as the arrow sailed past his target, missing by inches and travelling sixty-metres before dropping into waist-high savannah and pampas grass.

"Stop what you're doing!" The woman hissed, her accent was distinct. Stone thought Australian or South African. *"Can you hear me?"* She changed tack. *"All units, all units. The Saracen has a coms fault. Stop him from killing the target. We have commercial obligations to fulfil. Somebody give him a new headset."*

Stone fixed the second arrow and drew it back again. It was tipped with a wicked-looking head, both serrated and grooved in what looked like a titanium double-edged blade. He was steadier aiming this time, but the stiff draw still hurt his shoulder to the point of nausea. The arrow left the bow and found its mark dead centre in the corpse.

"No! Stop! We need to honour the bidding! All units, stop him!"

Four men appeared from savannah grass at the foot of the hill. They were waving and shouting animatedly. All were armed with side-arms in belt holsters, two carried pump-action shotguns. They were dressed much the same as safari guides in khaki and olive coloured shorts and short-sleeved button down shirts.

"Yo! Saracen! Take a chill-pill you rag-head prick!" the nearest man drawled. He was deep-south. Grits, biscuits and gravy for breakfast. "You've messed up bigtime!"

Stone fixed another arrow and walked forward.

"She's really pissed with you," another chided. He had the shotgun held in one hand, the barrel skywards, the butt resting on his hip.

Stone was only twenty-feet away when he drew the arrow back and fired. The arrow hit the man just left and low of centre. It stopped penetrating as the flights met the flesh, the point a good twelve-inches out from his back. There was a look of shock and bewilderment on his face, but Stone barely registered it. He was already bringing the FN pistol up to the second man with the shotgun. He double-tapped the man centre-mass and moved on. The other two men were in shock, and had only just remembered their pistols. They were attempting to draw them from their holsters, but they were no *Butch & Sundance*. Stone fired twice more at the furthest man. He fell backwards. Stone charged forwards, the muzzle of his pistol just a few feet from the remaining man who had the butt of his Sig P226 pistol in his hand, but had still not managed to get it free of the holster. "Don't do it! Stand still! Stand still!" The man did just that, raised his hands slowly above his head. The man who had been hit with the arrow was kneeling now, both hands clasped on the arrow shaft in front of him. He was grunting and sucking air in through clenched teeth. Stone moved his weapon quickly, fired at the man's head from no more than a metre away and had it back aiming at the last man standing in an instant. The three men on the ground lay still. Stone lowered his pistol, shot the man in the fleshy part of his thigh, avoiding the bone and femoral artery. The man dropped like a heavy sack, screaming. He didn't notice Stone take the pistol from his own holster as he held his leg and closed his eyes, sucking air through the pain. Stone looked down at the man and kicked his other leg. "Listen to me! Listen! You're going to tell me what I want to know.

If you don't, I'm going to shoot every bone in your legs and work my way up."

The man nodded. Stone pulled off the head dress and discarded it onto the ground, before helping the man to his feet. He then heard a burst of static in his ear. *"Every available asset to the bunker. We have a security breach. Repeat, every available man to the bunker. We have a security breach. Switch to second emergency frequency immediately."* There was a long pause, but Stone could hear muted background noises. And then a man's voice, deep and raspy filled the void. *"Congratulations Mr Stone. You've made it to the next level…"*

31

Stone shouted for Kathy to get down and went to push her to the floor, but she dodged him and made for a built-in floor to ceiling cupboard at the other end of the lounge. Stone drew his pistol and tracked one of the men, but he was too late and the man got away from the bay window and behind the wall. He took a chance and fired three shots, about ten inches apart, across the wall. The building was constructed from what appeared to be timber cladding and stucco. The chimney breast was made out of red brick, as were the gable ends, but Stone doubted that the brickwork extended any further, merely to have ended up being covered by wood. He was correct in his assumption, and the man staggered out clutching his stomach. Stone fired one more shot at the man's head through the double-glazed bay window and the man went down amid a mist of crimson and shattered glass.

The second man had darted towards the back of the building and Stone noticed a figure sprinting from the gateway down the side of the boundary. That made three. One down, two to go. He ran to the window but turned when the world erupted beside him. For a moment he thought one of the attackers had tossed in a grenade, but then he saw Kathy with the pump action shotgun and she racked another shell into the chamber. She had blown out the side window and was taking aim again. She fired and the recoil knocked her slight frame back at least half a stride.

"Got him!" she exclaimed. "He's fallen behind my father's old skiff!" The remaining part of the window pane shattered and she ducked down as the man she had shot at returned fire with a machine pistol. He was controlling his shots in bursts of three or four rounds. It was a professional response. Kathy crawled to the sofa and looked at Stone. "Damn, I thought I got him. He fell."

Stone darted over to the window and peered out. The man dashed out from the upturned wooden boat and limped back towards the gateway. It was a bad injury – if he had favoured the leg any more he'd have been crawling. "You did," Stone said to her. "He's been injured; you've peppered his legs." He aimed at the man's back, but as he was about to fire he heard gunshots and the sound of wood splintering in the kitchen. He turned and was about to fire, but Kathy had stepped in front of him and was wheeling the huge pump-action shotgun around. She fired and pumped, fired and pumped. The person in the kitchen was scrabbling on the parquet flooring. Stone could hear them slipping on empty brass shell cases, glass and wood, and now loose balls of lead bird shot. Stone pushed Kathy down onto the sofa and fired a dozen rounds out into the kitchen. The 5.7x28mm bullets from the FN travelled a flat trajectory and had tremendous penetration, capable of defeating bulletproof jackets. Which was one of the reasons he had recently switched to it.

Stone eased forwards towards the doorway. He glanced at Kathy, who was pushing herself to her feet and scowling at him. She shouldered the shotgun and turned around, covering the windows behind them. She wasn't a trained agent, but she was handy with the weapon and seemed to know the basics.

There was nobody in the kitchen. The door was wide open and swinging on its hinges. Stone turned to Kathy. "Stay here," he said. "Cover the door while I take a look."

"I'm coming with you," she said adamantly.

"No, stay."

"Bullshit! I'm coming with you! There's two smashed windows in there." She nodded back towards the lounge. "I can't cover two different directions at once and I only have three shells left."

Stone looked at the intensity in her dark eyes. They were almost ebony, but softer than the other woman who had been claiming to be her. He recognised when he was losing. "Ok," he conceded. "But stay close and watch our rear. I'll keep watch ahead." He changed to a new magazine and put the old one, with at least three rounds left, in his pocket. He now had twenty-one bullets in the weapon. He glanced out through the doorway and realised it wasn't going to be enough.

The wounded man had reached the grey Ford Taurus and backed it into the driveway. He was taking aim from behind the hood and another man had joined him, crouched by the rear bumper and pulling out the retractable stock of a Heckler & Koch G36 carbine. He noticed Stone, smiled and shouldered the weapon. Stone spun around, grabbed Kathy and hustled her back into the lounge. His eyes darted left then right, then settled on the cavernous fireplace. It had been cleaned out in the spring and arranged with dried flowers. There was room for two. Just. He barrelled into Kathy and they hit the hearth together, Stone pulling her into the protection of the brick surround as the bullets sliced through the building and tore up everything in their path. Stuffing spewed out of the sofas and chairs and the glass coffee table shattered, along with practically each and every item on the shelves, sideboard and walls. They both pulled their legs up and ducked their heads. The onslaught was terrifying and Stone realised the man must have changed magazines two or three times.

"We can't get out front to escape!" Stone snapped at her. The bullets were still tearing up the room. Stone knew that if the men were tactically trained, and he could see that they were, then someone would be flanking them as the man continued to fire. They could not afford to get bogged down. "We need to draw them out so we can get to my bike!"

"What about a boat?" she said, still shielding her ears, her head ducked down to her chest. "I have a dory with an outboard at the beach."

"Perfect! Is it in the water?" he asked. He had seen waves breaking on his ride down, a boat couldn't be moored in the surf.

"The beach ended half a mile up the coast. There's an inlet here, a few boats are moored inside."

The gunfire subsided. Stone wasted no time. "Let's go!" He pulled her up. She had dropped the shotgun, but Stone pushed her onwards towards the shattered bay window. "Lead the way, I'll cover us."

They both hurdled the body on the deck and Kathy sprinted across the sand-covered lawn. Stone realised she was faster than him and had to give it everything he had to keep up. Kathy looked like she was pacing herself. Gunfire started up behind them, but it was a different calibre than what had decimated the house. As Kathy darted through a narrow gateway, bordered by sand dunes and tufts of seagrass, Stone turned to see the wounded man standing on the deck. He was favouring his legs, leaning against the building. He raised his machine pistol, but Stone fired first. A burst of four shots, in two double-taps. The man darted back inside, glass shattering the window next to him. As Stone turned to run there was just enough time to see the man with the assault rifle run across the ground at the front of the house. Stone didn't stop to fire, he was outgunned and the distance was a factor, so he ran as fast as he could to where he'd last seen Kathy. He ran through the gateway and down a sand path. He could see a set of small, fresh footprints. The pathway wound round to the right then dropped steeply to the beach. A mixture of shale and sand with patches of rock, the shore spanned thirty-metres to the sea, which was calm and clear. Six or seven boats were moored up, tethered to the shore by ropes fastened to large boulders in the sand. It was only when Kathy untethered the rope to a small dory and pushed it deeper, that Stone saw their problem. The water was permanent – a lagoon, cut off from the rest of the Chesapeake by a breakwater, a groin of sand where large waves crashed onto the shore. The mounds of green water rose, sucking sand and stones with it, then broke into five-foot high walls of water before unleashing onto the sand with an audible crack. The lagoon must have been usable for about half the tide, and at low tide it would be completely surrounded by sand and landlocked.

Stone cursed loudly and jumped into the boat. Kathy had started the engine and reversed into deeper water. She looked at Stone apologetically. "We're cut off from the sea!" she exclaimed.

Stone looked up the sand dune and saw one of the men sliding halfway down the loose sand. It was the man with the machine pistol. He raised it and aimed. Stone caught Kathy's wrist and killed the engine's revs. He raised the FN and aimed. Even though he was armed with a pistol, he still had the trajectory, power and range advantage over the 9mm MP5. Stone fired, not expecting a hit, but to see the splash of sand near his target. He needed a marker. It was left by a half metre and low by one. He adjusted his aim, close to one-hundred-and-thirty metres distant. The machine pistol spat out some rounds and they splashed into the water in front of the boat's prow. Stone had recalculated and his next shot closed the range and width by half. His third, fourth and fifth rounds struck the man in the chest and he rolled the rest of the way down the dune and rested still on the rocky shoreline.

Kathy tried to protest as Stone took over the control and increased the revs, the boat shot backwards and Stone knocked it into forward gear and turned hard on the tiller at maximum revs as the man with the assault rifle ran into view two-hundred metres away at the top of the dune. Distance was of the essence, their survival depended upon it, and as the boat powered out towards the sandbar, Stone weaved left and right with no particular rhythm to hassle the man's aim. He heard gunshots, but did not stop. The boat was fairly quick, its moderately powered thirty-five horse power engine helped considerably by the boat's light weight and short length. The flat bottom drew little draught and the boat skipped playfully across the light chop of the deep lagoon. The steering was sensitive and Stone found himself making constant adjustments. He chanced a look behind and saw the man aiming. He was a long way off now, towards the effective range of the short barrelled G36 with its 5.56mm ammunition. But a trail of splashes followed them and then bullets pinged into the aluminium transom. Stone ducked and looked at the damage, but smelled the fuel and saw water seeping into the boat. The bullets had gone through the portable fuel tank. By the smell of it they would run out fuel soon. He imagined the man changing to another magazine, raising his aim so that the bullets rained down on them from three hundred metres away. He slew sideways, kept the revs on and watched the breakwater ahead of them.

"What are you doing?" Kathy yelled above the engine noise.

"Hold on."

"You can't be serious?"

"There's nowhere in this lagoon where we'll be truly out of range. Especially if he works his way closer. The water is giving him perfect markers when he misses."

"We can't go over the breakwater!"

"Hold on."

Kathy looked at him, then back at the breakwater. She tucked herself down into the boat and gripped a cleat with both hands. More bullets struck the boat and Stone twitched, sensing a bullet had come as close as possible to his head without hitting. He brought the boat to port and watched the wave breaking along the strip of beach ahead. There was a surge of water subsiding from the previous wave. It looked a little deeper in the middle so Stone aimed at it and kept the revs on full. The wave started to mound, drawing up sand as it peaked. As it crested, the tiny boat was no more than twenty-feet from it. The wave looked a lot bigger than it had from the shore of the lagoon. Stone guessed it was six to eight feet of pounding shore break. He held his nerve, ignored Kathy's scream as the boat ran aground on the shale and sand. The wave barrelled and seemed to slow for a moment before crashing down just feet from the prow of the boat. The prow rode up on the white water and the entire boat left the water and was airborne. The engine revved loudly, its reverberation echoing across the lagoon as the propellers spun freely in the air. Stone gripped the tiller and felt himself taking off, parting company with the boat. The boat landed stern first, at about thirty degrees and the propeller sliced back into the water sending up plumes of spray. When the rest of the flat hull thudded into the water, waves were thrown outwards on both sides. The boat landed at the base of the next green wave, the last of the set. The boat climbed, almost pivoted backwards, but pushed through at the crest and smashed down onto calm water behind.

Stone had slipped off the transom and sprawled into the boat. Kathy was picking herself up. The two looked at each other for a moment, then both of them grinned with relief.

"Awesome!" she shouted. "I never thought we'd make it!" She hugged him as he climbed back onto the bench seat.

"Nor did I," Stone replied. He revved the power control on the tiller and the boat moved through the calmer water parallel to the shore. He lowered the revs and the boat wallowed with the swell. "We need to get away. The fuel tank has taken a hit and it's leaking badly."

Kathy looked behind Stone at the beach. "The gunman has gone. Could we double back? He's seen us head up the coast. Maybe he'll drive up and try to shoot at us from the shore. He can travel on the road in his car faster than we can out here."

"My thoughts exactly," Stone said. "What's down the other way? Somewhere we can put in easily?"

"There's a nice beach a mile down from the house. There's a turning and parking area almost on the shore."

"I don't like the idea of walking back along the road."

"We don't have to," Kathy said emphatically. "It's part of the nature reserve, there's footpaths all through the woods and the dunes."

Stone nodded. "That will do." He pulled the tiller towards him and the boat turned out to sea in a wide arc.

"What if they're still there?"

"They won't be. Someone will have sounded the alarm, called nine-one-one." He thought of what Max had said. Maybe those police officers would be coming for him anyway. He needed to turn himself in, but he also needed to find out what was happening and who was behind this. And he needed to find the woman who had impersonated Kathy. The woman who had brought down the Secret Service.

32

The man had told Stone about the Jeep and Stone had pushed him on ahead. Stone had ejected the shells from one of the Remington shotguns and removed the firing pin. The man now used it as a crutch and limped ahead of Stone, who periodically shoved him in the small of the back with the muzzle of his own shotgun. Stone had stripped off The Saracen's robes. He was bare chested and wore just the Arabian style trousers. He took one of the dead men's pistols and three magazines and pocketed them. He then ditched the FN Five-Seven – there wasn't enough ammunition to make it a viable option. Instead, he had taken the other shotgun and mustered a dozen or so 00 buck shells. They were 3 ½ inch magnum loads with nine deadly ball bearings per shell, each ball bearing marginally smaller than 9mm pistol ammunition. They were fearsomely devastating loads. At close range, each shot was like firing nine handgun rounds.

Stone had elected to keep the bow and had slung it over his shoulder along with the dozen arrows in the quiver. He liked to keep his options open.

The Jeep was exactly that – an original Willys-Overland from world war two. Open-topped, seats for four with a small cargo deck on the back overhanging the rear axle. It was basic, but small and manoeuvrable in the terrain.

"Get in," Stone said sharply. "You can drive."

"But my leg," the man protested.

"Hell, this thing will shift without the clutch once you've got it moving."

"But..." Stone pointed the shotgun at the man's other leg. "Ok! Ok!" he pleaded and got into the driver's side.

"What is this place, an island?" Stone asked. The man nodded. "Where?"

"Off the west coast of Panama."

"Is this to do with Richard Anderson? Of Anderson-Lucas Holdings?"

The man shrugged. "I don't know them."

"It's a he," Stone said. "Richard Anderson. The company is called Anderson-Lucas and has a bank in Panama City. Payments to missing veterans were made from an account held with his bank. Is he behind this? Does he own the island?"

"Oh, wait, the banker guy?"

"English?"

"Yeah, he *owned* a bank in Panama," the man nodded. "He was here before you. His family also."

"Where is he?"

"Wasted."

"What?"

"Him and his family. They were wasted before you got here. Some Chinese bankers did some pretty high bidding to have them all fucked up. The guy apparently screwed them over years ago, they didn't forget. He nearly put them out of business, or knocked them a few dollars off of billionaire status. Who knows? Money is all the same to those guys."

"What happened?"

"Him and another guy were pegged out at the ponds. A couple of the guys in the game fed his family to the crocs while they were forced to watch. The bidding went insane. Wasn't the nicest thing done here, but not the worst either."

Stone shook his head, sickened. He had seen the stakes, used the rope to start the fire for his meal. He had assumed it was the remnants of a trap. "Who was the other guy they pegged out?"

The man shrugged. "No idea," he said. "Just some suit. Who the hell knows what goes on here, really."

"This, *concession*, you have here must have a generator for electricity. The cameras and Wi-Fi are running twenty-four-seven."

"There are stacks of generators and a solar array."

"Really?" Stone changed tack. "Tell me about communications. To stream live on the internet, you need routers and a network hub, but you also need a phone line. Out here it will need to be an antenna or a satellite dish."

"They have a satellite dish. A huge one," he paused. "Hey man, I'm helping you. You've got to help me."

"What do you want?"

"I want out."

"You're not free to leave anytime? I'm surprised."

The man started the Jeep's engine and shrugged. "I guess it's obvious really. Nobody has ever asked to leave. Most of the guys here really enjoy what they do, but they're pretty psyched up. All experienced combat veterans. They missed the killing." Stone remained silent. He had killed, but he had never once enjoyed it. Living with it could be difficult at times. He'd always made sure that the people he'd killed had been on the wrong side of the moral compass. He'd led them to Edwards, he knew that. The man's death was on him. This episode was going to take some dealing with, he was sure of that much. "I'm not a killer," the man continued, pulling away jerkily. He winced as the Jeep vibrated and obviously hurt his leg. "But…"

"But you turned a blind eye." Stone finished the sentence for him.

"I did what I did," the man said.

"Like German guards in the concentration camps," Stone commented. "They lined them up, marched them along. But it wasn't their decision. Is that it?"

"No, not really. Hey, don't judge me, man. When this shit first started it was vet against vet. Soldiers battling it out like gladiators. They knew what they were getting into. Their egos got them into it. Then the word spreads, throughout the net, through different walks of life. Then the betting and bidding escalates. People are actually having enemies abducted and dropped off here. They get to watch them scared and pleading, get to watch them die. All from the comfort of their snug, a brandy in one hand and a Cuban cigar in the other. This place turned rich men into gods in their own homes. Suddenly the people dying here aren't even mortal enemies, they're business partners, ex-wives, a partner's lover… Hell, one guy apparently got himself blown by a two-thousand-dollar whore while he watched his ex-wife hunted through the jungle. People are plain weird, whichever way you cut it. But the operation still needs clearing up afterwards." He thumbed his chest. "And that's by the people who keep this place running. The cooks, the cleaners, the maintenance guys. And the field support staff, like me and my buddies you just wasted back there."

"Well I hope the benefits are good. On more than Obama care at least."

"We do ok," he said quietly. "Or would if we ever thought we'd leave here to spend it."

"Is that the feeling in general?"

"Nobody says so, but we ain't *that* dumb. It's gotten too big. I guess we're all just riding it out, hoping there'll be an opportunity to jump."

"So how do you get rid of the bodies?"

"Use your imagination," the man said, swinging the Jeep onto a narrow stone track. "Where do you want to go?"

"The satellite."

The man drove onwards. "There's at least a dozen Black Caiman here. Big ones. The smaller ones have all been eaten. They don't get fed between killings, that way they're hungry and have to make do with a few catfish and turtles. The west coast of the island gets Great Whites passing through in spring and fall. I think they head somewhere to breed in the summer but hang around here for a few weeks. It's pretty bountiful ocean around here. There's bull sharks, hammerheads, white-tips and tiger sharks off the coast all year round. You get some blood and chunks in the water and when there's enough sharks competing for it you drop the bodies off the boat."

"You have boats here?"

"Of course. That's how we get supplies in. And the players for the game."

"Where?"

"The west coast. There's a natural inlet that almost curves back on itself like a double horseshoe. You can't see the boats or jetty from the sea, and the Pacific swells don't reach it. But it can get rough once you get out of the inlet. It's the least sheltered side, but the inlet is a natural harbour."

Stone thought of the breakwater in the Chesapeake. It couldn't be any more hazardous than getting over that. The man drove off the road for a short way and joined some tyre tracks that led up a hill. Stone realised that the hill he had first seen from the point was in fact a clump of five or six hills with trees in the valleys and savannah style grass on the top. He could see a large satellite dish and a cluster of smaller dishes in the distance.

"They'll know you're heading there by now," the man said.

"So what am I up against?"

"You'll finish this and get me off the island?"

"I'll finish this," Stone said. "You can make your own way off."

They neared the satellite dish and the man bounced over some rough ground and winced. He had a piece of material from one of his colleagues' sleeves wrapped around his thigh, but it was soaked through. Stone looked at the set up and went through his options. He had limited ammunition and wanted to conserve it. Ramming the dishes with the truck would seem the best option. He would take the wheel and simply ram and reverse the vehicle until everything that looked like a satellite dish, generator or receiver was smashed. He could then fire precision rounds through the generators and receivers. They may well be able to repair the damage, but it would take them weeks.

The man seemed to consider Stone's comment for a moment. "Ok," he said. "I'll help, but I want you to remember what I did."

"Oh, I'll remember *everything* you did, all right." Stone thought of the banker pegged out, watching his family torn up in front of him. A feeding frenzy of black beasts thrashing the water red. The screams of his wife and children… He had already decided this guy would never leave here. He wouldn't live past his usefulness. "So tell me."

"You've got Rodriquez. He's a Puerto Rican. Small guy but he's got like an iron core. He can hold onto a pole and push himself out like a flag."

"I know a bar where the girls do that for five-dollar tips."

"No, seriously. You won't hurt this guy in the stomach. I reckon he'd stop a nine-millimetre in his six-pack. He's an ex-recon marine. So you won't see him coming either. Then there's The Bull. Black guy, six-four, two-hundred-and-eighty pounds of muscle. Well, you know him."

"What?"

"Well, he brought you here, dumped you on the beach. Anyway, he played big-time college football. He was set for a great career in football but nine-eleven changed all that. He had two firefighter brothers die in the Twin Towers. He joined the marines and did as many tours as he could. He's a handy soldier in every way, but he's a slow mover and relies on his strength. He's not too smart either."

Stone said nothing. This man could have been, *would* have been, a brother in arms. His joining the marines because of the atrocity of 9/11 mirrored his own in joining the army. "How many are there?" he asked.

"There's four assets left altogether. That's the name they use for the killers."

"Who are the others?"

The man hesitated. He seemed to be struggling to answer. He looked at Stone, opened his mouth, but said nothing. He looked back at the satellite ahead and shrugged. Stone recognised the man had a change of heart, but not in time. "Why don't you ask them yourself?" The man pulled the key out of the ignition dived out of the Jeep, landing heavily in a pile of splayed limbs. He clearly hadn't expected to fall so heavily, or had expected to travel further, and was struggling to get up and away from Stone at a laughably slow pace.

Stone saw a movement behind the large satellite dish. He ducked down as bullets struck the front of the Jeep. The vehicle was stationary and without the keys, and wouldn't be starting anytime soon. Stone slid out, the shotgun in his hand. He needed to do some damage limitation. He needed the keys to the Jeep, so needed the man to stop crawling for cover. He aimed at the man from under the truck.

He was up on his feet now, half hopping and half running away with the inert shotgun as a crutch. He was making a better pace now. Stone fired and the man sprawled onto the ground screaming, at least a few of the 00 buckshot smashing the shin bone in his good leg. Stone wouldn't lose sleep over the man, too many bodies had been disappeared by his actions and he detested people who simply did evil and justified that they were only a small cog in a big machine.

He turned his aim back to the satellite dish. He couldn't see the person who had shot at him, but he decided a few volleys at the dish wouldn't hurt and would disable their operation, if only in the short term. He fired and pumped several times, aiming at the receiver which was located on top of the arm in the middle of the dish. He then reloaded the weapon with shells from his pocket. He glanced around, but the absence of attackers was somehow worse than seeing them. He knew someone was there, he just needed to locate them. He had felt the same way before in Afghanistan. In the mountains, the culverts and fields of maize. Being in a firefight and not being able to locate your enemy was a truly terrifying experience.

He backed up along the side of the Jeep and crouched down at the rear. The man with the ruined legs was thrashing about in the long grass. He was unarmed and of no further threat. He wasn't going anywhere anytime soon. Stone left him and shuffled down the driver's side of the tiny vehicle. He felt the hit of the bullet in the centre of his back. He dropped the shotgun and fell forwards, unable to break his fall. His face was turned to the right, his cheek in the dirt and his hands by his sides. He couldn't move, the pain in his back was crippling and had spread across his body into his limbs. The pain was constant. He had felt it before, though not for so long a period. It was as if he had been Tasered, but the operator wouldn't stop the shock... And then he realised it was a drug affecting him, like a tranquiliser dart.

Stone was paralysed. He could not move his head, but he could see a pair of black military boots on the other side of the Jeep. They made their way over to the man in the grass. Stone could see a thick pair of legs clad in camouflaged trousers as the otherwise unseen man moved further away from the Jeep. The boots roughly turned the injured man over. He looked upwards, held his arms outwards, his hands spread protectively in front of his face. Stone could not hear, but from the man's actions, he knew he was pleading for his life. There was a loud gunshot and the man's body jerked, as his head turned to mist and disappeared. His hands dropped by his sides. Lifeless, still.

The boots and legs made their way unhurriedly back to the Jeep, then all Stone could see was the boots as they drew near. And then they went out of view entirely and he heard them behind him on the ground. He knew what was coming. He'd had a good run. He'd danced with death many times and won. Now it was time to pay the band. Hopefully it would be quick. Strangely, he wasn't scared.

The feeling of paralysis started to fade and he felt the boot on his side, saw the blue of the sky come into view as he was rolled over. He looked up into the man's face. As black as coal, towering above him. This man could only be The Bull. He had the most curious features, aesthetically all wrong. It was a moment before Stone realised what it was. The man had no nose. Just two raw-looking holes and some fleshy skin that looked like an upturned limpet. The man was breathing hard through his mouth, exposing a set of brilliant white, but shattered teeth. Whatever had happened, it had been recent. He certainly hadn't been born that way, nor lived like it for years. Stone guessed it was merely a matter of days. Part of the featureless nostrils had started to scab over. He looked past the man's extraordinarily unpleasant face. Took in the white clouds scudding across the beautiful blue sky behind him. There was no fight left in him, because as hard as he tried, he could not make his arms and legs move. They were stiff and numb, atrophic. And then the man took out a strange-looking pistol with a cavernous diameter muzzle. He was smiling and Stone suddenly realised, like déjà vu, that he had seen both the man and the weapon before. Another time, another place. He saw the weapon point downwards, felt the impact of the dart, but only a whisper of sound, like a rush of air. He lurched on the ground, then, much like the pain in his back, he filled with heat and numbness and what he would have described as being drunk and sick and dizzy and hungover all at once. And tired. As tired as it was possible to be. And then his eyes closed and for the briefest of moments he remembered how he got here, the gaps filled in the chasm of uncertainty, and he took comfort in the fact that nothing else seemed a blur.

33

Getting the tiny dory to shore had been more difficult than Stone had imagined. He had judged the swells as best he could, but a large wave had broken over the stern and not only drenched them, but sent the vessel side-on to the subsequent wave. The engine had died and with no power to manoeuvre them into a better position, the boat had been swamped and overturned. They were only waist deep when they both resurfaced, but they had little choice but to abandon the boat and wade to shore. The water was cold and the air temperature was dropping fast. The boat had been left abandoned, bobbing with the swell, half submerged with the rudder scraping the sand. The next wave broke onto its prow and it disappeared entirely.

When they waded clear of the water, they stopped at the shoreline and looked at each other. Kathy's hair was stuck to her face and she was slicking it back. "Nice work," she said. "Remind me never to get into a boat with you again."

"The chances will be slim."

"Non-existent," she chided. "It wasn't insured either."

"The Secret Service will reimburse you," he lied. He had no idea how he stood with the agency, but he knew it wasn't good. If he got out of this and managed to keep his freedom, he'd buy Kathy a new boat with his own money.

"So what now?"

"Into the dunes," Stone said decisively. "We get out of sight, get dried off and get back to your house. If they're still there, we'll have the element of surprise." Stone took the pistol out of his holster and ejected the magazine as he walked up the beach. He upturned it and water ran out. He handed it to Kathy while he pulled back the weapon's slide and gave it a shake. It dripped with water and Stone blew harshly down the barrel and into the breach to remove any droplets. He took the magazine off of her and made the weapon ready again. Holstering it, he stopped and took out his cell phone. "Damn thing," he said. "This is how they got to me. This is how they found Edwards and how they followed me to you." He turned and threw it into the ocean. "I'm sorry. They corrupted my voicemail, intercepted my calls, I should have thought they would be able to follow my signal GPS as well."

Kathy didn't say anything. She touched his arm, then turned and carried on walking towards the sizable dune. It was steep and the sand was loose which made climbing it difficult and the exertion burned the muscles in their thighs and calves. At the peak, the dune dropped down ten-feet or so on the other side and the sand became firm underfoot. Sea grass sprouted and grew in large clumps and after fifty paces or so, small, gnarly trees formed the fringe of a wood made up from mainly large pines. The woods were not dense and had been well-managed. The visibility through the trees was considerable. There were stacks of logs in places and at first Stone thought they were the property of a logging concern, but as he studied them, rotting to the elements, Kathy had told him they were stacked in such a way as to attract insects and worms – a kind of feeding station for rodents and birds, which in turn attracted snakes and bigger birds such as eagles, owls and hawks.

The walk had dried them quickly. They had taken off their clothes and wrung them out, then redressed and kept moving. After almost a mile Kathy stopped. She had been limping for most of the walk.

"I need a rest," she said. "I've got blisters from my wet shoes." She pointed to her wedges. "These aren't exactly meant for cross-country."

Stone looked at her toes, noticing they were bloody. He motioned her towards a fallen tree. It had upended and the majority of the roots were clear of the earth, but a few had hung on and the tree was still alive, it's branches reaching upwards like individual trees. "Let me take a look," he said.

"It's ok, I just need to rest them."

Stone took out his Spyderco knife and whipped open the blade. He cut the lining from his jacket and folded it. "Here," he said. "Take off your shoe and wrap your foot in this. It's silk. It should soothe and cushion any cuts or blisters."

"You need a new jacket now," she teased, easing a shoe off and reaching for the material.

Stone gently brushed her hand aside and held her foot, wrapping it for her. He helped her on with the shoe, then sliced off another piece of the silk. "Give me your other foot," he said. She did so and he repeated the process. She had tiny feet, but then most of her was. She seemed childlike and vulnerable, her wet hair stuck to her scalp, her clothes damp and clinging to her body. When she put her foot back down, she smiled. Her smile was childlike too, almost innocent. It made him feel even more guilty that he had inadvertently led them to her. He had to remind himself that she was a grown woman in her thirties and not a teenager. She was vulnerable, yes, but not completely innocent. She had gone looking for a story, one with enough meat on the bone to feed the media and the public's appetite for a shocking story for a long time to come. A story that would potentially secure a book deal, maybe even television rights. She had trawled the worst of mankind to find what she wanted, and now she was running from it. She had brought much of this on herself. Even so, by his mistake, he still felt responsible.

"What's the plan?" she asked. "I mean, there could be police and a TV news circus there, for all we know."

Stone shook his head. "These people are well organised. They tapped your phone to establish your connection with Isobel, and in turn, her connection with me. Then they had the time and resources to put an asset into play and convince me she was you. They must be well connected. You don't learn this stuff in the private sector. They have government history for sure. They manipulated the law in Washington, tapped the lines, fooled me into thinking I was talking to a dispatch operator. Then they sent a fake cop to kill me…" he frowned, trailing off mid-sentence. It didn't make sense. The man impersonating the detective had drawn his weapon and fought with Stone, but Kathy – or the woman pretending to be Kathy – had tried to help. She had got herself punched in her face for her trouble, and that's when the two dogs had gone crazy. The man had been killed within seconds. But why would the woman try to help Stone, if another was trying to kill him? The man calling himself Detective Rawlins had to be another party. A competing organisation.

"Sorry, you were saying?" Kathy asked, uncomfortable by Stone's long silence.

"I don't…" he paused. "I think I've been played all along," he said. "Yes, this woman who impersonated you wanted to find both yourself and Edwards through me, but someone else has wanted me dead all the time. Kathy didn't want me dead. She used me as a stalking horse."

"A what?" she frowned.

"Hunters used to, maybe they still do, make a wooden cut-out of a horse and hide behind it moving it ever closer to their prey. When the time was right, they'd shoot. She used me to get to Edwards. The man, Rawlins, was another contingent. Most probably after the same thing."

"Two people hunting you?"

"Two different organisations, yes. One hunting, one using me to get to another target."

"Who else?"

"I have no idea. I don't know who Kathy is representing, let alone the other guys." Stone shook his head. "But how else would they really have got my phone details to start with? And the two gunmen, they tried to kill me as I left her place."

"Wait, what?" she frowned. "So how many people have tried to kill you?"

"Two men, after I met her for the first time. Then the cop who came to investigate. Then my computer tech guy was killed on his way in to help me with the information Kathy, or this woman, gave me. A car-jacking gone wrong is what the Washington DC police are calling it. Although I don't think it was a car-jacking, but a professional hit and it went very much as intended." Stone shook his head. "And Edwards was killed by Kathy, or the woman pretending to be you. I'm absolutely sure of it."

"How sure?"

"Positive," Stone said emphatically. "He had like a cherry or berry lipstick or lip gloss smeared on his lips. He'd kissed her for sure. I've no doubt he was under the illusion he was heading into the bedroom for sex."

"Well, how would you know it was her type of lip gloss?"

Stone hesitated. "I just do," he replied. "It was the same as she wore when I met with her."

"Oh," she said, sensing there was more to Stone's comment. She didn't push. "But Edwards knew me," she insisted. "He wouldn't have been fooled by her *Kathy* act."

"Well, maybe she had another angle. Either way, he had kissed her, and she got the drop on him. I'm sure of it."

"Ok. So who were these guys out here?"

"It could be either outfit. They looked professional. *Were* professional. They looked in-keeping with the two guys who attacked me on the road."

Kathy stood up. "Well, we better get going and see what we can find out."

They walked on, led by Kathy through the myriad of paths. Some were well-worn, most likely trails to the beach made by nearby residents or visitors. Others were smaller, most probably fox or rabbit trails. Thistles ran along the edges of the paths and they occasionally brushed the thorns with their ankles or shins. After several hundred metres Kathy stopped walking and turned to Stone. "There's a property coming up here, then my father's house is about a hundred yards further on."

"Ok," Stone said. "Do you know your neighbours?"

She shrugged. "Not *that* well. It's a holiday home. There won't be anybody here now until Christmas, maybe Thanksgiving, then after that they open it up from June to September. Weekends mostly."

"So we can go across their ground?" Stone asked.

"Yes."

They walked onwards and traversed down a steep dune. The ground that stretched out ahead of them looked rough and unkempt, but three strands of thick boat rope draping from posts denoted the boundary. It looked quaint, but a little over-thought. Stone would bet the owner had a skipper's cap that he wore for sailing. Most likely with a blue blazer. The ground gradually became more cultivated and the grass twenty-metres from the house had clearly been recently cut. The grass was full of sand though, and the plants in the garden looked like different varieties of seagrass. The view was stunning, an uninterrupted vista of the Chesapeake. The house was constructed largely of chrome and glass and old reclaimed ship's timbers. In front of the house, secured on a trailer, a sizable silver-coloured RIB with two notably large engines that had been covered with tarps, was attached to a pulley winch system that looked as if it could pull the boat all the way up the beach from low water. To the side, nestled into the ground between the beach and the garden, an ancient forty-foot wooden sailboat had been beached and turned into a child's climbing platform, complete with pirate flags and lengths of dangling climbing ropes and netting. Stone wondered how much the owner earned to justify such an expensive climbing facility for a child. Or how much was in their checking account. He smiled to himself. Ironic when he thought how much was in his own account after today.

The no-man's land of scrubland and dune between the two houses afforded them the perfect view of three-quarters of Kathy's father's property. Apart from the Jeep there were no vehicles in the driveway, nor in the road outside. The house blocked Stone's motorcycle from view. To all intents and purposes, the property appeared deserted. They only watched for ten minutes. They had been away from the house for over two hours. There was no point watching indefinitely, so Stone made a move.

"Wait here," he said. "I'll go ahead and check it out."

"No."

"What?"

"No, I'm coming."

"Look, just…"

"Don't waste your breath!" she snapped, but there was a good-natured tone to it. "I'm coming with you. I'm unarmed, so there's no way I'm staying here on my own. Besides, we're better in this together."

Stone considered this for a moment then nodded. She had a point. She was unarmed and it was better to stay together. She was a tenacious woman, and he had to change the way he handled her. In fact, he knew he was handling nothing. Kathy would do what she wanted and he had to live with it. Besides, she had been pretty handy with the shotgun. It would be beneficial to keep her close

"Was the shotgun yours?" he asked, pushing himself up out of the seagrass and brushing the sand off his damp suit.

"Dad's," she replied.

"You were pretty handy with it."

"I watch movies." She smiled. "Dad taught me to hit cans and bottles with it. He did some dove shooting a few times, but he softened with age. Didn't really enjoy killing them. He never was a big shooter, but he kept it for home protection. A cop friend of his said it was the best weapon for home defence, that people under duress tend to miss with pistols and a shotgun takes no prisoners."

"Can't argue with that," Stone agreed, then prompted her, "He's in a retirement home?" He held her hand and helped her down over a steep part of the slope. "That must be tough."

She nodded. "Mom died twelve years ago. The day before I graduated. That was a really shitty day. Dad insisted, along with the principal, that I attend the graduation the next day. All my friends and fellow students were so happy! Full of hopes and dreams and promises, and I was just..." She shrugged, her eyes glossy. "Anyway, Dad is seventy-five and physically fit, but his mind? Well, there's more and more they can do, close to good treatment, I guess. But the retirement home was always meant to be short-term. I want to sell this place and my apartment when it's re-built and get a ranch-style single storey on the outskirts of Washington DC for him to come live with me. If I could get things settled, get working properly again and without having to travel to see dad, then I could afford to hire a carer. But there are problems."

"Such as?"

"My job, for one. It's finished, this story was to be my trump card. Then there's getting power of attorney over his affairs. It's not been easy so far. Dad is what you would call in-and-out. He's fine one day, doesn't even know who I am the next, then angry that he's in a home, other days he loves it in there and he's cleaning up playing poker. I just don't know what to do."

Stone didn't mention what her editor had said about her employment prospects or status. Maybe her story would swing it for her with the paper. He felt for her. In a time when people regularly and selfishly turned their backs on family, Kathy was front and centre. He looked at her, not knowing what to say. They had reached the boundary of the property, so silence was both necessary and a somewhat convenient distraction.

Stone took the pistol out of his holster and held it out of sight down by his leg. He was coming up on the upturned skiff. He scanned the ground around him, turned to Kathy. "They've cleaned up. There's no shell casings and the guy you hit fired a dozen or so rounds from here."

"That's strange, isn't it?"

Stone nodded, his eyes on the house. "I've only seen it once before."

"When was that?"

"Last night. When two guys shot at me, tried to run me off the road. When I got back to the scene, it was as if it never happened." He shook his head, thinking of what had happened. Suddenly he realised how tired he was. "Jesus, these guys really have resources. I've been on the back foot ever since."

"It will be dark soon," she said. "Where are we going to go? I can't stay here, it's not safe."

"I'll find somewhere safe."

"What, your place?" she laughed. "What? Is that your standard *woman in distress* scenario? No thanks, I'll take my chances in a Days Inn!"

Stone hesitated. "No, I just meant…"

"I know what you meant!" she chuckled. "You won't be recognising *my* lipstick the next day, Agent Stone."

Stone looked away from her. He was annoyed. Not really at her, but at himself. He had fallen into a honey trap with Kathy's imposter, merely so she could take his mainframe computer log-in card. He had made mistakes, but he would be on it now. He would get Kathy to safety and go back to Secret Service headquarters and lay himself bare. It wouldn't be easy, and it would take time, but he would work towards clearing his name and making amends. Even if it ultimately cost him his career. Kathy would be able to add what she knew, if he could persuade her to help him, and that would lend credence to his report.

Stone positioned himself in front and to the right of Kathy as they approached the house. It gave him the best arcs of fire. He moved around the decked porch and peered inside. The house had been wrecked, completely riddled with gunfire. He walked around to the back door, Kathy following three paces behind as she was told to. When Stone turned to check her distance she clasped her hands together, bowed and shuffled like a dutiful geisha. He turned back, but she didn't see him smile.

Stone checked the rooms, but it was a largely open-planned building and obvious that nobody was there. He walked back outside, Kathy following him. "Go and fetch anything you may need," he said, then added, "If everything's not full of holes."

Kathy bowed. "Certainly, *Rob-San*…"

"Cut it out," he said as he stepped down the wooden steps and walked towards where the Ford Taurus had been parked.

"Yes, *Rob-San*!" she shouted.

Stone looked at the tyre tracks. They had clearly taken off at speed, digging two trenches in the sandy earth with the wheels of the Ford Taurus. The ground was littered with 5.56mm shell casings. There were hundreds of them. Nobody was going to stick around to pick them up, so why had the 9mm casings from the MP5 been removed? It puzzled him as he walked over and looked over Kathy's Jeep. The hood was undone, raised on its springs. Stone got down and peered inside. He did not touch anything for fear of a booby-trap or IED. There were leads and wires that had been ripped out and left to dangle across the engine block. He stepped back and inspected the wheels. The two front tyres had also been punctured, gouged with a sharp knife. He looked up as Kathy walked over with a tiny rucksack. It was garishly coloured and patterned with flowers. It was essentially a Hawaiian shirt turned into a beach bag. It suited her. She was an upbeat, ageless woman.

Perhaps it was her size and demeanour, or maybe her Asian features, but Stone could imagine her passing for eighteen in beachwear or look to be in her early-thirties in a business suit.

"You look confused," she said.

"Just trying to make sense of it." Stone pointed at the ground and the glistening brass cartridge cases. "What was the point in removing the cases left by the man you hit?" He waved a hand towards the house. "It's obvious what happened here. Unless the MP5 could be traced? If the man with the machine pistol was in government service and was using an accountable weapon, he may well have taken extra precautions."

"So someone working for the government, attempting to murder a Secret Service agent? That sounds pretty reckless," she said. "But if it was sanctioned to some extent, then it's terrifying."

"It means taking this to the FBI or back to my department could be playing into their hands." Stone shook his head dismissively. "No, I trust the Secret Service. I *have* to."

She looked at the ground, studied the shell casings littered at her feet, then pulled a face when she saw her truck's tyres. "Oh no! Look what they've done!"

Stone caught her arm as she started towards it. "Don't," he said. "I've had a quick look, but we don't know if they tampered with anything. The doors or door catches, or that bonnet lid. Linking it to a grenade through a wire would be child's play to these people."

Stone walked over to his bike. It had been kicked over. But being an open-framed motorcycle, Stone could see that nothing had been tampered with. He reached the handle bar and stood on the footrest. He pushed down with his foot, pulled with his arm and leaned backwards. The bike righted slowly, but the effort was considerable on Stone's part. Kathy stepped in and helped finish the manoeuvre and the bike rested back on two wheels. Stone rested it on its stand and crouched down to inspect the other side of the engine. He moved around the bike and checked all around. It looked ok, certainly not tampered with, but he needed to start it. He reached into his pocket for the keys, felt the fold of paper he had recovered at Edwards' house. He took it out an unfolded it. It was soggy and tore as he handled it. The ink had started to run. Kathy craned her neck to see.

"Do you have your phone with you?"

She reached into her ruck sack. "I do. It's my Dad's. Mine was recently disconnected, the paper paid for it," she said, taking it out. She thumbed the screen and handed it over to Stone.

"Fancy for a seventy-five-year-old."

She scoffed. "He's got Alzheimer's. He's not a klutz. And seventy is the new sixty, haven't you heard?"

"Can I get onto the internet with this?" Stone asked.

"Of course!"

It was a Samsung smartphone and he wasn't familiar with the screen. He eventually found the *Google* app and pressed. He typed the number into the search bar – 09008000. The first hit was an equation. Stone looked at it, then scrolled down. There were various sites involving all or one of the numbers. Three million hits in all. Stone spaced the numbers out. Nothing of relevance. He played with decimal points. Nothing.

"Where did you find that?" Kathy asked.

"I found it on Edwards and forgot I had it in my pocket. I tried dialling it on my cell phone back at his place. No success."

"Not enough digits."

"No."

"Safety deposit box?"

Stone shrugged. "If it is, then there is little chance of finding it."

"What about coordinates?"

"Of course!" Stone put a decimal point after the nine and the eighty. "South, north, east or west?"

Kathy shrugged. "South and west."

"I doubt it," Stone frowned at the screen. "About five-hundred thousand square miles of empty Indian Ocean south of the Maldives." He adjusted the search to North and East. All he got was a ship's blog, a log of their current course. He reconfigured the coordinates to 09.00N 80.00W and pressed the search icon. "Bingo."

"What have you got?" she asked excitedly.

"Panama."

"Any significance?"

Stone thought of the missing British banker, his bank about to go under amidst allegations of fraud and financial malpractice. "The payments made to the missing veterans was traced and terminated from an account held in a private bank in Panama City. The bank's owner is missing. I don't think it's merely a coincidence." He folded the damp and crumbling piece of paper and put it back into his pocket. He handed the phone back to her and put the key into the motorcycle's ignition. The bike fired into life and rumbled away at an idle. "Let's go," he said, swinging his leg over and settling into the seat. "Have you ridden pillion before?"

"I don't even know what that means."

Stone patted the rear of the seat. In fairness, there wasn't much for her to sit on. "Just lean when I do. Relax and don't fight the angle of lean."

"What happens if I fight the lean?" she asked. "I've never been on a motorcycle before."

"If we don't lean, we don't turn. It's alright at slow speeds, but once we get above twenty-five miles-per-hour we need to lean through the turns. The further down I take the bike, the faster and sharper we turn." He looked at her face in the mirror as she swung her leg over and nestled into his back. She looked scared. He took the helmet off the handlebar and reached it around to her. "You have this. It'll be a little loose, so just tighten the strap." He waited for her to get it comfortable, then he dropped the gear shift and eased forwards. She hugged him tightly and he smiled. It felt good. He'd always liked bikes, especially when he'd been in college. Carefree nights, buzzing through the traffic with a girl clung to his back on their way to a party. Snapshot moments. Then the Twin Towers fell. Patriotic duty called and life got a lot more serious. It was the life he had chosen, but he hadn't lived through many carefree days since.

The sky was darkening and Stone flicked on the headlight. The road was bumpy and the sand was still a consideration as they motored along. He didn't want Kathy to experience any skittish handling and make her nervous, he needed her to be relaxed for when the road opened up and he would be able to make swift progress along the forty or so miles back to Washington DC.

A car came down the road towards them. It was a black Mercedes SUV. When the driver saw Stone's light they switched theirs on and for a moment Stone couldn't see against the glare of full beams. The driver seemed to notice their error and dipped. The SUV drove past slowly. Stone saw an attractive middle-aged woman at the wheel talking to her two children strapped into boosters in the rear. He eased back out into the middle of the road when he was clear and accelerated until he neared the next pile of sand in the road. He slowed, and Kathy squeezed him a little. The road bent round to the left and Stone accelerated and leaned into their first real corner. Kathy leaned with him and they travelled through the apex seamlessly. He felt confident in her and built his speed as the road started to leave the coast behind and the sand became more infrequent, until he was confident there would be no more drifts. There was forest on both sides of the road now, the dunes far behind them. There were residential pockets, with houses built like a slice of suburbia and plenty of road turnings leading to cul-de-sacs, but no shops or street malls. The houses would thin out and then there would be nothing but woodland on both sides of the road for another half-mile until the next cluster of homes.

Stone caught a dazzle in his mirror and saw the vehicle behind them gaining steadily. The driver had their lights on main beams and hadn't dipped. Stone wound the throttle on and dropped a gear and the bike shot forwards urgently. Kathy gripped tightly, her hands linked together. A right-hand bend was dispatched quickly and smoothly and the bike was up and level again, a little light on the front wheel, and charging down the straight ahead. Stone noticed the car had accelerated rapidly too and its lights remained on full beams. He eased his speed for the approaching left-hand bend and they rounded as smoothly as they had through the previous corner. He accelerated and eased off when he saw the needle nudge way into three figures. The car behind had unnerved him, but it also had a good turn of speed. He would have to get into a dangerous road-race to lose the car, and the car could well have a higher top speed. It couldn't match the Ducati on acceleration, but it seemed to catch up quickly as Stone braked for the approaching corners and was forced to travel slower than the car through the bends. The next residential area was well-lit and as Stone slowed and took a sharp right-hand bend, he could see the front quarter and bonnet of the car in his mirror. It was a silver sedan. He would bet it all that the car was the same silver Ford Taurus that had been driven by the gunmen.

"What's wrong?" Kathy shouted into his ear above the wind and exhaust note of the Ducati. "You're going too fast!"

Stone half turned his head, keeping his eyes on the road ahead. "That sedan is following us, matching our speed. Or at least trying to."

Kathy turned around to look and the bike swayed half a car's width across the road. "Sorry!" she screamed back in Stone's ear. "Is it the same car they used back at the house?"

"I think it is," said Stone. "It's pretty distinct looking."

Stone had driven the three-hundred-and-sixty-five horsepower model Ford Taurus in his line of work. The Secret Service procured domestic vehicle brands and specified the higher performance models, and Stone knew how effortless its automatic gearbox was. It was an easy vehicle to drive fast and was making short work of the bends and straights, barely having to slow before the corners. The bike, in contrast, had to slow down and take the corners at a steady speed. The advantage they gained over the car from acceleration seemed to be countered by the corners. The result was an even distance between the two vehicles. A stalemate. Stone knew that in around five miles the road would join a two-lane and that would give him the opportunity to get ahead. It would also have more traffic, and that would seal the deal. If he could weave his way through the traffic and get some vehicles between them and the pursuing car, then he could lose them.

Ahead of them a large blue work van pulled into the road, forcing Stone to slow the motorcycle so suddenly that the rear tyre momentarily left the road. He could see the road ahead and it was clear of on-coming traffic. He dropped the shift down and accelerated hard. The Ducati roared at high revs and the speed in which it picked up pace was astonishing. Stone leaned left to get around the van, then canted the lean to the right to straighten up, when the van unexpectedly lurched across the line and into them. Kathy screamed as Stone slammed on both the front brake leaver and rear brake pedal, but it was too late. The side panel hit them, and they remained upright, but before the bike could slow enough, the van kept pulling out and the bike simply ran out of road. The front wheel hit the soft grass verge at speed and it was all over. The bike twisted, skidded and shuddered. One of the wheels, Stone did not know which, dug in and the sudden traction flung the bike upwards and forwards, sideways and downwards all at once. Only motorcycles could disobey all the rules of physics when they crashed, and the Ducati was no different. When it landed on its side and threw both of them off, it speeded up as it started to tumble down the road, wheel over wheel, increasing its velocity when all science would argue it should be slowing down.

Stone hit the ground hard and bounced high into the air. When he landed a second time on the road, he lost momentum and tumbled a few times before sliding a short distance and resting still. Kathy was thrown to the left and into the verge. She slid a good forty-feet on the grass, before her foot dug into the ground and she was catapulted high into the air. She landed heavily on her chest and stomach and lay still.

Stone was aware of the van near him. It had stopped in the road, its hazard lights flashing to warn oncoming traffic of the accident. He tried to roll over onto his side, but it was agony. He was grazed and bruised, and severely winded. He simply could not breathe. He fell back down onto his back. He could hear groaning and thought of Kathy hurt nearby, but then realised that the noise had come from him. He felt as if he were two seconds behind his actions, that his senses were delayed and that he was as much a voyeur to the scene as a part of it. Eventually, air filled his lungs and stabbed his ribs. He turned his head painfully and caught sight of Kathy, saw the man bending down and moving her. The helmet had split open and the man had removed it and cast it aside. Stone could hear himself shouting for the man to leave her alone. Not to remove the helmet, not to move her until the paramedics had arrived and put her neck in a brace. The man did not listen. He picked her up and carried her back to the open rear doors of the van.

The Ford Taurus pulled close, its tyres crunching to an urgent halt. Both front doors opened. The men were smartly dressed in black suits and white shirts. The man holding the silenced pistol stepped around the open door and brought the weapon up to aim. Stone did not recognise this man from the beach house, but the other man who stood by the open door shouted something and raised the G36 rifle, and Stone realised he was the same gunman who had cut Kathy's house to shreds. Stone did not hear what he was shouting above the hail of automatic gunfire that cut them both down. The man with the silenced pistol got off a short burst of fire before he fell. The second man was still bringing the rifle up to aim when he went down amid a mist of shattered glass and metal fragments from the door he had taken cover behind.

Stone tried to get to his feet but was pushed back down. He reached for the FN pistol behind his right hip, but rough hands clasped his arms and another man retrieved the weapon. Stone looked up at him. The man towered over him, half as broad as he was tall. His face was as dark as night. Stone could only see the whites of his eyes in the gloom. The man pulled out a strange looking pistol and aimed it down at the centre of Stone's chest. It coughed a virtually silent report and Stone arched his back as a large dart speared him between his ribs and he started to lose all feeling in his arms and legs. The man who had carried Kathy to the van returned, bent down and pulled up Stone's sleeve. He was a foul-looking man with bad teeth and ginger hair. He was rough, tearing the sleeve of Stone's jacket and shirt. Stone tried to fight it, but his arm would not move. He did not feel the hypodermic needle, but he saw the dose administered slowly emptying its contents, almost timed perfectly to release the dose entirely as Stone slipped into a lifeless, dreamless sleep.

Stone floors. Rough concrete walls. Cold air. A single bright light bulb. Shadows cast onto the floor and walls. Metal door. No windows. No sound. Except for his breathing. Sharp, short breaths. The sound of fear.

The drugs had worn off and his left side ached tremendously. A throbbing of bruised muscle and cracked bone, a rawness that he knew could only mean torn and shredded skin. The aching was the bruising and swelling developing, the brunt of the impact with the road taking its toll. His sleeve was pulled up, the hypodermic left hanging, the needle teasing at the vein. He remembered being drugged at the roadside, that hypodermic had looked smaller. He had been drugged again. He could see the tip almost protruding back through the skin. There was blood all around the track marks, so many needles had stuck in him, so many holes had been left after they had been roughly extracted. A tourniquet hung loose. It was a Velcro strap and he had seen the type before. British soldiers had loosely attached them to their limbs before embarking on patrols in Afghanistan. The practice had been adopted by US soldiers soon afterwards. With the amount of IED injuries that happened daily, the procedure had saved hundreds of lives in those first chaotic and traumatic minutes of catastrophe. This tourniquet, however, had been used to prime the vein in the forearm. Roughly pulled tight, the arm swelled and the vein popped. Although by the look of his arm and the multiple puncture wounds, it hadn't been too effective.

Stone had noted, in some semi-cohesive part of his mind, that no alcohol swab had been used, that the needles had been extracted from a plastic box with no sterile packaging. The man who had administered the drugs was rough, enjoyed inflicting pain. A little twist here, a scrape there. He was a sadist. Small and ginger-haired. A wispy attempt at a beard. Narrow eyes and bad teeth. Stone hated giving the man the satisfaction of seeing him in pain. It motivated him to control his emotions and pull on his determination.

The door opened and the ginger man entered. He had changed his clothes. Stone gleaned some satisfaction knowing it was a well-aimed glob of bloody spit that had inconvenienced the man. Although the beating he had administered to Stone had taken the shine off of it somewhat. During the beating Stone noticed that the man was wearing his watch. He knew it was his – he had scratched the black of the bezel at the twenty marker. The quote had been high and the watch would have to have been sent away to Switzerland for three months. He had never bothered with the repair.

Stone was bound to a chair. His feet had been duct-taped to the front chair legs. His right hand was tethered with duct-tape to his right thigh and his left arm – the one with the needle and hypodermic hanging loosely from the vein – was taped to his waist at the elbow and the wrist was taped to his knee. There was no give, and the entire forearm and inside of his elbow was exposed to do with as they pleased.

The ginger haired man stepped aside and the big black man stepped in, ducking his head through the doorway. He was the same giant who had shot him with the tranquiliser gun on the road. He held a bottle of water. He undid it and held it out for Stone. He shrugged when Stone didn't take it, pulled a face. He eyed Stone's bonds and smiled. The man then drank the contents down slowly. He almost finished, then held it the bottle out for him again. Stone stared at him coldly and the man grinned. He shrugged again and finished the bottle. Stone's mouth was as dry as hot sand. He could never remember having been so thirsty.

"You did good," the big black man said. "We got what we needed." Stone frowned. He couldn't remember having told them anything. He was certain he hadn't. He couldn't even remember being questioned. "You'll be wanting a new job after this, that goes without saying. A new passport might be a better option. Maybe you can go lie low in a cave in the Hindu Kush. That's about the outlook for you when we're done with you. They'll never stop looking for you, never stop hunting your sorry ass."

"What do you mean, *done with me*?"

The giant grinned, tossed the empty bottle of water into Stone's lap. "This is where your life is going to get a whole lot more interesting."

"Where's Kathy?" Stone asked. He didn't care what the man had to say. If he had talked and did not remember, then he couldn't do much about it. If he knew what they had planned for him, it might affect his judgement, lower his will to fight. He wanted to know where Kathy was, if she was still alive even. All he concentrated on now was trying to escape. "What have you done with her?"

"All in good time, my friend."

"I'm not your friend."

"That's right. You don't have friends, do you? Short term girlfriends, lovers, work colleagues. And you stepped over them all to get to the top of your game."

"Bullshit." Stone shook his head. "I was always first into work and the last to leave. I studied and passed every test, trained in my downtime. Everybody had the same chance as I did. You don't know shit about me."

"Oh, I know *all* about you. The *President's* man. The guy the rest of the Secret Service love to hate. Oh, they respect your abilities, listen to your judgement, but they hate the man." Stone was a little shaken. He had never been one for friends. His college friendships had faded out over the years. His army comrades had been the closest friendships he'd ever had, but like many who served, he lost contact with them in their civilian years. And he'd have done anything for his brother. Missed him daily. "Ah, did I hurt you?" the big black man said in a *boo-hoo* voice. He even exaggerated wiping an imaginary tear away using the knuckle of his index finger. "Oh, poor little middle-class white boy. Nobody wants to play with him." He bent down and put his face up close to Stone's. So close, Stone could smell onions and pickles on his breath. He pinched his cheek and squeezed hard. Stone concentrated on taking the pain, not showing the man any sign of weakness. The man grinned and twisted the skin. "Well, you'll soon know who your friends are. You'll need them, but will they be there? Don't bet on it Agent Stone. Life is going to get really lonely from now on…" Stone did not flinch, but he muttered something. The man frowned and said, "What?" Again, Stone muttered. The man turned his ear towards him. "Speak up, boy." Stone muttered again, then added a shrug. He glanced up at the ginger-haired man, who merely shrugged back at him. The black giant put a knee on the floor and leaned in. He stared at Stone, who more than matched the coldness of his stare. He was about to speak when Stone lunged forwards and bit the man's nose. He clenched his teeth down hard. It was hard enough for the man to start to submit, rather than lurch backwards. Stone tensed his jaw, evening out the pressure and keeping his grip, then bit down and shook his head from side to side like a shark sawing off chunks of its prey. There was a sickening sound of cartilage crunching, separating – like pulling apart cooked chicken joints – and the man screamed a blood-curdling cry of agony which filled the room and reverberated off the hard walls.

The ginger-haired man had been slow to react, but came up to speed and caught Stone around his neck with his arm, pulling backwards with Stone's throat in the inside bend of his elbow. He gripped his hand with the other and applied more pressure. Stone knew he would lose consciousness, or worse, if the man did not let go, and he steeled himself for a final bite. He ground down hard and the giant fell back onto the ground, his hands clasping at his face. The man was in shock. Stone recognised the signs, he had seen it before on the battlefield. People went quiet, into themselves. He was in no less agony, but he was unable to scream.

The ginger-haired man released his grip and backhanded Stone across his face. He reeled backwards as far as his restraints would allow. When he looked back at the giant on the floor he was met with an incensed pair of eyes, brilliant white against his jet black skin, and the man got up and lunged at him. Stone caught the first punch on the chin, but he did not have much distance to go and his head rocked forwards as the man punched again. He was angry and vengeful and had not thought out his attack.

Stone moved his head and the punch glanced off the top of his head and the man slipped in the pool of his own blood on the floor, lost his footing and fell into him. There was enough time to get his head back and at the last moment Stone snapped his head forwards and smashed his forehead into the man's front teeth. Two-hundred and eighty pounds falling helped build the momentum and the impact was tremendous.

The black giant fell onto him and knocked the chair backwards. He was out cold and rolled off of Stone and onto the hard floor.

"I told you to watch him! I told you to be careful. He kicked *his* ass, and he's taped to a fucking chair!"

Stone could hear the voice, raspy and deep. There was something familiar about it. He had heard it before. He turned his head, but could not see the doorway. He strained his neck, but still couldn't see who the voice belonged to. His own knees were blocking his view and the unconscious bulk of the giant stopped him from seeing to the side.

"Shall I dope him up now?"

"Yes. As much as you dare. I want him out cold so we can finish what we started."

"Do you want his memory wiped again?" The ginger-haired man glanced down at Stone, then looked back to the doorway. "He's not in as good a shape as he was when we did it the first time round back in Virginia."

"Do what you can. Give him a serious high. Then strip him and take him on a boat trip. Dump him on the east coast beach," the voice rasped. "And don't let The Bull beat the crap out of him when he comes round. I'm going to get somebody to meet him. Somebody who will confuse the hell out of him. The Zulu should do it."

"Now *that* would be a sight!" The ginger-haired man laughed and started to open vials and draw the drugs in the order he would need them. Stone could hear him, but couldn't see him. He struggled to loosen his bonds, but the tape was tough and only felt tighter the more he moved. The man stepped around him and pulled on the tourniquet. It cinched tight like a snare. Stone could see his veins building. He continued to struggle and looked up into the man's eyes. He smiled back at Stone, then jabbed the first needle into the vein and administered the drug. It burned like fire. Stone opened his mouth to scream, but closed it in time, not wanting to give the sadist the satisfaction. The next syringe spat out pure ice. The cold ached his arm and he felt the iciness work its way through his chest and into his heart. He started to sag and go dizzy, his chest heaved and he felt sweat run down his face and neck. There was another drug, thick and syrupy. He swore he could feel it clogging and sticking in his arteries. More fire, more ice and then he was dropping. Falling out of consciousness, and stopping himself with fitful starts.

His chest heaved and his heart raced. He was leaving this world behind, the door of another partially open for him to step through. To lay down and sleep. He was seeing his past, his present and the unknown all at once. He tried to move his hands against the bonds, but he was frozen. The blackness started to come and with it the image of a man's face peering down at him. A man he had thought dead, but knew he would have to face again. An inhuman man, the stuff of nightmares or unthinkable reality.

34

"I have Saudi Arabia bidding ten-million to view."

"Just to view? Bank it. Welcome them to the show."

"Will do," the woman said, her accent thick and twangy Australian. She tapped keys and laughed. "A consortium of ten Iranians is in now for five-million."

"Total?"

"Yes."

"To watch?"

"Yes."

"Give them one camera feed. If they want more, they'll have to pay more. That will teach them to be cheap. They can pay in oil if they want to have full coverage."

"Russia to claim it. Mafia outfit in Moscow."

"How much?"

"Twenty-million."

"*Niet.*"

"I've already told them."

"North Korea?"

"No reply yet."

"They're cutting it fine."

"They only have thirty websites in the entire country; I'm surprised they even managed to get down into the dark web."

"They want to hold everyone off, claim it when it's too late for others to up their bid," the man rasped. "Tell them they're out of the bidding. Tell them that Al Qaeda are in and it's at one-hundred-million."

"We haven't heard back from Al Qaeda yet," the woman said, then added, "But ISIS are at twenty-five."

"Twenty-five gets them involvement. We'll create a tenuous link. An ISIS training camp or something. But to claim it they have to merge with someone else fast. Boco Haram are at twenty. They're all Sunni Muslims anyway, merge and fifty-million buys the claim."

"They're all Sunnis, but they can't agree on what time of day it is, let alone broker a deal in such a short time frame. What about the North Korea bid?"

"Fuck them! They don't fit into the plan anyway. They're cash cows. We'll take their hundred-million and the world will laugh at their claims! Like they'd be able to make that kind of claim look remotely plausible," he paused. "Besides, there are bids coming in from potential viewers who want more middle-east uncertainty. The last thing they want is peace out there. It's good for western weapon contracts and oil reserve pricing. Bids have been placed taking oil pricing into account. The Saudis for instance."

"And Iranians with the sanctions now lifted."

"Exactly. Get onto the Iranians, talk oil and get their bid raised for more cameras."

The woman got back onto her keypad and worked away. Both of them had their back to Stone, who had taken a while to come round, but was now fully conscious, his eyes closed and his head lolled to one side as he took in all he could hear. He could feel his hands bound tightly in front of him, his legs either bound or taped to the chair legs. He eased his hands upwards, felt them pulling at his knees. He squinted and saw silver duct-tape wrapped around his knees and his wrists. He wasn't getting out of the chair any time soon.

He looked up and studied the monitors on the wall. Ten high and twenty wide. Two hundred HD television screens. Many were showing footage of the island, in particular the jungle and beaches where the game had been played out. But twenty screens at the centre were blank. At the console were ten computer monitors and a series of keyboards. There were telephones by each monitor and a switchboard in front of the woman. She was slim and had short black hair. Stone knew who it was before she reached out and touched the giant dog on top of its head. The animal sniffed her hand and whined. The dog looked at Stone and growled. Stone noticed a movement out of the corner of his eye and saw an equally large dog, its snout just inches from his elbow. This dog also growled, its teeth bared in a snarl.

The woman turned around, swivelled in her seat. She smiled, then looked at the door as the ginger-haired man walked in, gripping Kathy roughly by the arm. Stone could see his fingers dug deeply into her flesh, red marks underneath. The woman looked back at Stone. "Hello, lover," she said softly. "Wakey, Wakey…" She smiled as Stone opened his eyes fully and took in the scene. "Sorry to have run out on you back in DC…" She got out of the chair and walked over. The dog followed.

Stone looked at her, the change of accent a little unsettling. The southern-belle never seemed right to him, but that thick antipodean twang wasn't going to hide in a performed accent too subtly. "Did you? I can't say I noticed."

She stared at him, then looked at Kathy, who was smiling at the comment. Kathy stopped when the woman stared into her eyes. "Oh you liked that, did you?" She nodded to the ginger-haired man. "Bring her over here." She pointed at the floor between them and strode over quickly to meet her.

The man gripped her and she let out a wail. His grip did not relax and he dragged her over. Kathy was smaller than the other woman. But Stone noticed how much prettier she was. When he first met the woman he had known as Kathy, he had been awestruck at how attractive she had been. But compared to Kathy her features were harder and her eyes were predatory. It was as though she had been prettier back then, her features changing slightly as part of the act. Or maybe Kathy was so genuinely beautiful as to cast a shadow on this woman.

Stone did not see the slap coming and nor did Kathy, who recoiled clasping her cheek. She straightened up and was struck again with lightning speed. There was practised martial arts knowledge behind the move. A sort of straight punch that whipped sideways into an open-handed slap as it neared her face. The force was incredible. The third slap was just as fast and Kathy fell backwards into a work desk. A jug of iced water and tall glasses rested on a tray along with some paper napkins and a plate of sliced lemons, and the whole tray went with Kathy smashing on the floor. She rested on all fours, shocked and hurt and breathing hard. She pushed herself up slowly, carefully, her hands among the broken glass and chips of ice. When she stood she was glaring, her teeth gritted in determination. She took a step forwards at the woman. Both dogs growled.

"Don't!" Stone shouted. "It's what she wants!" Kathy hesitated and looked at the dogs. They were salivating, both coiled back on their haunches readying themselves to pounce. Stone looked at the woman, who was smiling sadistically. It was the same smile he had caught briefly when her dogs had killed the man impersonating the cop. She had changed her expression quickly then, but not now. Now she was enjoying it and was free to do so. "The dogs will kill you," he said. "She's let them do it before."

Kathy looked at her, held her stare. "I'm sure she has."

Stone studied the man who was watching the monitors. His back was to them and it was broad, well-muscled. He turned around slowly, stood up and walked over. His stride was uneven, he favoured a leg.

"Marnie," he said to the woman. "Go and get the Sunnis to confirm their bid. And get North Korea's money. Now's the time." He looked at his watch. "We have less than fifteen minutes."

She broke off her stare with Kathy, then bent down and kissed Stone on the mouth, her lips wet and open. When she pulled away, she patted his cheek and smiled. "Bye-bye, lover-boy," she said. "Sorry to have run out on you again, but business is business."

Stone said nothing, ignoring her. He looked past her like she wasn't there and watched the man, who was now leaning against the back of a solid wooden chair. The man was six-five and Stone figured him to be about two-hundred-and-thirty pounds. Twenty or so down on when he had last seen him.

The man looked down at Stone and smiled. "I've had fun with you this past week."

"What happened to your leg?"

The man pulled up his trouser leg and exposed a prosthesis. "Blood poisoning. An infection."

"You have to be careful where you step. Especially in the forest. All kinds of traps out there. Dumb prey just fall in and get stuck. Must have been a bitch to get out of. Sharp spikes, dirty."

"But I got out," he said sharply. "That's more than you've done in this trap I have set for you." He waved his hand elaborately around the room.

"It's not over yet."

"Oh, but I think it is. The end of the game, Agent Stone. The last act." He shrugged. "Well, maybe not the *last* act, but a pivotal one. With only a mere footnote to go."

"Your head looks interesting." Stone stared at the curious looking valley running through the centre of the man's head. It was a considerable inversion, almost devoid of hair and the hair on both sides of it was thick. "I should have hit you twice." He looked at Kathy. "This man and I have history. He was part of an experiment of freaks…"

"A project of elite special agents serving the government…" the man interrupted.

"Assassins…" Stone countered. "You never got to serve your country. Just some self-serving scum involved in the project and making money and gaining favours from running you."

"You did me a favour, as it turns out," the man smiled. It was the smile of a crocodile, full of menace and wishful opportunity. "That rifle butt you smashed against my skull woke everything inside me. All the drugs, the hypnosis, the implanted false memories; it all moved aside and gave me my life back. I can remember my real life, my family, lovers, friends. All gone now, they mourned me a decade ago, thought I'd died in a desert war, when really my life had been stolen from me by the government. But I can live my life now and I can make my own decisions. I discovered I was resourceful, ambitious and ruthless."

"Ruthlessness was never a problem for you."

"Your brother would know all about that," the man smirked. "If you could ask him."

Stone shrugged. "My brother's dead. I have dealt with it. Now you deal with knowing I beat you, and I could beat you again. Any time." He looked back at him. "I knew it would be you when the computer virus your pet bitch released into the computer mainframe was named Ares. The Ares Virus was far too big a coincidence."

Marnie started to protest at what Stone had called her but the man snapped at her. "You got North Korea yet? One hundred million. Get it done!" He looked back at Stone. "I've had a fun two years. I managed to find my handler's files on the project. He had all sorts of contacts, bank accounts for my taking and assets for me to make use of. A little research and tweaking and I set up something new. Completely new. Something that my particular set of skills could create ownership over."

"A game of death," Stone said. "Gladiator games for the internet age."

"At first," the man said. "But it's evolved. It's so much more than that. Since I made you my target. We've managed to tap into a wealth of world-wide contacts and have a unique auction in place as we speak. My god, what an opportunity!" He laughed, it was maniacal and Stone realised that the blow he had struck him in the forest two years before hadn't cured him, it had merely made him worse. "I brought you here to finish you off, to have you hunted to the point of exhaustion. I have watched you, almost constantly for three days. Our virus, *The Ares Virus…*" he grinned. "Has taken down the Secret Service, the agency which shut down my handler's plans…"

"Your handler was using you!" Stone raged. "He would have pulled the plug on you as soon as he made his money from the anti-virus and there was no more use for your skills!"

"As I was saying…" he continued, unflustered. "Not only have I shut the Secret Service down, but I have drained their accounts, and left you with your hand in the cookie jar. Killing you would have been the icing on the cake, but two separate projects have overlapped and I can think of nothing better than to bring you into the second project. It's genius, really it is." He looked at his watch and smiled. Then he turned and waved a hand to the screens. "Marnie, let's go live!"

The bank of blank monitors in the middle flickered into life, some of the screens were split-screen with multiple camera angles, others were single images, some magnified on the same image. One of the screens was a series of colours. Stone recognised this as thermal imaging. The blue areas were cold, the red and yellow denoted higher heat sources.

The man looked back at Stone. "Recognise this place?"

Stone did. He recognised the speaker as well. Luke Cheney. Vice President of the United States. The man had lost his son in the first of the Twin Towers to fall. Stone admired the man. Not because he was a career politician. But because speaking from the auditorium at the memorial he was standing on meant that he was standing in the last place his son had been alive. The place where his son had taken his final breath. The site where his son and four souls short of three-thousand lost their lives on September 11 2001. It would be an emotional experience and the man was holding up well.

"Over to assets," the man said. "Position one, check?"

"Check."

"Position two, check?"

"Check."

"Position three, check?"

"Position three compromised. Relocated to tier three."

"Further problems?"

"None."

"Standby." The man looked back at Stone. "My masterpiece. And you're here to watch it happen."

Stone watched Vice President Luke Cheney speak. There was a low volume audio running. Stone knew when he had finished speaking then the President would enter the stage, take the auditorium and stand at the podium. He would make his speech about the years since 9/11. It was a fine speech, Stone had heard parts of it in the West Wing, but it would concentrate on the building of international relationships, especially with Islamic nations, and not the rhetoric of US and coalition forces battling extremism around the globe. That wasn't working out so well lately. It was time for a different approach. The President was on his outward journey, nearing the end of his second term. Cheney was tipped as the man to run the most successful presidential campaign, and was more or less a shoe-in for the presidency. As much as politics could dictate. And Cheney would carry on the stance of building over battling. It could be a new era.

Stone's heart raced, a sinking feeling in his belly. He looked at the man, studied the expression on his face. "What is this?"

"Progress," the man said. "I watched some television when I regained my memory. I failed to see what all the fuss was about. I watched pay-per-view boxing and saw an opening. With the internet as it is, a growing and evolving entity, it was possible to up the game to a platform without rules and regulations, without censorship. Pure visual freedom. The people who started experimenting with this, by auctioning methods of execution…"

"The ISIS terrorists in Syria," Stone interrupted. He looked at the man's surprised expression. "We know all about it. We know more than you'd think."

The man scoffed. "You know nothing. Clawing your way in the dark, no doubt," he said. "Well, the ISIS people were taken out swiftly. Afterwards, I took their efforts and gave them new audiences. And then a whole new format."

"You killed them?"

"I leaked their whereabouts to serving CIA contacts of my former handler. The agency did the rest from the comfort of Nevada and a drone armed with Hellfire missiles." Stone watched Cheney on the screens. Then he saw a screen with the aperture of a riflescope. The cross hairs were on Cheney's chest. There were distance increments running down the side and a digital compass in the bottom left-hand corner. Directly below that screen another, from a more acute angle the same kind of aperture was visible. He looked back at the man, who was smiling at him, then looked back at the bank of screens and noticed a third screen. Much higher, the angle opposite from the second screen. Three sights, all focused on the same target and all covered from different distances and three separate angles. The man seemed to know what Stone had seen. He nodded. "The direct image is a camera feed through a recording enabled riflescope, placed at five-hundred metres with an elevation of three-hundred and twelve feet. It's a .308 calibre. The image on the bottom screen is from a weapon placed at one-thousand-four-hundred and fifty metres with an elevation of five-hundred and fifty-seven feet. It's a Barrett .50 calibre. To Vice President Cheney's left is a 6mm long-barrelled assault rifle at three-hundred metres and eighty-eight feet of elevation. When all three weapons are fired simultaneously, the ballistic variables, distance and elevation will see all three bullets strike at the same instant. Three different weapons at three different distances and fired from three different locations. Utter confusion. Like I said, my masterpiece."

"You're sick," Stone said quietly. He looked at Cheney, knew the man's speech would end when he quoted a poem his son had once written about world peace in elementary school. The man would shed a tear, perhaps more. He wouldn't be acting. Stone felt bile rise in his throat. He didn't want to watch, averted his eyes, but looked back almost instantly.

"Like driving past an accident," the man smiled. "You can't help but take a look." He looked at his watch again, then said to the woman, "Marnie, are we there with ISIS and Boco Haram?"

"It's transferring as we speak. PDRK are close, they're at eighty-million to claim it for North Korea."

"Do it," the man said. "Get their money and start it bouncing round the globe. They will look like idiots. Like North Korea could organise something like this!" He looked up as the giant black man with no nose and shattered teeth, and a wiry, compact Hispanic man walked in, both carrying assault rifles on slings and wearing pistols and combat knives on their belts. He nodded to them and they stood silently beside the ginger-haired man, who was still gripping Kathy firmly. Stone noticed his watch gleaming in the light and felt a flush of anger. For some reason the watch was taking his focus. He didn't want it on the hideous sadist's wrist a moment longer.

"It's in!" the woman said triumphantly. "Islamic funding and organising to claim responsibility for the assassination. That's the icing on the cake, with what we have lined up." She tapped the keypad and said, "It's started its journey through the accounts. They can't get it back."

"Terminate the transaction in the South African account."

"Ok."

Stone looked at Kathy. Their eyes met and they shared a look of utter despair, but she turned back to the bank of screens. The ginger-haired man had a grip on her arm, but he was staring at the screen also, his grip loosening. Stone watched Cheney as the man got towards the end of his speech. He was talking about his son. He wiped a tear, started to recite the poem. It was hypnotic, the voyeurism strangely gratifying. He wanted to look away, but couldn't. It may *not* happen, and he watched for that reason more than any other. Stone felt nothing but fluttering in his stomach and a heaviness in his chest. He willed the Vice President to break down with emotion, leave the stage. Step out from behind the lectern with its microphones from thirty different news networks. But he knew he wouldn't. His tears would be real, but he was not prone to histrionics. He was not one for show-boating and could care less about public opinion. No, Luke Cheney would stand and finish the poem, and he would do so with dignity.

"How the hell have you got the snipers in place?" Stone asked. "Security is as tight as it gets."

"Perhaps you should have been there, Agent Stone. Perhaps if you hadn't requested to abstain from the nine-eleven memorial this year, then you would have been able to stop this from happening." The man shook his head. "Poor Agent Stone… finding it hard to stand there, year after year, thinking about your poor fiancé with the second tower coming down on her. Your knee-jerk reaction to it all by turning your back on an engineering career and joining the army, going off to fight in Afghanistan. Your sense of duty taking you to the Secret Service…" He laughed. "Oh your face! I do hope you don't play poker! Yes, I know everything there is to know about you. I've been doing my homework!"

Stone shrugged. "Ok," he said. "So tell me how have you got three guns into play?"

"Networking," he said. "People in low places. Your precious Secret Service for one. NYPD's finest for another. They're *always* corruptible. Plenty of people have taken money to walk the other way. A *lot* of money."

"You have someone inside the Secret Service?" Stone said incredulously.

"I have two things, Agent Stone," he paused. "I have a disgruntled and discredited, once high-ranking agent inside the Secret Service who made a deal with the devil…" The man smiled, he seemed to like the analogy. "And I have a star agent that was ripe for the picking. Someone that people wouldn't mind sending down the river. You are a respected agent, but you have no friends there. Funny, your brother had exactly the same reputation at the FBI. People always refer to you as a *hell of an agent*, but they don't invite you to their Christmas parties."

"I like my sleep," Stone commented flatly. The man checked his watch, rubbed a hand through the thin strip of hair, the ravine that was his head. "That must have knocked a hell of a lot loose in there," Stone said. "And the leg? That *had* to hurt."

"Pain is merely weakness leaving the body. I am much stronger now."

"I still bet I could kick your ass," Stone said. "If you cut me free, that is. How about it? How about I rip off that peg-leg and beat the rest of your head in with it?"

"You know I had you beat up on that ridge. You know your silly little knife throwing trick stopped me from killing you. That and your boy scout trap."

"You were going to shoot me. I'd say I had you beat. Five inches of height and sixty-pounds of weight over me and I still kicked your ass. So much so, you had to pick up a gun."

The man ignored him, checked his watch and smiled as Cheney finished his speech. His wife walked on and hugged him. The two parents, still mourning after half their son's lifetime, walked out of camera shot hand in hand. He looked up and smiled at Stone before turning his back on him. "Countdown," he said. "Position one, ready?"

"Check."

"Position two, ready?"

"Check."

"Alternative position, tier three, ready?"

"Check."

He turned to the woman. "Marnie, ready to call the Secret Service desk and warn them?"

"Yes."

"He needs to be at the lectern. He needs to be into the flow of his speech."

"I know, trust me."

Stone watched the President walk out, clasp the lectern with both hands. He bowed his head, closed his eyes and took a moment of silent reflection. A screen on the displays showed the crowd do the same. He raised his head and started to talk.

Stone tried to fight against the tape, twisting his arms and legs. He leaned forwards, then to the side.

The Bull walked over and punched Stone in the face. He slumped and the man hit him again. He bent down, his raw, exposed nostrils wet and flared. "Sit still and watch. *Watch* your life go down the shitter," he sneered, then grabbed Stone's jaw and squeezed, the flesh of his cheeks disappearing into his mouth as the man gripped so tightly, his fingers met, touching Stone's cheeks together inside his mouth. "Watch!" He released his grip and Stone shook his head, blinked and looked back at the screen. His mouth was numb and he could feel a molar had been loosened.

The woman turned and smiled. "You'll like this part Agent Stone, do try to stay awake for it." She was dialling a number on the telephone, then she pressed a button and replaced the receiver.

"I am former Secret Service agent Rob Stone. I have been the President's bodyguard and worked both on his security detail and on special projects for him during his two terms of office," the recording paused. *"On my first tour of Afghanistan I was taken prisoner. During my incarceration I came to sympathise with my captives, my Islamic brothers. I converted to Islam back on home soil. I have been committed to their cause ever since. I will strike at the heart of America, the Great Satan, at the September Eleven Memorial and Museum. And I intend to do it now, in front of the press and the eyes of the world..."* The recording cut off.

"Assets," the man said, looking at his watch. "In five... four..." Stone fought in vain against his bonds. He could picture the switchboard operator. Another crank call, another of America's nut-jobs making threats – it happened daily. Would they replay the recording? All calls were recorded, but only upon further investigation would they know the time significance, the validity of the threat. Later they would use voice recognition software to confirm it was one of their own who had made the call. Stone struggled, draining every ounce of strength he could muster. He tried to tip the chair backwards, maybe it would shatter and he could gain leverage. He caught the ginger-haired man smiling at his efforts. "Three…"

"No!" shouted Stone. He could barely hear his own voice over the thudding of his heart, the pulsating in his ears.

"Two..." The images on the screens changed. They left the President and centred on the President's wife and their two children. Each riflescope centred on a separate target. Marianne, the First Lady, her arms around the shoulders of their two sons; Elijah, aged eight and Daniel aged twelve. "One…"

"No!"

"Fire…"

35

Keeping his emotions in check was like navigating through dense fog. He wanted to scream and shout, wanted to weep at the barbarity of what he had just witnessed. The carnage and chaos, the screaming of the crowd, the President – unable to kneel beside the bodies of his family as the Secret Service agents had scooped him up and rushed him away, the look of pain and anguish and despair on the man's face. Above all, utter disbelief. The camera stayed with him. This wasn't CNN or Sky News; this was filming without remit. Voyeuristic, intentionally cruel. People had paid millions to see this and they would not be disappointed. The cameras were fixed on the bodies. Many cameras at many angles.

Stone had kicked a soccer ball with those two boys. He had shown them how to shadow box and the trick of autorotation to get out of wrist locks and put an attacker into one. He had played hide and seek with them. He had seen their excited faces at Camp David on Christmas morning, had seen them hunt for Easter eggs on The White House lawn. He had talked freely to Marianne, drank coffee with her and escorted her to fundraisers. He had taken her aside and trained her to use her father's old service Colt .45 she carried in her handbag. He had seen the four of them as a family, because that's exactly what they had been. He had talked to the President about life after The White House. The man was looking forward to normality, to being a father and husband again, to making memories. He had talked of taking Stone, and some other key security personnel, sailing off Montauk in the boat he had been building before taking office.

The end had been quick. Stone was sure of that. He had seen what he had seen and it could never be undone. He was aware of Kathy sobbing. He could hear the jubilation of the Australian woman and the three men nearest him. The man at the bank of screens was silent, savouring the moment in isolation. There were whoops and high-fives from the three men, Stone was barely aware of them, a fog enveloping him. It was almost as if it were an out of body experience.

"You read out that statement under hypnosis," the man said, turning around. "Voice recognition software will match it one-hundred percent."

"They'll know I was coerced. I'm not even in the country for Christ's sake!"

"But you soon will be. And you won't remember any of this. The same drugs and procedures of mind control that kept me automaton for so many years will be used to nail you to the wall. You'll be tried and convicted. Fifteen years on death row…"

"No!" Kathy screamed and pulled away from the ginger-haired man. She threw herself at Stone, hugged him tightly, squeezed his hands. "They won't get away with this, Rob! There's no way they'll make this stick on you…"

"Get her away from him!" the man shouted.

The Bull caught hold of her by the hair and dragged her back. She yelped and fell, was dragged back to her feet, kicking out and screaming. He raised a hand and brought it down hard on her neck in a classic karate chop, or *shuto-uchi* meaning knife-hand-strike. She was knocked out cold and slumped at his feet.

Stone stared at him. "That was big of you. How about untying me and trying that?"

"You'll get what's coming to you soon enough," the black giant said. "The FBI will be getting you, but they don't need you with your nose or all of your teeth. I'm going to bite your nose off your face and see how *you* like it. Then I'll knock your teeth out and feed them to you so you'll shit like a slot machine paying out the jackpot."

The Australian woman had been bent over a series of tower computers and she stood up having retrieved a USB drive. The man held out his hand and smiled. She gave it to him and then she called her dogs. Both animals lurched over and sat obediently in front of her.

"Dose him up for transportation," the man said. "And start the memory wipe. More than last time."

"It's a fine line," the ginger-haired man protested. "He could be left a cabbage if it goes the wrong way."

"So be it. Alive and with the evidence we've got pointing to him is all we need. We'll get his finger prints on one of the weapons, the empty shell case and his DNA all over the scope. But, I *would* like him coherent enough to suffer in his incarceration." He turned to the black giant and said, "Do what you've got to do, but we need him alive. A corpse isn't going to cut it." He looked back at Stone and shook his head. "Goodbye Agent Stone, I've enjoyed our encounter even more this time round. I'll be taking great interest in your case, from afar." He bent down and picked up Kathy's unconscious form like she was a bundle of laundry. Stone had seen the prosthesis, the incredibly deep, but almost comical ravine in the man's head, noticed he had lost a good deal of weight in the past two years, but was reminded of just how big and strong the man was. The man flung Kathy over his shoulder and walked out of the room, followed by Marnie and her two obedient hounds.

"Fun time!" The Bull grinned at him. "One of you pussies going to hold him still for me?"

"Fuck, he's tied up!" Rodriguez said. He walked over to a counter with a table-top refrigerator and helped himself to a can of soda, perched on a workstation and pinged the tab. "But I guess he was tied up last time and *still* kicked your ass."

"Fuck you, spic." The Bull snapped, then looked back at the ginger-haired man. "How long have I got?"

"Well the boss wants him dosed up and his memory wiped. A partial lobotomy. I'm going to start pulling the syringes now. So do what you've got to do and then we can get off this fucking island."

The Bull walked over and bent his huge frame down, his eyes level with Stone's. "Let me tell you, pussy, when I bite your nose off it is going to hurt so bad…" He opened his eyes wide, his sentence cut off by the jagged piece of glass, half the base of the broken jug Kathy had managed to press into Stone's hand when she had made a scene of crying and hugging him close. Stone had worked on the bonds of his right hand with it while everyone had pontificated and recounted the cleverness of their plans.

"Don't hit him about too much, or he'll choke on his blood when he's unconscious," the ginger-haired man said. He looked at The Bull, on his knees, his head close to Stone and blocking the Secret Service agent from view. "I've got the first dose ready, get on and bite the fucker's nose off!"

The Bull was close to dying. His legs were weak and his breathing rasped, gargling on the blood in his throat. His carotid was severed from the slash and Stone kept him pulled close to him, while he worked on cutting the bonds of his left hand. It was awkward just using his left hand, but he'd already managed it with his right. When he felt the man had lost enough strength, he let go of him and started to slice through the tape with the glass using his free hand. He noticed the knife on The Bull's belt and drew it from the sheath, dropping the large piece of glass onto the floor.

The ginger-haired man stopped pulling the syringe and looked over at Stone, who caught his eye. Startled, he looked to Rodriguez, who was tipping the remnants of the soda down his throat. "Rodriguez! He's…"

Stone cut him short with a 9mm bullet to the forehead from the Glock 17 he had drawn from The Bull's belt holster. He pushed the dying giant away, and he slumped to the floor, both hands clasped to his bloody neck, his legs starting to twitch wildly as he went into shock. Stone aimed at the Hispanic across the room, but the man was quick and had his M4 rifle off his shoulder as he flung himself to the ground. Stone bent down, sliced at the tape on his ankles, chanced a look and saw the man up on his knees and aiming at him. He pushed backwards, taking the chair to the floor as Rodriguez opened fire and computer screens, jugs of water and glasses and telephones were all cut down and turned to shattered plastic and shards of glass as he emptied the thirty round magazine at Stone.

Stone had one ankle free, but had dropped the knife. The pistol was in his hand, but he could not see his target. He could hear the man changing to another magazine. Stone spun around on the floor and went for the knife. He grabbed the handle and turned back to his tethered ankle. It sliced through easily and Stone rolled away from the chair and took cover behind a workstation. He heard the M4's receiver spring forwards with a loud click, making the weapon ready. He pressed himself low, looked under the workstation and saw a pair of feet thirty-feet away. He aimed the pistol and fired six rapid shots. The man fell onto the floor screaming and Stone followed up with multiple shots until one cracked open the man's skull like a watermelon.

He got up and surveyed the scene. The silence which followed close quarter combat was always unnerving, but nevertheless, exhilarating. The Bull was as good as dead, but Stone fired a round into the man's head and his quivering legs went still. He took no pleasure in it, but he didn't linger to pay his respects either.

Stone looked at the bank of monitors. He scanned them quickly until he found what he was looking for.

Movement.

36

The horseshoe bay was rocky and the sea was rough. Huge swells generated thousands of miles away in the southern Pacific unleashed their load on the northernmost point of the bay, pummelling the rock with a sound akin to distant explosions. The waves peeled across the entire bay eventually crashing to the jagged shoreline in a surging shore break that washed through the rocks and up onto the sand. At the southernmost tip of the headland, another horseshoe cove within the bay provided a perfect natural harbour. There were two boats moored in the cove and they gently rocked on their moorings, the water rolling from the backwash of the waves which had crashed ashore and now surged back to sea and faded away in the deep water.

A jetty had been built from sturdy, but rustic timber and sealed empty forty-gallon oil drums, each chained in place to keep the structure afloat. The jetty would rise and fall with the tide as well as with the gentle swell. The largest of the boats was a cabin-cruiser of well in excess of a hundred feet. It was a modern and well-appointed vessel with smoked glass, white fibreglass and teak decking. There was a cluster of satellite dishes, a sonar array and a cluster of cell-phone and radio antennae. The smaller of the two boats was a narrow wooden work-boat around thirty-feet in length and powered by twin three-hundred horsepower outboards. It was constructed from wood with sit-up-and-beg wooden bench seats. The boat was extremely basic, but massively powered. Stone had seen such boats used by drug-runners in the Caribbean. They were fast, agile and easily scuppered in the event of capture. Their low profile and wooden construction made detection from both satellite and sonar more difficult than modern fibreglass sports boats. Stone supposed the boat had been used here for similar reasons, only the cargo had been quite different indeed.

Stone watched, but he still couldn't see them. He knew that there was no other way off the island and he was sure he had beaten them to the bay, but he was paying for it now. He had run at a sprint for almost twenty-minutes, and was seriously hot and dehydrated. So much so that he felt light-headed and his vision was starting to blur.

Stone had acted quickly back in the bunker. He had taken back his watch from the ginger-haired man. He had then helped himself to the man's loose shirt as well. It turned out The Bull's feet were closest in size to his own, so he hastily removed his boots and put them on. Weapons were not a problem and he kept the Glock pistol because he knew it worked, and he took Rodriguez's spare magazines and tucked them into his pockets. He then picked up the Puerto Rican's M4 assault rifle, again because he knew it worked, and took the bandolier that the man carried his spare magazines in. He searched the men and found his Spyderco knife in Rodriguez's pocket. There was a thousand dollars in The Bull's vest pocket, the same in Rodriguez's and two-thousand in the ginger sadist's. Stone took it all and tucked the bundles of fifties and hundreds into his pants pockets. If he could get off the island he would need funds and figured that if he'd just been set-up for the deaths of the President's family, then walking into a bank and giving his account details to draw some funds wasn't going to be the best idea he'd ever had.

The cameras had shown the man carrying Kathy over his shoulder in a fireman's lift to the back of an old open-topped Land Rover. The woman and her dogs had followed and the dogs had dutifully and obediently hopped into the back of the vehicle and stood over Kathy while their owner opened the driver's door and got in. Stone studied the cameras and could see the cove. He knew they were going there, where they would be waiting for the three men to arrive with Stone, drugged and incoherent. Most likely comatose. That gave him time, at least. But surprise would serve him better.

He got onto one of the computers and opened it up. There was a password verification, which he did not bother with, merely went to the next terminal in the row and moved the mouse. After three computers, he stood back and looked around the room. Marnie had retrieved the USB from a machine. He went to it, moved the mouse and sure enough she was still logged in. He opened the email account and could see a long list of accounts and email. He scanned down the names. Many were repeat messages, conversations in snippet format. The names meant nothing to him. Except one. He opened the file and read, opened more and saw the messages, the progression of a conversation. He selected them one by one, entered his email address and forwarded them to his account. Then he changed his mind, selected what amounted to a month's worth of emails from around the world and forwarded them to his account as well. Something for a rainy day. Or a courtroom no doubt. It was a vast selection, and there was much that could be gleaned from the accounts of the various users, as well as contacts they themselves had emailed in turn.

Next, Stone scanned his eyes over icons on the homepage. He saw *Google Maps* and opened it. The island, or what he assumed to be this island was on the screen. He controlled the arrows on the screen and found what he recognised to be the two headlands in relation to the hill. He found the pond, saw that there were actually two smaller ones further west. He could see the overgrown hill where he had outsmarted The Saracen, changed his direction to flank him. In the centre of the island, which looked smaller than he imagined, he could see a cluster of buildings and a gravel roadway. He could see the road which led up to the satellite array where he had been hit with the tranquiliser gun. The road terminated at a cove on the other side of the island. He looked at the key running down the side of the screen. It was a little under a mile away. That was, if he was in one of the buildings in the cluster on the screen, which he had to assume he was. The compass showed it was due west from the buildings. He looked at the hill and the satellite dishes to get a bearing, then made his way outside.

There were no other vehicles and no sign of life. But if there were no other vehicles, then how were the three men going to have transferred him to the boats? Perhaps one of the other two was going to drive back and pick them up after they had secured Kathy. But that seemed a waste of resources. Unless there was another vehicle somewhere. He couldn't see one and the place looked deserted. There was the Jeep, but Stone could not see it and neither of the three men had keys on them.

Stone kept the M4 rifle shouldered, the muzzle lowered a few inches. Safety off, finger touching the edge of the trigger. He could get the weapon on target, wrap his finger completely around the trigger in a few hundredths of a second.

The huts were set deep in the ground so that the roofs were all that was visible, which meant that each one had a dozen wooden steps leading down to them. Stone knew he needed to check each one before he left for the cove, but safely searching a building was a time consuming process. He made his way down the first set of steps and tried the door. It opened and he could see as soon as he pushed the door inwards that it was a sleeping quarters. There were a dozen military-style cot beds and each was covered by mosquito netting. He could see it was empty. There was a bathroom at the far end, the door left ajar. He called it clear and made his way up the steps to the next hut. Again, it was unlocked and the door pushed inwards. This was a cookhouse and rec-room. There were tables and chairs, a serving hatch at the far end and along one side of the room there were vending machines. Mainly soda and confectionary. Empty calories for people waiting around. One quarter of the room was given over to a lounge area with a large flat-screen television on the wall. There was a pool table that had been abandoned in the middle of a game and an Xbox hooked up to a smaller television in a cosy nook with a selection of games and magazines scattered on the floor. It was more civilised than most of the army barracks he'd spent time in.

Stone walked through, having already seen that there was no place for somebody to be hiding and waiting to ambush him. The kitchen was empty. There was a bowl of fruit on the counter and he ripped the skin off half a dozen bananas and practically inhaled them. He ran the faucet and filled a coffee mug with water, downing it and another two right afterwards. There wasn't time to eat more, and he could tell without opening the fridge or cupboards that the kitchen had wound down. Whoever had the kitchen duty had known that the operation was drawing to a close. There was nothing prepared for dinner, no sign of food waiting either to be cooked or defrosted.

Back outside in what he termed in his head as the compound, he looked for the landmarks he had seen on *Google Earth*. Satisfied he was heading in the right direction, he ignored the winding track the vehicle would have taken and ran at a fast pace west.

The terrain was thinner, long savannah and pampas grass, tall banyan trees and tight thorn bushes. The air was cooler than it had been in the dense jungle of the eastern side of the island. At the fringe of the coast, the jungle started again, but it was lighter and less dense. Stone realised that he was at around a hundred feet of elevation when he caught sight of the coast.

A rugged outcrop of rocks gave him some cover. He crouched down and saw the two boats in the bay. He recognised the cruiser as a Sunseeker. He liked boats but they were something to enjoy with friends and family, and Stone didn't have many of either so never had any real aspirations of ownership. But senators and politicians liked boats and Stone had flicked through enough boating magazines whilst waiting around on security detail to know what the boat was and how much it would have cost. He recognised the other boat as a utilitarian craft, most likely made locally, although it had powerful engines and would probably match the big cruiser for speed.

Stone moved from his position and made his way around the outcrop of rocks. He worked his way lower down the slope, placing his feet carefully on the shale surface. He could see a pile of the scree at the bottom near the water. He didn't want to take the ride down; it was only a degree or two off vertical. He crossed over to where the rock looked firmer. Below, he could see the vehicle parked on the beach. He realised that the track went to the other end of the beach and the last two hundred metres had to be driven across the sand, which was why he had not seen the vehicle before now. He edged closer to the cliff and peered down to his left. He could finally see them, joining the walkway to the jetty. His heart was pounding and he felt a dramatic relief well within him when he saw Kathy walking in front, prodded in the back with the muzzle of a compact Kalashnikov assault rifle held by Marnie. He could only assume they had plans for her regarding her story into their affairs and still needed her for damage control. The man followed, struggling on the last few feet of sand and pebbles with his prosthesis. The two dogs brought up the rear, sniffing the air and whining. Marnie looked at them and stopped walking. She seemed distracted, then turned and stared up the cliff directly at Stone. He went to duck down, but it was too late. He simply raised the weapon and took aim.

"Hold still!" he shouted.

"Seek!" she shouted. "Attack!" She pointed directly at Stone and the two dogs took off, disappearing from view under the lip of the cliff.

Stone corrected his aim, but Marnie had the weapon aimed at Kathy and was moving swiftly towards her closing the gap that had opened up when she had spotted him. The man was aiming a large handgun up the cliff at him. The weapon was huge, comically so. A gunshot rang out and Stone fell backwards, the rifle ripped from his hands by the bullet. He checked himself over, dazed by the impact. He went to pick up the rifle but stopped when he saw the twisted and buckled frame. The bullet had passed straight through, punching a thumb-sized hole through the receiver.

He wondered how long it would take the dogs to get to him, and he thought back to what he had remembered about the night they had taken down the man impersonating the cop. The night they had eaten out a man's throat.

He got his answer almost instantly as the first dog bounded up the slope and stopped dead at the top. Stone drew the 9mm Glock. The dog was huge and seemed even more muscled than it had been on that night. Suddenly, he felt under-gunned. The dog was standing head-on, and at fifty-feet it was a small target. Stone brought the weapon up to aim and waited for the dog to make its move so he could make the bullets count.

It remained still, its eyes staring at Stone, its teeth bared. And that's when the other dog, silent and still just a few feet behind him, made its move.

37

The strength of the animal was incredible. Its teeth tore into Stone's shoulder and he dropped the pistol as he involuntarily raised his hands to cover his neck. He bowed his head and wrapped his arms around his ears and head. Survival mode was kicking in, the instinct of self-preservation. Already the dog had savaged his right hand and was working at getting its jaws into his throat. Stone felt the other dog bound onto him and was thrown down onto his side as the dog, weighing at least one-hundred-and-forty pounds attempted to get its jaws into his throat. Stone rolled onto his front and struck out a blow, but his fist simply hit hard muscle and bone and did nothing to slow the animal down. Keeping his guard up to his head, he struggled to his knees but was pushed back down by one of the beasts. The attack was frenetic, a flurry of claws and jaws, wailing, barking, growling – savagery at its most basic, primal instinct.

He pictured the man lying on his back, his throat ripped out. The image had been with him throughout the attack. But he was unable to fight like this. He couldn't see what was happening, he needed to get himself into a better position. He still had the knife, but couldn't draw it from its scabbard. Stone took a chance and started to roll over. At once he caught one of the dogs by its throat and he squeezed until his fingers met behind its windpipe. The dog seemed shocked and stopped its attack, but started to push and jerk itself backwards. Its strength was too much for Stone and it jerked free, but instead of continuing its attack, he coughed and choked on the spot, attempting to clear its throat. It was obviously taking in little air and its own survival instinct had kicked in. Stone grabbed the dog's tongue and pulled it clear by almost a foot. The dog froze, its jaws still for fear of severing its own tongue. The second dog was still attacking with all its vigour but Stone managed to keep it at bay using the point of his elbow, as he fumbled for the knife. The other dog's tongue was hot and wet, and the attack from its companion meant that Stone lost his grip. The dog shook its head, stunned and confused. It watched on as the other dog kept up its relentless attack. Stone managed to get a good grip on the knife and with his other hand now free to grab a handful of skin around the other dog's throat, he slashed it across its ankle joint and it practically jointed the creature's leg there and then. The dog slowed its attack, howled and tried to back up but with the partially severed leg, lost its footing, enabling Stone to grab harder at the skin of scruff of its neck. He got the knife under its throat and sawed vigorously as he pulled the dog closer. The knife was a razor-sharp military K-Bar, the blade honed as sharp as a scalpel. There was a massive release of air and blood as the blade slashed through the arteries and windpipe and the dog lolled on the spot, its legs shaking before it flopped down and rested still.

Stone backed up, sitting on his backside with his legs tucked in, the bloody knife in his hand. The other dog was still coughing and spluttering, its tongue hanging limply where muscle and fibre would have ripped at the back of its throat, but seemed to be getting enough air to remain standing. It looked at Stone, then at its dead companion. It walked over, sniffed the body and pawed at it. Stone edged towards the pistol on the ground. He picked it up tentatively and aimed carefully at the dog. The animal no longer seemed interested in killing him, but Stone didn't want to take the chance. He aimed at the dog's head, tightened his finger on the trigger and watched as the dog held up its head and howled like a wolf. Stone lowered the weapon. The dog then laid down beside the body of its companion and rested its chin on its bloody neck and let out a long, eerie whine. As Stone got to his feet and edged cautiously away, the dog watched him through the corner of two of the darkest, saddest eyes he'd ever seen.

38

The power cruiser's engines started and reverberated around the bay. Stone looked down from the clifftop and saw Marnie casting off the forward and aft ropes, the man controlling the boat at the helm. The boat had two steering platforms. One inside with the cabin comforts and the other on an elevated platform for enjoying the sunshine and being seen by people in smaller boats.

Stone watched as the boat moved seamlessly away from the jetty powered by its bow and stern thrusters - a transversal propulsion device fitted front and rear on both sides for effortless mooring. Once the boat was clear, the bow rose as the power was applied harshly to the rear engines and the boat surged away developing a tremendous wake that lifted the work boat high out of the water and smashed it repeatedly into the jetty.

Stone could see the boat lean hard to starboard as the man spun the wheel and cleared the edge of the horseshoe, perilously close to the jagged rocks. The boat then leaned hard to port, its cabin getting considerably close to the water as it hugged the headland and straightened up for open water. Stone looked around and saw the scree. It was practically vertical, but he ran for it and jumped, digging his heels in as he landed twenty-feet further down and rode the shale down the cliff like a surfer dropping down the face of a monster wave. He trailed his right hand in the scree to help slow himself down, but with little effect. He dropped so fast, he could feel his internal organs rising, his stomach playing catch up. He skidded at the bottom, his feet digging into the pile of flat shale and he was flung out across the beach and landed in a heap in the sand and pebbles. He looked up but could no longer see the power cruiser. It was out in the open ocean. He could hear it though and the craft's engine emitted a base thrumming that was echoing off the cliffs around the bay as it headed away at full throttle. Stone got to his feet and limped across the short distance of sand and onto the jetty. The log platform rocked with the wake of the cruiser, making it tricky to run across. Not only that, but both of his ankles felt tight and he was favouring them with every step. He had been lucky not to sprain or break them when he landed. He put some thanks into the tightly fastened military boots he was wearing.

The work boat was rocking on its strop, the line fastened to a large cleat on the jetty. Rubber fenders hung from the prow and stopped the boat from becoming damaged by rubbing on or striking the platform repeatedly. Stone unfastened the rope, just keeping it looped once around the cleat. He wrapped the length around a bow cleat and looked at the control panel. As he suspected from a work boat with multiple users, it was a simple ignition switch and push-button start to negate the problem of people losing or forgetting a set of keys. He knew the battery would have a cut-out switch to avoid discharge, but he needed to locate it first. As a tester he switched the ignition just in case, but nothing happened. He got down on his knees and looked along the sides of the boat and under the control panel, where he saw a tool kit and flares. He went back to the rear bench seat and lifted the cover. There were four large removable fuel tanks and located between them was a dial with three settings: Battery 1 – Off – Battery 2, written on the transom at the quarter-to, twelve and quarter-past positions. He selected position 1 and went back to the control panel. The two engines fired into life immediately. The boat was equipped with two batteries which would charge each other during use. The user simply had to alternate the batteries.

Stone flicked the rope from the jetty cleat and dropped the line on the deck. He reversed out and pushed the throttle forwards a quarter of the way. The boat lurched forwards and Stone took the rocks close, just as he'd seen the man do in the Sunseeker. As he rounded the point of the second horseshoe bay he could see the white cruiser a long way off on a northerly heading. Stone slammed the throttle forwards and the prow climbed. He adjusted the trim and tilt setting on the throttle and the nose of the craft came back down again and the wake lessened. The boat now seemed to fly across the water. Every now and then the boat would hit a swell and would leave the water entirely and crash back down on the surface with a tremendous spray. There were no dials other than a temperature gauge so Stone had no idea how fast he was going. All he knew was that he'd never been faster on water, even in the US Navy SEAL's attack boats, when he'd done a water insertion course with them and learned all about pain and being cold and wet for two weeks.

Stone didn't really have a plan, but he could see that he had a speed advantage over the cruiser. That said, the Sunseeker was an exceptionally fast boat. But what the power cruiser had over this roughly made, over-engined work rocket was fuel capacity. Stone had no indication of how much fuel he was carrying, but he knew the four tanks would last minutes rather than hours at this speed and he had not checked whether they were full when he had left. And nor could he leave the skittish controls to go back and check the levels and adjust his speed accordingly. It was simply time to do or die. Only if he ran out of fuel, it was Kathy at risk, not himself.

The boat ahead had quadrupled in size now; the work boat had caught up quickly. Stone estimated there to be a thousand-metres in it. He had trained as a sniper and reckoned the man, who he knew to be six-five, was about the right size for a thousand-metres. After a few minutes that distance was down to seven-hundred. And then five. And then three. And that's when the man casually turned around and started shooting at him.

Stone didn't worry too much for the first couple of shots, but a bullet whizzed past his head and he ducked down. He'd had close calls with bullets before, and this was in his top five for as close as it got. He felt the wind from the spinning bullet brush his face. He heaved the wheel to port and the boat leapt over a four-foot high breaking white horse from the Sunseeker's wake. The man turned and fired again. Stone didn't even bother taking out the 9mm Glock for an unsteady three-hundred yard shot at forty-knots. It would simply be a waste of ammunition. Instead, he concentrated on drawing the man's fire. Hopefully he'd run out of bullets. But the man did not fire anymore, and Marnie did. She hunkered herself down on the transom and opened up with the short model Kalashnikov. It was good for three-hundred yards or so, and the bullets clattered into the hull of the boat spitting splinters into Stone's face. He wheeled to starboard and the rounds tracked across the water sending up plumes of spray and then tracked back and found the boat again.

There was some respite while the woman changed magazines, but Stone kept the boat slicing through the water, matching the Sunseeker's speed as the woman fired rapid bursts that mainly went wide or dotted the heavy prow of the boat. She casually took out the curved magazine of the Kalashnikov and bent down for another, and that was Stone's cue to make his move. Holding his distance, he had a good amount of throttle in reserve and he slammed the lever forwards and swung the boat across the power cruiser's wake and into the frothy water directly behind. The boat surged forwards, the aerated, agitated water offering less resistance to the craft's twin propellers and the boat gained rapidly on the cruiser. With his increase in speed there was a closing difference of twenty knots, and Stone kept the throttle jammed forwards, even when the prow rode over the Sunseeker's swim platform and powered up into the rear and higher onto the second platform. The man turned and looked, but it was too late. The wooden work boat rose out of the water, the swim platform and transom acting as a ramp, and slammed into the cockpit. The man had enough time to shield his face, but the boat hit him hundredths of a second later and crushed him against the wheel.

Marnie had got out of the way and fallen onto her back. She was scrambling for the Kalashnikov, but Stone had the Glock in his hand and shouted above the engines, which now clear of the water, whined in a high-pitched, frantic crescendo.

"Hold it!" he shouted. "Do not touch the weapon!"

She rolled onto her back, her eyes burning into him. "What did you do to my dogs, you bastard?"

"You don't want to know."

"I'll kill you…" she said coldly. Stone could barely hear her over the revving of the engines. Then the boat shifted slightly and dropped backwards, the propellers eating into the deck, chopping fibreglass and seat covers into pieces, the engines now overheating and smoking badly. But he was on the port side, his weapon aimed at her. He couldn't switch the engines off and she was too close to the Kalashnikov. "Get up and put your hands on your head," he ordered.

She rolled onto her side and pushed herself up, but as she did so, she swept up the weapon and rolled out of Stone's line of sight. He lunged over the portside and found himself staring into the muzzle of the assault rifle. It was check-mate, because the barrel of the Glock in Stone's outstretched hand was a mere eighteen inches from the woman's face.

"I'll kill you for what you've done to my…" she did not finish her sentence. Stone had pulled the trigger and the bullet smashed through her teeth and severed the synapse behind her throat. The point where the spine met the brain stem. There was no faster recorded method of killing somebody.

Stone got up and cut the engines. The power cruiser was still ploughing on at speed and Stone climbed down from the boat and made his way to the cockpit. There was blood on the deck, but the man was not there. It was impossible. But then again, he had history with him and he had survived the unthinkable once before. He pulled both of the chrome throttle levers back and the cruiser slowed quickly. He turned around, his arm half outstretched with the Glock in his hand, but it was too late. The heavy stainless pistol slammed down on his wrist and the Glock skittered across the deck. The pistol came back up with great force and whipped him in the face. Stone was falling, there was nothing he could do. His head went light and his feet felt like lead. His face burned and when he hit the deck, his cheek felt as if a sharp implement had been driven into the bone. He knew his orbit had been shattered, his cheekbone had cracked at the very least. He rolled over, his instincts telling him to keep moving, but as he looked up he saw that the pistol was aimed steadily down at him. The man behind it was contorted in pain, his shoulders sagged, but he still managed to hold the Smith & Wesson .500, his aim unwavering. This was an over-sized revolver that made the once infamous .44 magnum look like a peashooter. The man kicked out and Stone caught the blow thankfully just short of his groin. He winced, made the impact seem worse than it was. You could never show enough pain to your captor.

"Get up!" the man shouted. He rammed the handgun into Stone's face. The barrel was still too hot to touch from firing and it sizzled on his perspiration. The weapon was a hand cannon. A toy for gun enthusiasts with no combat effectiveness. Except that it was looking pretty effective from where Stone was standing. "Walk to the side of the boat." He switched off the engines using his left hand, and struggled to keep the weapon steadily aimed. But the muzzle was still too close to start heroics. Stone could see the man was badly injured. It was an effort to do just that simple task. "You've been a thorn in my side. Like your brother before you. He begged, you know…"

Stone yawned. "You've already told me." The boat pitched and rolled in the swell, and he rolled on his feet unsteadily. He lowered his hands to keep balance.

"Well I'm telling you again!" he snapped. "I cut that bastard's throat!"

"Get on with it."

The man raised the enormous handgun, it hovered just in front of Stone's face. Stone dipped with the roll of the swell, then swiped the barrel out of the way with his left hand, his right hand already scything towards the man's belly. The gun clattered to the deck and Stone stood still. There was a look of confusion on the man's face. He backed up a pace, his guard ready. Stone's punch had amounted to nothing, he looked pleased they were going to fight it out. They'd been there before. Stone slowly raised the Spyderco knife with its wicked-looking diamond-sharpened serrated blade. There was blood on the blade, a few droplets had run over the back of his hand and dripped onto the gleaming white deck. The man looked down hesitantly, and that's when everything inside him seeped out from between the folds of severed skin and muscle and fell out onto the deck. He fell forwards onto his knees, his expression one of disbelief.

Stone walked around him and stamped on the prosthesis. It wrenched off, held on only by suction and rubber. Stone bent down and yanked it easily out from the man's pant leg. He looked at it, hefted it for weight and balance, holding it by the metal ankle. "Hey," Stone said down to him. "Caught out by me twice, and both times with a knife." The man grunted, but he was fading fast. "Remember when I said I'd beat your head in with your own leg?" The man grunted as Stone raised the leg high above his head. He brought it down as hard as he could. He did it twice more and the man stopped moving on the last blow, the thudding sound of impact giving way to a wetness much like the sound of breaking eggs. Stone looked at the body, a sense of relief washing over him. He'd had history with him, and now it was over. Stone looked out across the ocean to the island. He could see another in the distance. He turned, swaying unsteadily as the boat rocked with the swell. There were two large shark fins in the water. They popped up and down, occasionally covered by a swell or some chop. Stone realised it wasn't two sharks, but one big one. He thought back to what the clean-up guy had said to him after he had killed The Saracen:

The west coast of the island gets Great Whites passing through in spring and fall. I think they head somewhere to breed in the summer but hang around here for a few weeks. There's bull sharks, hammerheads, white-tips and tiger sharks off the coast all year round. You get some blood and chunks in the water and when there's enough sharks competing for it you drop the bodies off the boat...

He looked down at the man who had killed his brother. The man who had made millions from killing. Who had taken money to kill the President's family and film it like a reality show. The man who had treated lives as commodities. The man who had fed another man's family to the black caiman and forced him to watch.

And it gave him an idea.

39

Kathy had been tied to a fixed table in the galley. Her eye and lips were swollen from the slaps Marnie had brutally administered back in the bunker. She had been shaken and scared, and as pleased as it was possible to be to see Stone standing in the sliding glass doorway.

Stone cut her loose and she hugged him tightly. The hug lingered for a long while, relief was an exhausting emotion to move away from. After relief came the unknown, and Kathy had not wanted to leave this moment and move forward. Stone knew how she felt and had been happy to reciprocate.

Back outside, there was a considerable amount of blood on the deck. Kathy stared at the patch and Stone asked her to fetch water from the galley and sluice the area clean. She had to be involved, had to be a part of it. Not only would the action keep her busy, but she would own it. She would move forward after this experience and she would have a filter when she came to write about it. There would be a line she would not cross because of her involvement.

Stone looked at the water where he had dumped both the man and his entrails and Marnie's body. He had seen the shark, a beast of about eighteen feet in length and as wide as a European hatchback car. The shark had rammed the man's body, torn into it and taken it below the surface. Stone had not stopped long to look. He didn't want to be a voyeur, just needed to know it was over and that the man had gone for good. Marnie's body had simply sunk below the surface. Stone was in no doubt as to what was happening under the boat at that moment.

Stone tried, but could not shift the work boat from the deck. The Sunseeker did not seem to be suffering from the damage caused to the stern. He took control in the cabin cockpit, put the engines into reverse and the boat lurched backwards. He increased the power until he was at maximum revs, then slammed the throttles forward and the engines wailed at the transferal of power and the inertia made the workboat shoot off the stern. It slid down the shattered swim platform and plunged into the water. The angle was steep and the heavy outboard engines entered the water first and water flowed over the transom and filled the stern. The boat started sinking and within a minute had disappeared, lost to the sea.

Kathy stood at Stone's side as he looked at the navigation display. Stone took out the USB he had retrieved from the man's pocket. "When we get to Panama City I'll find somewhere to get this copied. I'll give you a copy for your story," he said. "I need a copy to investigate this, and another two for both the Secret Service and the FBI."

Kathy rubbed his shoulder. "I get the impression you're not coming back with me."

"You're right," he said. "I'm on the back foot now. I need to get out in front. I'll be the most wanted man in the world right now. And there'll be a lot of people who want to take me down. Dead or alive. I need information. That's the only power I'll have to fight this and clear my name."

She rested her head against his chest, her body swaying with the motion of the boat as it ploughed through and over the swells. "I'll help in any way I can," she said.

Stone smiled. "I'll contact you somehow. Take it as read, your phones will be tapped. Especially when your story is published and the world finds out what happened here and why the President's family were assassinated."

She shook her head. "I can't believe what was going on, what they did for the money."

Stone shrugged. "I've come to realise that there are people in this world who have no limits."

"And what are you limits, Agent Stone?" she asked, her head resting back against his chest.

Stone thought for a moment, his mind awash with images of the past few days that he knew he would never forget. "I suppose if it's a matter of personal survival, or perhaps knowing morally I'm on the right side…" he paused, images of black caiman taking a man into a death roll, of shark fins thrashing, white teeth slashing and tearing and water turned crimson on the bubbling surface. "Then I have no limits either."

40

Eight months later

There are few places on earth that rain as much, or at least as frequently as Seattle. Few metropolitan inhabited places at least. Most people stick around, decide whether it's worth investing the time and money in before they get a township up to city status, but the settlers in the Pacific Northwest decided there was much to Seattle that outweighed the near constant precipitation. The gateway to Alaska, shipping hub to Asia and the Pacific Rim and the third largest port in the United States had sprung up and grown thanks to mining and logging and the opportunity to exploit it. Stone guessed the pioneers could cope with the weather, and so could the people who had flocked there ever since.

A cultured city, arguably famous for its coffee houses and the chains and franchises that had been conceived there. Stone preferred independent coffee houses, and it was in one of these that he had sat most afternoons for the entire week. He had taken a window table in a sofa booth, and he had worked his way through the largely Java and Columbian blends and seen his way through many oversized cookies and brownies. He would need to abstain and hit the gym when he was finished here. Or maybe just run. He'd been running a lot lately, but not to work out. He was the FBI's most wanted. He was running for survival. He was a step or two ahead, but those steps were getting shorter. He had engineered it that way.

Stone had grown out his hair more than usual. He had grown a beard too. Seattle favoured beards – a place where hipsters and full mountain-men met ironic facial art. There was a beard on every other man under the age of forty-five. Stone's spoke of mountaineer more than hipster. He had pulled off the look with cargo pants and a checked shirt, hiking boots and a windcheater. He neither stood out nor entirely blended in, which was the key to undercover work. And being on the run as America's most wanted criminal and terrorist was as good as undercover work.

Financially, Stone was comfortable. His assets had been either frozen or seized, and he did not have a possession to his name, apart from the watch on his wrist, but he had accessed an account on the USB drive he had taken and stashed the hard currency in various rented lockers at bus stations around the country. He had also buried some in locations he knew he could find again and access easily and discreetly. He wasn't intending on living a luxurious lifestyle, although he was sure there was enough for him to do that for the rest of his life, but the money helped him towards getting back his name, his freedom. And he was closer to that now than he had ever been since leaving the island. Identification had been an issue at first but he had secured a fake driving license for two-thousand dollars in Chicago and cash spoke at cheap motels around the country, especially in the small cash-strapped towns, the towns that were still victims of America's ongoing recession and poverty. Bus journeys gave him anonymity and the train was an easy way to travel vast distances. He had bought some junk second-hand vehicles, usually choosing family mini-vans or station wagons – nothing flashy or in any way similar to the cars he would have driven in his previous life. Staying under the radar meant he had to sever any behavioural or habitual ties he had once had. He abandoned the cars each time he arrived somewhere new. That was until this morning. This morning he had rented a vehicle from Hertz. The car hire company was even offering a deal on the new Corvette Stingray. A 6.2 litre, V8 beast. American muscle capable of taking on Italian supercars. He had taken the opportunity, given the car a good thrashing up to Snoqualmie Falls then driven back crossing Mercer Island and through most of Seattle and parking it two blocks away in a public car park. He had fed the meter and called into The Gap and spent five hundred dollars on a new outfit. Like the hire car, he had presented his own credit card, and almost smiled when it was declined. He knew it would be. He tried his debit card next and then gave the sales assistant some story about payday problems at work. When that too was declined, he used cash.

He made sure he took his time when he left the store, checked the buildings, even stared up at the CCTV when he crossed over the street and headed for the coffee shop across the road from the building he had been watching for a week.

Stone looked at his watch. Eleven-fifty-five. Each day the receptionist came down the steps to the Georgian brownstone building at twelve. Each day she had taken one-hour and five minutes' lunchbreak. The target did not take a lunch hour. He had seldom been in all week, his work taking him all over Seattle and Washington State. But Stone knew he would be in for the next hour because he had made an appointment. Or rather, he had paid a waitress who he had built up a rapport with, one-hundred-dollars to make the appointment for herself.

He walked to the counter and handed over his debit card. The sales assistant pulled a face when it was declined. Stone told her it was a pay issue, that he could go across the street to the offices where he had a meeting and get some money. She pulled a face again, and he made a thing of patting himself down and smiled, acting surprised and relieved when he took a twenty-dollar bill out of his pocket. He walked out into the foyer and into the men's room. He ran the sink with hot water and splashed it over his face. He used the travel shaving gel and foamed his entire beard. Shaving was uncomfortable and even though it was a new triple-bladed razor, it pulled and pinched the facial hair. He soaped up again, a trick he had learned after patrols in Afghanistan, and with another new blade he had a comfortable and effective shave. Nobody else came into the men's room, but he went into the cubical and changed into a shirt, trousers and a retro leather jacket. He swapped his boots for brown leather brogues and stuffed his old outfit into the carrier bag. He checked himself in the mirror, smoothed his hair down and walked out through the foyer and crossed the road, dumping the bag into the bin he had noticed earlier in the week.

He figured he'd have twenty-minutes, maybe less.

The building housed six offices, all separate businesses. The one he wanted was on the second floor. He looked at the plaques and pressed the buzzer for Dwight & Engle Law Firm, on the third floor. They were a firm of lawyers and would take special deliveries all day long. A voice came back. "Yes?"

"DHL couriers, ma'am," Stone said. "Signed package."

The door clicked open and Stone walked through. He took the stairs and noticed the CCTV system. He was sure to look into the camera for long enough as he reached the top of the second flight of stairs. He would soon be growing the beard again, but he needed to be seen to be as close to the records and files held on him.

The door to the office read: *Andrew Reece, Specialist Solutions & Private Security*. Stone opened the door and saw the empty desk belonging to the secretary who was on her lunch break, and the small waiting area with a two-seater sofa and a coffee machine. The only other door was closed. He opened it, drew the 9mm Beretta from his waistband and stepped inside.

Reece was fast, but Stone was faster. The man had gone for his weapon, but Stone crossed the room in three strides and kicked the desk. The force pushed Reece backwards in his chair, pinching his gut and cannoning him into the wall where framed photographs and credentials dropped and smashed on the floor. Stone pressed the muzzle of the pistol under the man's chin.

"Don't do it," Stone said calmly. "You know what the triggers are like on 92's. I've already got two pounds of pull, it's hit and miss whether it can take an ounce more…" Reece raised both hands and Stone reached inside the man's jacket and retrieved a Smith & Wesson .357 magnum. It was a snub-nosed model with rubber grips. A professional's choice. Stone pocketed it and stepped around the desk. "Got any other hidden surprises? I'm fresh out of patience and this gun is a Saturday night special. No links to anybody."

"No."

"Just the one weapon?"

Reece shrugged, shook his head. "9mm short in the filing cabinet. A Walther."

"That's more like it," Stone pulled the desk back out, keeping the weapon aimed at him. "So, you got out," he stated flatly. "Private security. You always said you might go do that. After you messed up that currency case. So now it's Andrew Reece, PI."

"Don't knock it. I make twice what the service paid."

"And how much did you make out of killing the President's family?"

"Fuck you!"

Stone raised the pistol. "How much, Reece?"

"I never signed up for that!"

"But you betrayed the Secret Service."

"I took money to fuck *you* over, sure."

"You sold me down the river," Stone said. "You got them into my cell phone, sold them the details they needed to work on me."

Reece shook his head. "It wasn't like that," he glared. "I got shafted, took the rap for an operation that went south and spent the rest of my career on a desk. On a nightshift. A fucking nightshift! Do you know what it's like to be standing at the President's shoulder one minute and manning a telephone the next?" He shook his head. "Of course you don't. Rob Stone, the President's Man! Drop him in shit and he comes out smelling of roses…"

"So you sold me out?" Stone asked. "Because you fucked up and I hadn't?"

Reece sneered. "Commendations, secret assignments," he paused. "Tooling around in that stupid car of yours. You're a tough act to follow. It wasn't so hard to take some cash and wave you goodbye."

"I don't buy it," Stone said. "There's more to it. You said you never signed up for the killing of his family. What then? The people who took me weren't the same people as those trying to kill me. I only knew for certain when they ran us off my bike and gunned down the men in the Ford Taurus. They were government men. I've dug about and they were with the Secret Service. Were they in it with you? Did your deal go wrong?"

Reece laughed. He scratched at his stomach, his fingers reaching under his jacket. Stone moved sideways, but not fast enough. Reece had a retractable baton out and flicked it as he swung and caught Stone on top of his hand. He dropped the weapon, his hand recoiling involuntarily. Reece was out of the chair and onto him with the baton. Stone blocked, felt his forearm almost shatter under the blow. He kicked Reece in the knee and the man flinched. Stone kicked again and then got his hand into Reece's throat. He was strong and gripped tightly. But he knew the secret to completing the move was to drop the man's head forwards using his other hand as leverage. Reece

346

knew this too and was leaning his head out of the way. Stone countered using the man's momentum and pushed his chin hard, smashing the back of his head into the wall. Reece sagged to the floor amongst the broken frames and glass.

Stone stepped backwards and picked up the pistol. He could see that one of the photographs was of Reece standing beside the President. He shook his head. "You're not fit to display that."

Reece looked up at him rubbing the back of his head. The man looked beaten. "I took money to sell you out, Rob. I'm not proud. I knew you were getting set up for something, but I had no idea it would be that. I had no idea they were going to assassinate his family. They promised they'd set you up with something, that they would give me the details and that I would be able to make a connection, arrest you for something big and get my career back."

"And they didn't tell you what?"

"I guessed it was bad," Reece relented. He shifted and winced, some glass cutting into him. "They wanted to know so much about the nine-eleven memorial that I guessed what they were planning. Well, I figured they were going to try and kill the President. I never thought in a million years it would be his family. I told them I wanted out. Then they came for me one night. They shot me up with drugs and I woke up tied next to some Brit who was having his entire family fed to fucking alligators! They said my family would get the same. They drugged me and I woke up at the back of a bar in DC with an almighty hangover. I wasn't even sure it had been real, that I hadn't really dreamt it, but they sent photos to my phone. The sick fuckers! I got docked two weeks' salary for going AWOL on what human resources thought was a massive bender."

Stone shook his head. "But you had a change of heart," he ventured. "At Kathy's beach house. The men attacking us were contacts of yours with government connections. That's why one of them tried to cover himself by picking up the spent shell cases."

"I thought that they were planning to assassinate the President. I wasn't going to let that happen, but I wasn't going to risk my family's lives either." Reece looked at Stone. "Let me get back up, Rob." Stone aimed the pistol between the man's eyes and nodded. Reece shifted awkwardly on the glass, got back to his feet and collapsed into the chair. "I'm not proud of it, but I had taken enough money to know I wouldn't be giving it back anytime soon." He shrugged. "I'd spent so much of it, anyway. I thought that if I could get rid of you, then I could halt their plans. I'm sorry, but it was worth the collateral damage."

"Thanks," Stone said dryly. "So the guys at the beach…"

"Before that," Reece interrupted. "The night you called in the killing at the house. The two guys in the Audi. They were private security. An ex-FBI agent and an ex-marine-turned bodyguard. Both as shit as each-other, so it turned out. The third, the guy impersonating the cop was one too. He was an ex-CIA hotshot, apparently. The people putting pressure on me knew that Kathy Newman had contacted you, they'd had your phone tapped for weeks. They knew that the time was right to make a move on you. It was a personal vendetta for the freak, the guy with the caved-in head and the artificial leg. He wanted you burned. It was so close to memorial day that I just knew it was POTUS. I never assumed it would be Marianne and the boys…"

"So you launched your own hit?" Stone shook his head. "So what then?"

Reece shrugged. "The security outfit wouldn't play ball. You wasted three of their best men, so I made alternative arrangements. The men at the house were Secret Service, as you said. They followed you and the other lot wasted them on the road."

"I never saw them before though."

"You don't walk the lower echelons anymore," he paused, looking at him contemptuously. "I don't think you ever did."

"So they turned guns for hire, just like that?"

"A two-hundred-and-fifty-thousand dollars to share as they saw fit, they turned pretty damned quick. Even joked that there might be a promotion or two in the chain once you were six feet under. One of them used his own civilian rifle. Generic ammo and no registration made it quite safe, but the other idiot used his service machine pistol. I think they thought it would be a quick in and out. Fire a few shots and they would be out of there."

"What about Ramirez? I got the poor guy out of bed and into the office to help me with the internet data. Was he simply collateral damage?"

Reece shrugged. "I guess so. Sometimes it's necessary. I needed to buy some time."

"You did that?"

He nodded. "I was in deep."

"His wife is due to give birth this week," Stone said coldly. "She was five weeks pregnant. Now she's got no husband, her child will have no father."

"She was a good looker from what I remember. She'll get her Puerto Rican claws into some guy sooner or later. It won't take her long."

Stone clenched his fist. The knuckle clicked. He wanted to break the knuckle on the man's face. "How much did they give you to sell me out?"

"Three million," Reece said. "They managed to hack a million back out of my offshore account when they guessed what I'd done. I paid those guys two-hundred-and-fifty-thousand, the first outfit two-hundred-thousand, then spent a fortune on relocating my family the three-thousand miles out here after leaving the service. That and setting up this venture."

"That should still leave you a nice nest-egg," Stone sneered. "What the hell did you think was happening on the island?"

"I don't know. But that was some crazy shit they had going on there. The guy's family were ripped apart. Those alligators were damned hungry."

"What did they want from him?"

Reece shook his head. "Nothing. They didn't ask him a damned thing. He told them he would sign over his bank, give them everything he had, but they weren't interested."

"His competitors wanted him to suffer," said Stone. "They tendered bids to get the job done, have it streamed live to them through the internet. They would have sat in their snug with beers and popcorn. Or wontons and rice wine, whatever Chinese billionaires eat and drink in their snugs."

"Jesus…" Reece trailed off. He looked at Stone and asked, "If you're here, does that mean they're shut down?" He seemed more confident at the thought of the prospect. "Look, I *do* have a nest-egg. There's three-quarters of a million in an off-shore account. It's all yours if you walk away and say nothing."

Stone said nothing. He kept the pistol on him, but edged towards the window where he could see a collection of shiny black sedans and SUV's pulling up outside the coffee shop. He was down to just a few minutes now. He reached into his pocket and took out the Taser. Without a further word he fired and two darts attached to wires shot out and stuck into Reece's chest. He arced the current and Reece jolted in his chair, his feet kicking out wildly. Stone took his finger off the trigger and the current ceased. He put the Taser on the desk and took out the handcuffs. Stone cuffed his right wrist, pulled his arm around his back then cuffed the left wrist. He then used two cable ties on the man's ankles and secured him to the chair. Reece was starting to protest and Stone picked up the Taser and shocked him again. He dropped it back down onto the desk and thumbed the screen of his iPhone. It was a non-contract phone, and there were only three pieces of stored information on it. One was the recording of his entire time in the office through the concealed fish-eye lens and built-in microphone in the button of his shirt. The second was a video recording of his full statement accounting for the events through to leaving the island. In the statement he gave details of a locker where he had stored a USB drive containing the bank details and IP addresses of those involved in the dark web bidding. It was his defence, proof of his innocence. The iPhone had already automatically backed up the film to iCloud. Stone had contacted Max Power and given him the passcode to retrieve the information and set about uploading it to various websites. The film of

Reece's confession was to be loaded to *YouTube* multiple times, under various guises. Max's work would be done from a laptop Stone had purchased solely for the task and using only Wi-Fi from places Max would reconnoitre first. Max had been adamant about maintaining anonymity, and Stone had both agreed and respected that. The third piece of information on the iPhone was a detailed video report by Kathy Newman. This was also destined for the same treatment and Max had already uploaded to a pulse server where it would complete the upload when a metatag used in Stone's upload was activated. Kathy had not only corroborated his story on film, but had agreed to tell everything she knew in person to the FBI and the Secret Service when the time came.

Reece was unconscious. He was perspiring and his breathing was shallow. Stone looked back at the street. Agents wearing blue vests with *FBI* written on them in yellow were gathering, and two plain clothed agents were crossing over the street, both talking animatedly on cell phones. Stone took out the envelope and dropped the iPhone inside. He had already addressed it for the attention of the FBI lead officer and he sealed it with the pre-sealed tape strip.

He slipped the pistol back into his waistband and left the office without looking back. He had earlier reconnoitred the rear of the building and had noted the fire escape and drain downpipes. He knew he needed what he had assumed to be a lavatory window on the third floor, so he crossed the corridor and climbed the flight of stairs and made for the rear of the building. The lavatory was mixed sex and consisted of three cubicles. Stone figured it was a communal affair, one on each floor. However, he needed to put some distance between himself and the FBI, and it had been a good call as he could already hear several sets of feet bounding up the stairs and voices shouting orders on the lower floors.

Stone opened the window, and this was the other reason for choosing this floor. This window backed onto the fire escape and looked large enough to climb through. The lower two floors were half-tilt windows. He eased himself out and onto the metal fire escape. He walked to the end and climbed over the rails, caught hold of the stanchion and slid down a floor. Next, he got his feet onto the lower window sill and climbed hand-over-hand to the drain downpipe. It was a thirty-foot drop to the alleyway below, and he kept his feet against the wall and lowered himself down, part climbing, part sliding until he dropped the last few feet to the ground.

He unlocked the eight-year-old Ford pickup truck and climbed inside. Behind the seats were two holdalls. One full of money and the other with everything to his name. He was going to lose himself in Alaska for the summer. There was every chance he would be vindicated soon, once the FBI and Secret Service had the USB and the video confession of

Andrew Reece and the corroboration of Stone's statement by Kathy Newman. But for now, he needed to put distance between himself and the life he once had. He couldn't face the President yet. Doubted he would ever return to his previous life. He had recalled once hearing that everyone in Alaska was running from something. And the thought was appealing to him more and more. Even if deep down he knew he was only running from himself.

Hi – thanks for reading and I hope you enjoyed the story!

Before you go, if you could please head to Amazon and leave a review it will help no end in keeping my work visible. This link will get you there, just click on the relevant book – www.apbateman.com You will also find the links to other books in this series, as well as news of new releases and can sign up for my newsletter.

Also, to win the chance of a signed paperback mailed to you simply email me and tell me which book you'd like. I will randomly draw a name each week. If you're drawn, I'll reply to you for your postal address. It's as simple as that and I'll add you to my contacts so you can receive info and updates in the future.

authorapbateman@gmail.com

Thanks for reading!

A P Bateman

Made in United States
Troutdale, OR
12/16/2023

15745908R00217